Print ISBN: 978-1-7398552-2-2

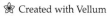 Created with Vellum

DAVID B. LYONS

THE MURDERS THAT KILLED AMERICA

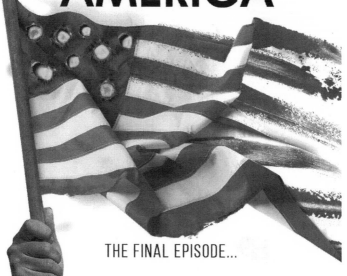

THE FINAL EPISODE...

THE AMERICA TRILOGY

★★★★★

"Extremely powerful and thought-provoking"

— The Book Literati

In memory of my great friend,
Thomas Healy

A better storyteller than I'll ever be.

—AMERICA FUTURE—

In the future, technology will exceed humanity.
Of that there is no doubt.

1

Sarah-Jane wrapped her fingers firmly around the stem of the crystal cake stand, then swiveled on the spot before striding toward her famous kitchen island. When she placed the cake stand carefully down on to the olive-green marble top, she glanced over the top of Phil's balding head toward her daughter and sucked in a deep inhale. As soon as Erica's eyes met hers, Sarah-Jane nodded once, and then they both instantly began to sing. Not in unison. And certainly not in key. Yet each of them sported a gratified grin while they murdered the world's most sung song.

Phil was sat between them, lurched forward on a high stool, his forearms leaning on the marble top of the island, supporting his considerable weight. He could hear how bad the racket was either side of his ears. Of course he could. He just wasn't listening. The golden flames swaying tall and proud above the cake had enveloped him—his bloodshot eyes flickering in unison with the repetitive snaps of yellow and blood-orange.

When the racket finally stopped, Sarah-Jane held a hand to Phil's shoulder and gently squeezed it, causing him to glance at her hand, then up at her beautiful face. She could tell he was studying the wrinkles that were edging away from her heavy green eyes—as though it was the very first time he had seen them. Then his glance blinked away… back to the tall, flickering yellow and blood-orange flames.

'Go on then, make a wish,' Sarah-Jane said, squeezing his shoulder more firmly this time.

Phil's throat gently gurgled. But that was all he offered up. A gurgle.

'Blow 'em out, Phil,' Erica said, nudging him from the other side.

When he continued to remain still, Erica glanced over his balding head at Sarah-Jane to catch her biological mother puffing up her own cheeks before audibly exhaling. Erica squinted at her, before mirroring her—inhaling deeply, then exhaling audibly. Phil's eyes — one heavily bloodshot, the other less so — glanced at his lover first, then at his daughter before he began copying them; filling his cheeks with air before blowing the air out as loudly as he could. Sprays of Phil's spittle showered the top layer of chocolate on the cake, but the flames remained tall and proud. Swaying and flickering.

'Go on, harder,' Erica said, sliding the cake stand slightly closer to Phil.

He continued to replicate the blowing of the two ladies either side of him, before his feeble exhales suddenly stopped — as if somebody had removed his battery — and his bearded chin receded into his neck, while his heavy eyes zoned away from the flickering yellow and blood-orange flames.

'C'mon, Phil,' Sarah-Jane said, slapping his shoulder. 'Blow.'

She began to huff in and out noisily again, and after slapping him on the back, Phil's chin lifted, and he repeated his spittle-spraying technique—but to no avail. Erica, for whom patience had never been a virtue, blew hard out of the side of her mouth, swaying the two flames, and then harder again, finally extinguishing them with one forced blow. As two streams of gray smoke stretched toward the high ceiling of their penthouse, the two women clapped and screamed in celebration.

'Yaaaaay, well done, Phil, you blew them out,' Sarah-Jane said. 'Happy birthday.' She leaned down to kiss him on the cheek, before Erica mirrored her on the opposite side, leaning in too, making his bloated, jowly face the filling between their smooch sandwich.

'Sia,' Sarah-Jane muttered into Phil's cheek, 'take a snapshot of this moment.'

A mechanical noise could be heard, zooming and sizzling, and when it fell silent again, a holographic yellow dot appeared in the top corner of Sarah-Jane's kitchen. She winked her right eye to accept the saved memory and even though her face was still pressed into Phil's she rolled her eyes to watch the holographic 3D snapshot of the smooch sandwich. Phil's eyes were closed in the shot, but the wrinkles webbing away from his eyes were pointing upward, which made Sarah-Jane feel content that he was happy in that moment. So, she winked her left eye once to save the snapshot into her memory bank forever, and the 3D hologram of the smooch sandwich swiped itself away.

'Can't you take your Sia band off for two minutes, Sarah-Jane?' Erica said from the other side of Phil's fat face. 'We're supposed to be having a human moment here.'

Sarah-Jane scoffed, a dose of irony heavy in her tone, for it was she who had often lectured Erica with such a complaint. But before she unclasped the band from her forehead, Sarah-Jane blinked, then scrolled her eyes to the left, accepting the holographic purple dot that had been blinking in the top right corner of her kitchen for most of the morning.

She sighed, then shook her head before squishing her cheek firmer against Phil's, trying to envelop herself back into the human moment. But by then, the moment had passed. Phil was staring down at the green fleck in the marble top of the kitchen island again, his bearded chin sunken into his neck, and on the opposite side of him, Erica's eyes were shifting, scrolling left and right, then up, and down. She was lost inside Sia, as she usually was, flicking through a holographic news feed.

'Holy fucking shit!' she spat suddenly. Erica leaned away from her father and stood upright. 'Zuckerberg and Ziu are staying in the same hotel in San Francisco tonight. Some reporters are speculating they're meeting up…'

Sarah-Jane's lips popped open.

'That's why the President's been trying to reach me,' she said.

'The President? Why didn't you tell me the President's been trying to reach us?'

Sarah-Jane subtly shrugged.

'It's just… y'know. There's just so much going on here and-'

'Birthday cake,' Phil said.

Sarah-Jane and Erica snapped back to the aged man in between them. His bloodshot eyes had refocused. And he was staring at the glistens of spittle he had added to the top layer of the chocolate cake. Sarah-Jane dropped her Sia band on top of the marble kitchen island, then proceeded to slap her two hands to Phil's jowls, twisting his face toward hers.

'Phil… Phil, can you hear me? It's Sarah-Jane. Phil… Phil, it's your birthday. You're eighty-five today. Erica's here, too.'

She twisted his jowls over his opposite shoulder, toward his daughter.

'Happy birthday, Phil,' Erica said. He was always "Phil" to her. Never 'Dad.' They were forever 'Phil' and 'Sarah-Jane.' Her partners. Not her parents. Despite sharing the same blood, they never felt like family to her. Not like Mykel had. Mykel was the only family Erica had ever known — or Aimee, as she was known back then. But ever since Aimee had transformed into Erica back in 2022, Mykel had been left by the wayside, forever wondering what had happened to the 'sister' he had grown up with in foster care who seemed to abandon him without notice or farewell. Erica had managed to track Mykel down some years later, but she only observed him from a distance, much like her biological father used to observe her from a distance way back when.

Her biological father subtly grinned.

'What were the numbers like last night?' he asked, his voice hoarse.

Sarah-Jane pushed a laugh out of her nose that almost became a sob.

'Great,' she said, nodding. 'They were great, Phil. Thirty million. The show got thirty million viewers last night.'

She was lying. *The Zdanski Show* wasn't even on last night. It hadn't been on for three months. It was on hiatus. Between seasons. But the last episode of the last season only managed to attract eight million viewers. Sarah-Jane didn't want to burden Phil with the boring subject of their dwindling viewer figures, however. Not when it was becoming more and more rare that Phil would become lucid. These moments were way too infrequent.

'Phil,' she said, squeezing his cheeks even firmer, making him resemble an oversized chipmunk, 'I need you to listen to me. Sally W. Campbell is President now. I need to talk to you about the Release Bill. I think she wants us to sign the Release Bill…'

Phil sniffed out of his hairy nostrils, then his chin fell back into his neck, and he stared directly downward, to the sharp points of Sarah-Jane's Manu Atelier ankle boots.

'Phil, Phil,' Sarah-Jane said, shaking his face, causing spit to spill from his lips. But it was too late. The moment had already passed. Phil was gone. Back to wherever it was Phil spent most of his time these days.

Erica sighed, stutteringly and shakily, as a chill ran through her. Then she shook her head out of her reality and began to move her eyes to the left, then downward before blinking them twice.

'Okay… well, let's… let's call the President back,' she said.

'Oh, do we really need to deal with all of this right now?' Sarah-Jane sighed.

'Sarah-Jane,' Erica said over her father's balding head—a head she had begun to notice was producing an elongated fresh liver spot every time she peered at it. 'If Zuckerberg and Ziu are meeting, this is fucking huge.'

'It's just… with Phil and everything else… it just seems now is not an appropriate time.'

'There's never been a more appropriate time,' Erica said. 'Sia, call the President and AirDrop it to Sarah-Jane.'

The trill of a ringtone sounded as Sarah-Jane reached onto the marble kitchen island to retrieve her Sia band. When she clasped it to her forehead the ringtone eventually cut and a 3D hologram of an overly tanned middle-aged man, wearing a sharp lemon-colored three-piece suit appeared on the opposite side of their kitchen island. Kyle Borrowland—the President's squirm-inducing communications director was beaming his usual cheesy grin.

'Miss Zdanski,' he said, nodding at Sarah-Jane. 'Miss Murphy.' He pivoted to nod at Erica.

'President Campbell has been trying to reach me, Kyle,' Sarah-Jane said.

'She certainly has. Allow me to get her on the line right away for you,' he replied.

Kyle bowed, then his hologram blinked away. Sarah-Jane and Erica stood motionless, staring at the far side of the kitchen island, waiting on the President to appear where Kyle had just appeared. Between them, Phil's head was hanging low, a string of drool stretching from his bottom lip. When the President blinked on in front of them, she was wearing a purple microsilk North West-designed dress suit that seemed to glow in tandem with the sheen of her flawless brown skin.

'Sarah-Jane, thanks for getting back to me… eventually,' the President said.

'All due respect, Madam President, but I'm a little tied up here at the moment,' Sarah-Jane replied.

'I know. I'm sorry to hear about Phil. Can't be easy for you… How's he doing?'

'Worse every day,' Erica said, being her usual blunt self. 'Hard to believe six months ago he was so normal, and then… it just takes hold.'

'I know. I've been through Locked-in Dementia with my foster father,' the President said. 'He was cognitive one day. Then the next day his dementia started to take hold and, before we knew it, he just fell silent. Insular. As if all that was happening in his world was happening inside his own head.' Sarah-Jane pursed her lips, then pushed a knuckle into her throbbing temple. 'I wish I could give you a hug,' the President said.

'Me too,' Sarah-Jane replied. They both reached their arms out and wrapped them around thin air for a silent second.

'So, is it true?' Erica decided to ask, swerving through the niceties and driving straight toward her reason for the call. 'Are Zuckerberg and Ziu meeting each other in San Francisco tonight?'

The President nodded once.

'We believe they've met twice over the past month,' she said. 'Max Zuckerberg has pursued Sterling Ziu ever since my inauguration and we now believe he has persuaded Ziu to sign the Release Bill. Which means that all humanity needs right now is you… you, Sarah-Jane. Your signature. If you sign the Release Bill, we can take America out of this mess.'

MADISON MONROE

America's a mess.

That's what I wanna say.

But I won't.

I can't.

Not out loud.

Not to them.

Not to freshmen.

I'm not supposed to share my personal opinion with students according to the contract I signed with the college. My opinion would be considered too "radical" by the powers that be anyway. Even if my opinion is accurate. I know it's accurate. I saw the mess coming a mile off. We all did. We just did fuck all about it… We still do fuck all about it.

I glance up at the nine heads dotted sporadically around the rows of empty benches, each of them staring blankly forward, their fingers tip-tapping against thin air. Only one student's here in person. The other eight are holograms… likely sitting up in their beds.

'Okay, final minute,' I shout at them. The one student who's here — Neve — looks up at me. And smiles. So, I wink back at her. The rest of them don't bother to acknowledge my shout-out. It's a trend I've noticed in holographic students. It's actually a trend I've considered measuring and writing in an academic essay. If only I could find the time to give a shit about education anymore.

I flick my eyes over my students' heads toward the stained ceiling of my lecture room in anticipation of the pulse of a yellow circle. Thoughts of a yellow circle pulsing inside my Sia have been making my stomach roll for the past forty-seven hours—which is one hour shy of the deadline they said they'd be in touch if my bid was accepted. I've been feeling petrified since I placed that bid. Even though I thought it through for three long months before deciding to place it. But I only did it because I was desperate; desperate to get away from my own mess; from my own misery. Sometimes I feel that I hold such a strong belief that America is miserable just because I, myself, am miserable. As if I can only view the world around me through the haze of my own desperation, my own depression.

'Okay; and fingers stop!' I shout.

Three of them glance up at me. So, I pause, taking the time to click the roof of my mouth with my tongue… until all nine students are glancing up at me and their fingers have stopped tip-tapping against thin air. Then I clasp my hands and take one step forward to the marker in front of my desk, like the obedient robot I've been trained to be.

'When you go home this evening… although,' I push a laugh out of my nose, 'most of you are already at home, but… when you have time this evening, what I want you to do is this… read over the news report you have just spent the last twenty minutes typing up and ask yourself the five Ws and one H. What are the five Ws and one H?'

Neve's hand shoots up. None of the holograms bother to attempt an answer. That's no surprise.

'The What. The Where. The Who. The When. The Why. And the How,' she responds back to me.

'Correct, Neve,' I say, nodding at her again.

'Okay guys, type these notes down under the news stories you've just typed up: *The What. The Where. The Who. The When. The Why. And the How.* And as you read back over your news story tonight, I want you to mark each of these five Ws and one H off your list as you come across them. Have you missed any of these? If you have you need to write it in. It's imperative that all news stories incorporate all five Ws and the one H. If you haven't missed any of these elements, congratulations, you've just written your first news story. But anything else you've written, other than to answer any of those five Ws and one H, is redundant. Insignificant. Bullshit,' I say.

All nine of them snap their heads up at me, even the ones at home in bed. That's one thing that hasn't changed. Students have always been more shocked by a teacher swearing than they are upon hearing the stark home truths about the news industry. Swearing is frowned upon by the college. But it's not specifically written in my contract. So, I skirt it every now and then. Just to get the students' attention.

'But, uh… if you're only answering the five Ws and one H,' the blond mop of hair at the back of the class whose name I can't recall because he never turns up in person, says, looking perplexed, 'how are you supposed to fill a story?'

'Well, you're not supposed to *fill* a story. You're just supposed to inform your audience of the story. And the five Ws and one H is all the story the audience needs. Are you talking about the padding? The insignificant details? The redundancies reporters we watch include, such as their own slant? Their own rhetoric? Their own opinion? All of that will be dictated to you by whichever news organization hires you in the future,' I say.

Neve chuckles. She's the only one who does. When I first started teaching six years ago, that line used to kill. It's only funny cause it's true. But it shouldn't be funny. It should be tragic. It's a travesty that we accept news organizations sharing their opinions.

I shift my eyes into the top left corner of my holographics to catch the time. 12:57. Then I blink my eyes to refocus, taking in my students again.

'Three minutes until the bell pierces our ears,' I say. 'Any questions?'

'Miss,' Neve says, shooting her hand up. 'All that's been talked about on the news recently is the story about the Three Zs meeting up. Do you think something big is happening?'

'Well,' I say, before scratching at my matted afro, pausing to suck on my own lips. I'm not hesitating because I don't know an answer to that question. Of course I know an answer to that question. I obsess about the answer to that question. I'm hesitating because I'm not quite sure how to answer it for her. For a fresh-faced freshman, six months into a four-year degree in Media that will lead her nowhere unless she is willing to compromise everything she stands for. 'I'll tell you what's more significant, in my opinion, Neve,' I decide to say. 'Not so much the Three Zs meeting up, but more the fact that Sally W. Campbell is President. The Three Zs simply wouldn't be meeting if it wasn't for her.'

Neve frowns her lips downward and nods her head, kind of impressed, but not totally convinced by my vague answer.

'Do you think, Miss Monroe, that the news is making America miserable? A lot of people are saying that in my socials. That Americans are miserable.'

I cough politely into a balled fist. Twice. Buying myself a moment to conceive my freshman answer to such a grown-up question.

'Maybe,' I say.

'Maybe?' Neve asks, her eyebrows knitting together.

'Well, the President has released papers compiled by three scientific experts that say the rise in depression and ailments such as ADHD and even dementia are caused by an addiction to technology.'

'But that's just three people's opinion, right?' Neve says.

I lightly cough again, then punch at my chest, trying to dislodge an answer that won't get me cancelled by the college.

'It's not the opinion of three people,' I say. 'It's the opinion of three experts, led by Professor Theodore Wickle. Besides, what you'll find, as this media course evolves, Neve, is that what is most important in news is not what is being reported, but what is *not* being reported.'

She squints at me. Shit. Maybe that answer's a step too far. For freshmen. For anyone, in fact. Anyone who doesn't want to know the truth.

'Wouldn't that make you a conspiracy theorist?' Neve says.

I laugh. I think I like her. Neve reminds me of a young me. A curly-haired, ginger, white me.

'Well,' I say, before sighing, because I'm not sure how far I should push this. 'Ask yourself, Neve, would the media report that it is indeed the media's fault that America is miserable?'

She turns her lips downward again and nods. Impressed. I think. I'm not sure. I'm not sure about anything anymore. There used to be a time I enjoyed stoking these debates within students' minds. But teaching these days is like tiptoeing around eggshells. Nobody wants to get cancelled. I can't afford to get cancelled. Literally.

'Do you believe the conspiracy theories then, that Sia makes us miserable?' she asks.

I sigh — a kind of half-sigh, half laugh — just as I'm placing the pens I didn't use today back into the satchel I didn't need to bring with me today.

'Well…' I say, before pausing, buying myself time to form my freshman answer. I know my real answer. Of course Sia has made us all miserable. Life was so much better before we had a whole universe worth of information and misinformation clasped to our foreheads like a third eye. 'I guess. I uh…' The bell rings, saving me from being brutally honest to an eighteen-year-old girl who is only here in hope of one day becoming another cog inside an industry I despise. The eight holographic students blink off one-by-one and suddenly it's just me and her. Me and the only student who bothered to turn up in person today. Neve. The curly-haired, ginger, white me.

'Maybe you can answer next class for us?' she says, swinging her bag onto the bench in front of her. 'About whether you think it's Sia that makes us miserable?'

I grin at her.

'Maybe,' I say.

As she packs the pens she didn't use today into the backpack she didn't need to bring today, a hankering to hug her consumes me. To hug anybody, in fact, who isn't a cat. But Neve throws both arms into the straps of her backpack and then spins on her heels to walk the length of the lecture room's light-gray carpet and then, eventually, out the swinging door and into the hallowed hallways of the college, leaving me enveloped in a silence I should be used to by now. But I'm not. Silence is an impossible energy to embrace when it is all consuming. Especially when it's all consuming all the time.

I think I might like her. Neve. She's made me think of me. The old me. Well, the young me. The full-of-questions and frowning-at-teachers-because-I'm-not-impressed-by-their-answers me. I smile. A smile for myself. For my younger self. The tiny afroed Black girl who wouldn't shut up in class. Then, as I'm smiling at myself, the yellow light in the top corner of my Sia begins to pulse. And I immediately drop to my knees and grab for the wastebasket—so the vomit doesn't splash the light-gray carpet.

'Holy shit!' I gasp, after the first heave of vomit splashes against the base of the bin. 'They've accepted my bid.'

BOBBY DE LUCA

The doctor takes one step back, peels the Sia band from her forehead and shakes her wavy hair at me.

'It's not Locked-in Dementia,' she tells me. I gasp out loud. Adrenaline rushing through me. 'I see no sign of peculiar activity in the temporal lobe, Mr. De Luca.'

Relief washes out of my mouth with another deep exhale. But I still feel a little confused. If I don't got LiD, why the hell do I keep forgetting what I walked up the stairs for? Why do I keep forgetting why I went into the kitchen in the first place? Why do I keep thinking somebody is in my house, when I am the only person who's ever in my house.

'Could it be regular dementia, Doc?' I ask her.

She shakes her wavy hair again.

'There's no specific way of determining dementia, but in truth, Mr. De Luca, I think you're fine. We're experiencing so much placebo and false information when it comes to Locked-in Dementia.'

'Placebo?' I say. I know I've heard that word before. I just can't remember when. And I can't remember what it means.

'Yeah, people thinking they have LiD just because they are hearing so much about LiD. I promise you, Mr. De Luca, if you had LiD, there would be signals in the temporal lobe. In the 3D holographic X-ray I've just examined of your brain; you are as intelligent as any sixty-year-old man I've ever examined.'

'Sixty-six,' I say, correcting her.

'Well, definitely the brightest sixty-six-year-old I've ever examined.'

I laugh the thick, gruffy, Italian-American laugh I inherited from my pops at her. But I'm still a little confused. If she had have told me today that I was showing signs of early LiD, then that would have made sense. But all she's telling me is I'm fine. When I'm not sure I am. I've always feared I'd get dementia. My pops got it. In his late fifties. He used to talk to me as if he was back in the 1980s, still head of the family—the Mafia Don.

'Hey, you,' he used to say to me from his hospital bed, not realizing I was his son, 'you go git them muthafuckahs, ya hear me?'

'I'll go get them, boss,' I'd whisper back to him knowing all of his Mafia minions used to call him 'boss,' then I'd leave his ward and spend the next twenty-three hours upset that I had to go visit my pop in the hospital for another hour the next day, where I would stand in the corner of his room in silence with him scowling at me, not knowing I was his son.

'I'm gonna get engaged, y'see,' I tell the doctor. 'I'm gonna ask my girlfriend to marry me. So, I uh… I didn't want to ask her to marry me if I was going to trouble her with a husband who had LiD.'

The doctor's eyebrows lift.

'Oh wow, Mr. De Luca,' she says, stretching a hand toward me to rub my shoulder. 'What great news. She sure is a lucky woman.'

I look down at myself, at my rotund belly and short legs, aware the doctor is just doing what she is paid to do—be considerate. And caring. And nice.

'Hey, Doc,' I say. 'One more question… is it true you're

supposed to spend three months of your wages on an engagement ring or is that y'know, one o' those myths?'

She laughs. She's pretty when she laughs.

'I wouldn't know,' she says, holding up her left hand.

'I don't know why you haven't been swept off your feet,' I tell her, flirting with a woman thirty years my junior. But that's what we do, us Italians. We charm our way through our lives. We pride ourselves on it, even me; even somebody with four chins, who weighs two hundred and thirty pounds.

I reach out to squeeze the doctor's shoulder as I stand, just like she squeezed mine, then I pick up my coat and get on my way, trying not to feel confused about why I keep forgetting stuff. I just need to listen to what the doctor said. It's probably placebo. Me just imagining I'm losing my mind, because everyone is talking about people losing their minds.

'Thank you, ma'am,' I say when I reach the pretty little thing at the front desk.

'No problem, Mr. De Luca, that will be eight hundred and ninety dollars, please.'

She pushes a button on the small machine on her desk and when she holds the machine up to my face, I wink my left eye twice, sending the payment her way.

'How's business been lately?' she asks while she waits on the beep confirming receipt of payment.

'Busy,' I say. 'April is one of our busiest times, but we're doing good.'

'Awesome,' she says.

The machine beeps and a red dot appears in my Sia, informing me the receipt has landed in my account.

Which is very handy. But it's also annoying. I hate wearing this Sia band. I prefer life the old-school way. The way it used to be before everybody strapped a third eye to their forehead like a fuckin' mug. I try to live without Sia, but it ain't easy. I still have an old computer in my house that I use to run my business, even though everybody I encounter along the way tells me I should be using the latest technologies. Ain't no catering business needs the latest technologies. All we gotta do is provide the best food we can. That's what *De Luca's* has been doing since my pop set up the business as a front for his Mafia ways back in 1988.

'Okay, bye, Mr. De Luca,' the pretty girl at the front desk says.

'Bye, sweetie,' I reply, before pausing because I really shouldn't call a gal 'sweetie' these days. Even if when I was growing up all the men called the girls 'sweetie.' But they say we need to treat women the same way we treat men. No pet names. No telling them we find them pretty. I don't mind times progressing. I just find it hard to keep up is all…

'Hey,' I whisper, spinning back around, 'Guess where I'm off to now?'

She glances up at me and smiles, even though I know I am distracting her from her work. It's just I want to tell people. I am so excited that I just want to tell everyone.

'Where's that, Mr. De Luca?' she asks.

'To a jewelers. I'm gonna buy an engagement ring for my girlfriend.'

She makes an 'O' shape with her mouth.

'Good for you, Mr. De Luca,' she says. 'Many congratulations…'

'Hey,' I whisper, leaning even closer to her so the patient sitting in the waiting room can't hear me. 'They say you're supposed to spend three months' salary on an engagement ring… is that true?'

VIKTORIA POPOV

I have never been to the capital city before.

Not in all twenty-five years I have lived in America.

I arrived in this country on the fifth of July in the year 2022. On a rickety plane with fifty fellow Ukrainians all fleeing from the war. They kept telling us we were the lucky ones. That is still the stupidest thing I ever have heard in all my life.

Three days before I arrived in America I was happy. I had a bit of fear. But I was happy. We didn't think the Russians would come to our little town of Shyskove. There was nothing there for them to take. But they didn't care that there was nothing for them to take. They only cared that they were killing Ukrainians under the orders of Vladimir Putin.

I was out buying groceries at the store when they arrived in three tanks, shouting at the people of our town before throwing grenades at them. They threw four grenades in total. Killing sixteen. One of those sixteen people was my husband. Another was my little baby boy, Ivan. Ivan had the same name as his father. He had the same eyes as his father, too. The same smile. He was only two and a half years old. He only lived for nine hundred days. That was his life. Nine hundred days. I counted all the days he had lived for while I was on the rickety airplane to America. And I tried to remember as many of them as I could while I cried. And cried. And cried. I wasn't the only one crying on that airplane. We all were.

It was the Red Cross who swept me up the morning after my Ivans had been blown up. I was just walking around my town, calling out their name—hoping that they would run up to me and hug me and tell me everything was good. But I knew even as I was calling out their name that they were gone. That their bodies had been blown up and that I would never, ever see them again. Three days later, the Red Cross pushed me on to that rickety plane and I was sent off to America—where everybody tried to tell me I was one of the lucky ones.

I think somehow that people telling me I was lucky helped. Because it stopped me from crying. Instead of being sad all the time, I started to get angry. Really angry. That is when the daydreams started. I kept daydreaming, and daydreaming, over and over again, about killing a Russian soldier. I just wanted to wrap my fingers around his neck and squeeze as hard as I could, until his life choked away.

When I got off the airplane at Boston Airport, I was brought to a shelter that had about one hundred other Ukrainians in it, all fleeing from the war. I stayed inside the shelter at the back of a church in Dorchester for three months before I went outside for the very first time. I would lie on the mattress they gave to me day and night. Awake and asleep. When I was asleep I would dream about killing a Russian. When I was awake I would daydream about killing a Russian.

I had only been walking around the streets of Boston for about two weeks when I saw him for the first time. I knew he was Russian just by his walk. But when I overheard his accent in a store buying cigarettes, I knew... I knew I had to wrap my hands around his neck. And squeeze as tight as I could.

So, I did.

I followed him as he walked, with my fingernails digging into the insides of my hands. If he had not walked into the alleyway, I think my whole life in America would be different. But he did walk into the alleyway. So, I followed him.

I walked up behind him and wrapped my hands around his neck without thinking. He was moving a lot. But I didn't release my grip. I couldn't release my grip. I was doing this for my Ivans. I squeezed and squeezed and squeezed so hard until his moving stopped. Then his body collapsed to the concrete, and I ran. I ran as fast as I could all the way back to the shelter.

Two days later, a big black car pulled up outside the shelter and four men dressed in black coats got out. I knew they were looking for me. I thought they were the police, coming to arrest the murderer, until I heard their voices.

'We're looking for a tall blonde woman, maybe five foot ten inches tall. You got a girl here matching that description?' I heard one of them say. He didn't look like a policeman. He didn't sound like a policeman.

When a Ukrainian at the shelter walked them to my mattress and pointed at me, I knew my life was about to change forever. I knew I could no longer be Elin Chenko.

'What's your name?' one of the men in black coats asked me.

'Viktoria,' I lied. 'Viktoria Popov.'

It was the first name that popped into my head. And now I've been living with it for twenty-five years. I have now lived as Viktoria Popov longer than I lived as Elin Chenko.

'Well, Viktoria,' he said. 'You're coming with us…'

TIMMY BUCKETT

'Hello Timmy,' Sia says, getting in the way of my news feed again, 'we feel you would find a Coca Cola Kiwi really refreshing right now. You have been walking for sixteen minutes and Coca Cola Kiwi is proven to quench the thirst you will be feeling within the next five minutes. Coca Cola Kiwi, for only three dollars, ninety-nine cents at the store one hundred steps from where you are right now, or, of course, you can order at Markt and have it drone delivered within five minutes. Coca Cola Kiwi—to reinvigorate, refocus and refresh.'

'Oh, fuck off,' I tell the advertisement.

It drives me insane, but I have to go through thirty seconds of ads every quarter of an hour on this fucking Sia band. I can't afford the ad-free version. It's an extra sixty dollars a month. And I just don't have that much credit.

I look around after shouting 'fuck off.' But people don't stare no more. When Sia first came out a few years back, it was a little crazy to see people walking around talking and shouting to themselves. But nobody bats an eyelid no more. Because everybody walks around talking to themselves. As if America is just one giant crazy-ass nut house.

'Hi Timmy, we've noticed you haven't played *Gregory Psaki*

Golf Tour in twenty-five days. Why don't you instruct me to pick your favorite course to play this evening when you get home?'

I step into the road, causing an electric pod to brake really hard. I love doing that. Because I know electric pods can't knock me down. They brake as soon as they sense a person walk out in front of them. I grin at the old guy in the front seat. His face is beet-red, and I hear him shouting for his window to roll down.

'What the hell were you thinking walking out in front of me like that?' he shouts at me.

'Fuck you,' I snap back at him, holding my middle finger up.

Then I hop onto the pavement on the far side of the street and continue my walk as Sia tries to convince me to get back into playing *Gregory Psaki Golf Tour*. I probably should have a game this evening. It's been too long. Way too long. And I guess I'll need to relax after this dinner. I'm dreading this fucking dinner.

'Okay Sia, download a round of eighteen at Augusta for me later this evening.'

'Download beginning, Timmy,' Sia says.

Then she pulses at the sides, letting me know the advertisements have ended, and I can continue scrolling through the news headlines.

That's what's genius about Sia. The holographics are see-through, so you can always see where you are in the real world while you are lost in the virtual world. All it takes is the squint of the eye to refocus us to the real world, the real streets I am walking down. Then a subtle refocus of the eyes lightens the 3D holographic for me and I can get lost in my AI.

'According to CSN,' Sia tells me, 'Max Zuckerberg and Sterling Ziu were photographed in the same hotel last night, sparking rumors that the two met up to discuss proposals forwarded to them confidentially by President Sally W. Campbell.'

'Oh, fuck off, Campbell,' I shout.

She's a witch. She's no Republican, that's for sure. I can't believe they allowed someone like her into our party, let alone on the ticket. Wyatt was just trying to get more votes. That's why he asked her to be his vice. I bet he hated her. With every fiber of his being. Just as much as I do. I am certain she had Wyatt killed. I'm working on trying to get to the bottom of it. She put that cancer inside his brain. I know she did.

I scroll my eyes… to the next story.

'President Campbell says she will address the issue of women having to disclose their menstrual cycle — a Bill passed by her predecessor, the late President Jarod Wyatt — but says she may not get around to reversing that Bill within her first year as president.'

I tut while I scroll my eyes down to the next story.

'Veteran actor Timothée Chalamet has been confirmed as an early guest on *The Zdanski Show* when it returns to our screens in two weeks. It is not yet known when the five-time Oscar winner will appear in Sarah-Jane's kitchen, but we have been told he will be one of the first guests of the new season.'

I scroll my eyes down again.

'The LA Lakers have failed to deny reports that they have made a bid of one hundred million dollars for the services of current Chicago Bulls point guard Harold Rumini.'

'Fuck Rumini,' I shout to nobody.

I blink my eyes twice, already tired of the news. It's boring these days with Campbell in charge. When Wyatt was in the White House, the news was always fun. He was getting rid of all the Mexicans and the Blacks—doing what he promised us he would do when he ran for office. That witch Campbell has put the brakes on those deportations, though. That's how I know she's no Republican. She doesn't care about America. She has no interest in America being the greatest country in the world ever again. It's people like her who make Americans miserable. She's the worst of the lot of them. Because she's a left-wing nut dressed up as a Republican. And I see that as fuckin' treason.

'Fifteen more steps,' Sia says to me.

I squint into the real world, to see I'm being led up a garden path. It makes me sigh really loudly. I'd rather be in Hell than at this dinner.

'Hey, baby,' Caggie says, opening the door. 'Come in… come on. My dad won't bite.'

I lean in to kiss Caggie on the cheek as I step into the house, and when I lean back I see him over her shoulder. He's massive. I've never seen a belly like it.

'Hello, Mr. Harlow,' I say, putting on my classiest accent.

He reaches his fat hand toward me.

'Is that a red Sia band you've got on your forehead, young Timmy?' he asks as he's gripping my hand tight.

'It, uhhh… it is, yeah.'

'A Republican, are you?' he asks.

'I, uh…' I feel Caggie's finger stabbing me in the back.

'As it happens, I am, Mr. Harlow, yes. Have you got problem with that?'

I notice him glare over my shoulder at his precious little daughter.

'Oh, hello, you must be Timmy,' a woman crows out as she steps toward me, her hands wide open. The fat hand lets my skinny hand go and the woman grips me in a hug. When she leans back I can see she looks just like Caggie. Only thirty years older.

'Wow, I didn't know Caggie had a sister,' I say.

Mrs. Harlow grins at me. As if I've just made her year.

'Oh, ain't you adorable?' she says. 'Come in, Timmy, take a seat around the table. A drone will be delivering dinner in the next ten minutes.'

POTUS. SALLY W. CAMPBELL

The Oval Office sofas are a rather uncomfortable and ill-fitting environment to host the nation's most critical meetings. I'd rather we were around a conference table, slamming our fists on it to portray our impatience and frustrations. Right now, I'm sitting, awkwardly, with my two hands wrapped around one of my knees, squinting across to the sofa opposite me at my communications director. I know Kyle Borrowland is a world-class spieler and has brain cells to burn. But I've never quite worked out if he likes me or not. If he rates me or not. But for some reason, even though he has the appearance of a car sales-person, he is the only member of the ex-president's staff that I implicitly trust.

He was Jarod Wyatt's pick for the most important role a president has to decide upon. Communications Director. The deliverer of the president's message to the masses. My Communications Director holds more power than my White House Chief of Staff, or even my Military Chief of Staff.

I kept Kyle Borrowland on when I got sworn in. I didn't want to appear to be extinguishing President Wyatt from the White House. I'm President by default, due to his death. It would have been a total misjudgment for me to clear away everything my predecessor had set up; especially when all I truly care about is the Release Bill. That'll be disruption enough for the American people.

'Our intelligence tells us that the American people would welcome such a move,' Borrowland tells me. 'Right now, seventy-nine percent of Americans admit to spending too much time inside their technology. They want out. We know that. We've known that for a long, long time. Even before Sia was invented. Once we begin to push the rising figures on dementia, on ADHD, on suicide, that seventy-nine percent will rise into the high eighties. The American people won't be our problem. The biggest issue is Congress. If we want this Bill to pass, we've gotta convince both sides of the room. Red and blue.'

'We will,' I say, reassuring him.

'You've always been confident of that, Madam Vice President... I mean Madam President,' he says.

'I've spent my entire political career toeing this line... trying to bring the red and the blue together. That's why they call me the purple president, right?'

'Yeah, but...' Borrowland pauses to scratch his temple. He always does that with me. Yet he never seemed hesitant with Wyatt. They were like blood brothers. Always in cahoots. Always in agreement. 'These congressmen and women, Madam President, they will say anything to your face. Then they'll vote the other way.'

'Trust me, Kyle,' I say. 'Congress will pass this Bill. I've spent the majority of my political career getting inside the ears of each and every member of Congress about the overuse of technology, going way, way back... way before Sia was even a notion inside Sterling Ziu's brain. Trust me; I know where Congress stands on this Bill. I could tell you how each and every individual member will vote.'

'You're sure?' he says, his brow frowning at me the way men only frown at women. I bet he hates it more that I'm a woman president than a Black president.

'I'm sure,' I say, nodding at him. 'Which means, given that Sterling Ziu and Max Zuckerberg had a very positive meeting the other night, all we need to do is convince one person… then America can get back to where it belongs.'

'She'll never go for it.'

'She will,' I say.

'With all due respect, I've dealt with Sarah-Jane Zdanski for over two decades, Madam President. She might look bright-eyed and bushy tailed. But she's the toughest nut I've ever had to crack.'

'Kyle,' I say, offering him the type of stifled smile we women only reserve for arrogant men, 'I've known Sarah-Jane a lot longer than you…'

He nods… awkwardly.

'Of course, Madam President,' he says. 'But with all due respect, allow me to approach her first. I know her weak points. I know how to seduce her.'

I scoff, waving my hand dismissively at him.

'Please, Kyle,' I say. 'With all due respect to you… no man has ever been able to seduce Sarah-Jane Zdanski, so…'

'No… what I mean is…'

'Listen, Kyle,' I say, interrupting him. 'I probably shouldn't share this with you, because I was passed this news confidentially, but given that you have clearance I guess it's suitable to fill you in. Philip Meredith — Sarah-Jane's right-hand man — he's out of the game. He's got dementia. And he looks locked in. When I holocalled Sarah-Jane the other night, I caught a glimpse of him. He's gone. I know he's gone. Because I've seen that look before. If Sarah-Jane is witnessing him going through what I witnessed my foster father going through, then she'll want to sign this Bill. She'll have no choice but to sign it.'

'Philip Meredith's locked in?' Borrowland says, his eyes lighting up. 'That's huge.'

'I know. It's why I've got to call Frank Quilly right now. I need to get moving. You're dismissed, Kyle,' I say. 'I'll holocall you in the morning for a larger-scaled update on how the American people will react to this Bill when we announce it.'

'I'll have all the sources up-to-date, Madam President,' he says, nodding at me.

I wave my hand toward the hidden door of the Oval Office, and Kyle neatens the pleats on his lime green satin trousers before standing. Then he spins on his heels like a disciplined soldier and walks toward the hidden door. When the door shuts behind him and I'm left in the echoey silence of the most infamous room in America, I stand up and step gingerly around the eagle on the blue carpet to reach the most infamous desk in America. I pause to suck in a breath, before snatching my Sia band from the Resolute Desk and slapping it against my forehead.

'Sia, call Frank Quilly.'

Sia's sides pulse, before my pilot's bushy eyebrows pop up in front of me.

'Madam President,' he says, tipping the peak of his cap.

'Frank, I need to get to New York City stat.'

'Air Force One is prepped, and ready, Madam President.'

2

SARAH-JANE SAT ON HER OVERLY LARGE DRESSING-ROOM CHAIR with her elbows resting upright on her makeup dresser and a curled knuckle rolling a tight circle into each of her temples.

The dressing room, that was originally a guest bedroom until Sarah-Jane began producing her own visual podcast from her home a quarter-of-a-century ago, was where the country's most powerful media mogul spent most of her time. Which was odd, given that the dressing room was the tiniest room in a penthouse that boasted nineteen other rooms. Yet the dressing room was where she felt most at ease. Most secluded. Most serene. She'd spend hours of her day sitting in the velvet pink sofa behind the makeup chair she was now propped up in, flicking her eyes left and right and up and down and winking and blinking. When Sarah-Jane was lost inside Sia, she was most often navigating the never-ending maze of news she, herself, had created. She lived, breathed, drank and ate news. News. News. News. And more fucking news. News from the east coast. News from the west coast. News from Washington. News from Florida. News from Europe. News from anywhere around the world. Breaking news had been the oxygen Sarah-

Jane had survived on from the moment she first set foot inside her local PBS network a half a century ago.

The migraine she was attempting to knuckle-massage from her temples was partly due to the imminent meeting she was due to host, but mostly due to Phil's dwindling health. As well as her shows dwindling viewership figures. Though she knew only too well that those two headaches were intertwined. If Phil was still cognitive, the viewing figures at the tail end of her last season would have remained as high as ever.

When she opened her marble green eyes, she squinted them into the lit mirror in front of her and began to study her aging face. When she finally removed her knuckles from her temples she pulled the skin taut at the sides of her eyes, trying to erase her skin of the growing web of wrinkles. She knew she looked great for her age. Of course she did. That was hardly a secret. For somebody three-quarters-of-a-century old, Sarah-Jane still looked to be in an age range that began with a five. Yet she hated that she even looked like her age may begin with a five, for she was no longer the most lusted-after news anchor in the country. Those days had long since passed her by thanks to an array of hot new anchors she herself had signed to her own media channels. Though not being the most lusted after didn't mean she wasn't the most powerful. She was. By a long stretch. Sarah-Jane Zdanski owned the majority of media in America. Which is exactly why her signature was needed on the Release Bill. The Release Bill was pretty redundant without three signatories. Those of Sarah-Jane Zdanski, Max Zuckerberg, *and* Sterling Ziu. The Three Zs. The most powerful and influential trio in America.

She sucked on the tip of her finger, then rubbed away a dry patch of skin above her angled eyebrow before huffing and storming her way out of the sanctuary of her dressing room, ready, but not ready, for the imminent meeting she had been dreading. After strolling the length of the long hallway of her penthouse, she stopped suddenly, to stare at the back of the nurse Erica had hired to take care of Phil. The nurse was casually sitting opposite his patient, his legs crossed, his eyes darting and dancing, and winking and blinking. Phil's bloodshot eyes, however, were glazed over and zoned out, and a bubble of saliva was glistening in the white and gray strands of his wispy beard.

'Wanna mop up his chin?' Sarah-Jane called out.

The nurse uncrossed his legs, then sat bolt upright before leaning toward his patient to brush a curled finger through Phil's beard.

Sarah-Jane audibly tutted before stepping closer.

'How's he been today?' she asked.

'Same,' the nurse replied. The nurse was nice looking. Not good looking. Just nice looking. As if he cared about people. Even though Sarah-Jane had noticed, more often than not, that he preferred to sit opposite his patient lost inside Sia. She didn't think him a bad nurse for this. She understood the reality. There was no healing Phil. Not really. LiD was a death sentence. A painfully slow and debilitating death sentence.

'Did he become lucid?'

'Sorry. Not today. Not yet,' the nurse said.

'Well, why don't you try to do something to make him lucid? Rather than sitting around watching whatever it is you're watching in your Sia?'

'Yes. Of course, Miss Zdanski. Absolutely. Yes. I uh… let me uh… let me go get one of his favorite books.'

Sarah-Jane tutted audibly again and opened her mouth to say something before a rattle of knuckles on the front door of her penthouse startled her. She paced down her hallway, fixing the blunt edges of her angled bob as she went and when she opened her front door, a very tall man, wearing a black suit and tie and black Wayfarer sunglasses nodded at her.

'Ma'am,' he said.

She stood aside, and another tall man — not as freakishly tall as the first but dressed in the same attire — passed by her and walked into her penthouse. Sarah-Jane looked outside the hallway of her home, up and down the long corridor that leads to her front door, before turning around on the spot and traipsing back down the hallway after the two black suits. By the time she had caught up with them in her famous kitchen, the two of them were squinting, blinking and winking their eyes.

'All clear,' the freakishly tall one said. Then they both stomped their black leather shoes into the large living room, where Phil was slouched in his favorite armchair, a fresh bubble of saliva clinging from his bottom lip.

'All clear,' the same suit said again. Then they shuffled off, to find more rooms to shout 'all clear' in.

When the nurse arrived back in the hallway with a battered copy of George Orwell's *1984* gripped firmly between both of his hands, he nodded at Sarah-Jane, then raised one of his eyebrows with suspicion.

'What's going on?' he whispered.

Before Sarah-Jane could answer him, an unmistakable figure silhouetted in the light of her doorway, causing the nurse to almost curtsey.

'Oh wow,' he said, 'Good morning, Madam President.'

The President nodded at the nice-looking nurse dressed in green faux-plastic scrubs, then strode past him, to make her way to Sarah-Jane so she could envelop her in the hug she had promised her the last time they spoke via Sia. They held each other for a long moment, breathing in each other's hair products, before the President leaned away to grin at the media mogul.

'Let's sit,' she said.

'How about here?' Sarah-Jane said, pointing her hand toward her famous kitchen island.

The President pursed her lips, then shrugged a 'why not?'

'You're not going to interview me, Sarah-Jane, are you?' she said, pushing out a laugh.

'Course not,' Sarah-Jane said, returning a laugh before perching her famous ass on to her famous high stool where her famous surname was flashing behind her in neon lime green. The President sat on the opposite side of the island, the picture-perfect view of New York City framing her. It wasn't the first time she had sat in that stool. Sarah-Jane had interviewed Sally W. Campbell seven times over the years. The first time back in 2033 when Campbell was running in local elections in Sarah-Jane's home state of Kansas. And most recently, just three months ago, two days after President Jarod Wyatt had lost his battle with cancer and his vice president had been sworn in as the fifty-second president of the United States of America. The second female president the country had ever had. The first female president of color.

Her presidency wasn't meant to be. Sally W. Campbell was as aware as anyone in the country that she had only been appointed Wyatt's running mate for the 2044 presidential race simply because she checked a lot of the boxes the polls suggested the American public were growing most interested in. She cornered the Black vote for him. As well as the female vote. And she had long stood against the brainwashing of modern technology—just like a growing majority of the popula-tion. She had risen through the Washington corridors while calling for social media to be more stringently regulated. Online surveys and polls were beginning to show that most of the American public supported her in this effort. So, Jarod Wyatt put her on his ticket. Just so he could ensure the keys to the White House. He would get those keys in November 2044, only to last a little over two years in office. He was diagnosed with untreatable brain tumors in October 2046 and passed away three months later.

'Sarah-Jane,' the President said, interlocking her fingers before resting them onto the cold flecked-green marble top of the kitchen island, 'I know we go way back and there's so much we could talk about. But I only traveled to New York today to discuss one thing with you.'

Sarah-Jane leaned into her marble tabletop, mirroring the President.

'I... I...' she stuttered, before glancing toward her open-plan living-room, to where Phil was slouched into his favorite armchair either listening to, or not listening to, the nurse reading from his favorite novel. 'Before we start talking about the Release Bill, would uh... would you like a drink, Madam President?'

'Sure,' the President said.

'Sia, bring us two glasses of nutrient water,' Sarah-Jane called out.

The platinum faucet in the kitchen began to flow, before a mini drone hummed and rose from the kitchen counter, collecting two iced-glasses from a freezer cupboard before running them under the platinum faucet and then flying them to the kitchen island, landing one in front of each of the two women.

When the women gripped their cold glasses, they each raised them toward each other, and mock clinked them from a distance. After taking a swift swig, the President placed her glass back down on the marble kitchen island and prompted the media mogul with a wave of her hand.

'The Release Bill, Sarah-Jane...' she said.

Sarah-Jane glanced toward Phil again, before turning back to the President.

'With all due respect, if you just wanted to discuss the Release Bill, couldn't we have simply done this over Sia?'

The President raised an eyebrow.

'Don't you think that'd be a little ironic, Sarah-Jane?' she said softly. 'Discussing decreasing the amount of technology we consume, literally over that technology? I want to do this in person. I want to look you in the eyes, Sarah-Jane, while we speak about the Release Bill. Not at a digital holographic you. But the real you. The human you.'

Sarah-Jane looked down at the marble top of her kitchen island while agitatedly flicking at the blunt cut of her sharp-edged bob haircut just above her left ear. The right side of her hair was cut at a sharp-edged diagonal that fell beneath the right shoulder. That was the latest fashion. A lop-sided, sharp, blunt bob. Not many could carry it off better than Sarah-Jane Zdanski, even if it was no secret that she was seventy-five years old.

'Talk me through it. The Release Bill. I want you to talk me through it,' Sarah-Jane said. 'I know it is a big secret, and you're not making it public until you ratify it. But I want you to talk me through the specifics of what's inside that Bill.'

The President sighed subtly, deciding in her mind to start at the very beginning to win over the most powerful woman in the country.

'My step-family were Irish,' the President said. 'They told me one day that in Ireland the news only ever came on at six p.m. That was it. That was when the nation got their fix of news. For an hour at six p.m. every evening. And it was all the news anybody ever needed. They had other things to do. Better things to do. They had lives to live.'

Sarah-Jane sniggered, before glancing toward Phil and the nurse again. In the midst of her laugh, she was certain she noticed Phil's eyes unglaze, then he leaned forward, and his mouth popped open.

'Phil, Phil,' she shouted. She stepped down from her stool and was striding toward the living room when the nurse first held up his hand.

'He's just yawning,' the nurse said. 'It's just a yawn.'

'Phil, Phil,' Sarah-Jane said, before stooping down and placing a hand on either side of her lover's jowly face, twisting it toward her. 'Can you hear me? Phil!'

Saliva spilled from the small gap between his chapped lips.

And his bloodshot eyes glazed again, as if he had already resettled back into his own internal world.

'It was just a yawn, Miss Zdanski. That's all,' the nurse said. Then he picked up the worn copy of *1984* again and recrossed his legs as he sat back into his chair.

Sarah-Jane twisted her face over her shoulder to stare at the President sitting with perfect posture in her kitchen—the New York skyline blinking pretty colors behind her. When she let go of Phil's jowls, she spun around to walk back, slowly, and almost zombie-like, toward her special guest. After she had sat back onto her stool, the two most powerful women in America each took a cold, heavy breath in unison while they glared across the famous kitchen island at each other.

'I've been there,' the President said softly. 'Desperate to soak in those rare moments my foster father blinked himself back to life. I kept consoling myself with the fact that the consensus tends to be that Locked-in Dementia is better than original dementia.'

'Better for the patient,' Sarah-Jane said.

The President nodded once, before taking another sip from her nutrient water.

'It's all because of Sia,' she said, as she was placing her frosted glass back down.

'There is absolutely no proof of that whatsoever,' Sarah-Jane snapped back. 'LiD is just an evolution of dementia. Diseases evolve. They've always evolved. For centuries.'

'I agree,' the President said. 'LiD is an evolution of dementia. But it's an evolution brought on by Sia.'

'There is no definitive proof that Locked-in Dementia is linked to Sia,' Sarah-Jane said, flicking at the curl of her blunt bob. 'Locked-in Dementia existed before Sia. Dementia has been a diagnosed condition in humans for over two-hundred years.'

'Dementia used to exist in one out of every one thousand people,' the President said. 'But today, in 2047, Locked-in Dementia is hitting one in five-hundred people. By 2050, our scientists say it will be one in two hundred people. That's how fast this strain of dementia is multiplying.'

'Those research papers are speculative at best,' Sarah-Jane said, folding her arms. 'And they're only the findings of a team of three scientists led by Wickle. It's too early to suggest Sia causes LiD.'

'It's common sense that Sia causes LiD, Sarah-Jane,' the President said, matter of factly. 'And you know it does. But it's not just LiD. Mental health issues are up eight hundred percent over the past decade. The line in the suicide graph is practically vertical. People are lonely. People are miserable. They're insular. Humanity is craving humanity, Sarah-Jane.'

'With all due respect, Madam President, that's all wildly hyperbolic.'

The President released a slow exhale, then picked up her nutrient water again and took another small sip, just to whet her whistle before launching into her planned monologue. When she placed the glass back down, she clasped her fingers and rested them on the marble top.

'When cell phones first arrived in our pockets at the start of the century, Americans were using them for a total of forty-two minutes a day. By twenty-ten, and the start of the smartphone, that dialed up to two-and-a-half hours a day. By the twenty-twenties Americans were on their phones for five hours every day... By the twenty-thirties, and the evolution to Sia, Americans began to spend nine hours a day inside their technology. But today we're almost always inside it, Sarah-Jane. Every hour we're awake. Sia only ever turns off when we fall asleep.'

'I'm aware of all these stats, Madam President. But people live inside Sia because they love living inside Sia. It's part of who we are now. Anytime you need directions, Sia leads the way. Wanna play any golf course in the world? You can do that from the comfort of your own home. Wanna have dinner with your best friend who lives on the other side of the world? Grab a chair. Wanna store memories of your life to be called upon anytime? All you gotta do is ask Sia.'

'I know the benefits of Sia, Sarah-Jane, but I also know about all the torture and loneliness and mental strain people are going through. We're losing humanity. We're losing the human touch. We're in the midst of a humanitarian crisis—and we need to do something about it as soon as we can.'

Sarah-Jane glanced again into her open-planned living room, to witness the nurse leaning nearer to Phil so that he could stretch a finger to his beard and brush away another bubble of spit, before relaxing back into his armchair, re-crossing his legs, and continuing to read from the battered paperback.

'You need to break down the Bill for me,' Sarah-Jane said, turning back to her special guest.

The President glanced down at her clasped hands and held her eyes closed for a silent moment. When she looked up, she wasn't staring at Sarah-Jane across from her, but over her shoulder, down the hallway where the two tall suits were standing by the front door. When she raised a hand and wiggled a finger, the freakishly tall Secret Service man walked toward her, gripping a thick, bound contract. He placed it in front of the President, then walked away, back down the hallway to stand next to his slightly smaller colleague at the front door.

'This…' the President said, staring across the kitchen island at Sarah-Jane, 'this right here is the Release Bill. It encompasses everything I have mentioned to you over the past two years since I became President. We reduce access to Sia to one hour a day—at six p.m; when folks have gotten home from their workday.'

'Just like your old pal used to get in Ireland, right?' Sarah-Jane said, almost pushing out a snide laugh. 'One hour's access to news every day.'

'Exactly,' the President said. 'One hour at six p.m. every

weekday. Up to five hours on each of the weekend days to enable advantages of the technology…'

'I'd lose billions,' Sarah-Jane said.

'I know you would,' the President said, tapping her finger-nails atop the thick contract in front of her. 'About nine hundred Americans will lose billions. Four million Americans will lose millions. But over four hundred million Americans — ninety-nine percent of this great country — will gain in every way. And all that's required for that to happen is your signature, Sarah-Jane.' The President slid the contract the length of the kitchen island, to where it came to a stop against Sarah-Jane's clasped hands. 'Sign it, Sarah-Jane. Sign it so that America can get itself out of this mess.'

MADISON MONROE

I blink twice, then roll my eyes up to accept entry into the room. Suddenly my tiny living room disappears, and I'm sat in a dark-wood setting — like an old library — in the middle of a semi-circle of strangers, all facing Harriett. I know Harriett. I've been in her room before.

She taps her finger and thumb together silently at me, noting my arrival while she continues to nod at the middle-aged man with the pointed mustache sitting at the end of the semicircle as he drones his melancholic monologue.

He's talking about losing his wife. Not to death. To Sia. While he pauses to press his forefinger and thumb into his eyes to hold back the tears, I glance around at the other attendees. All holographs. Some of them are nodding, in sympathy. Others are rolling their eyes. Either with boredom, or because they're lost inside Sia. They're likely contemplating blinking out of the session. Which is what I'm contemplating myself. Even though I've just arrived. I don't even know why I join these rooms anymore. They don't do anything for me. I'm only here because the doctor said I should attend a group session once every week.

Clause leaps up onto the sofa next to me, then onto my lap,

before purring her nose into my sweaty armpit. I begin stroking her while the mustache continues sobbing about his wife. I don't blame him. Of course I don't. I pity him. Just like I pity everybody in this room. It's just... this process... of having to holocall into a chat room and listen to everybody else's problems... It's torturous. For everybody involved. Including Harriett. I bet she feels the same way about her career choice as I do about mine. As if she feels hollow and helpless.

I sigh, slowly and silently, through my nostrils, and just as I'm about to blink myself out of the holocall, Harriett's head snaps toward me.

'Don't blink off. Not just yet,' she says, holding her index finger up at the mustache man, but staring at me. 'It's, uh, it's Madison, right? You're a teacher. You've been in my room before.'

I nod and smile at the same time. But inside I'm not smiling. I'm cringing. Because I can feel the entire semi-circle glancing my way.

'I have, yeah. I, uh, I...' I stutter.

'Go on...' she says, rolling her hand.

'My name is Madison Monroe. And I am depressed,' I say. 'I have been depressed for five years, and seven months, but my depression has really taken hold of me recently... because I live in fear that life is never going to get any better.'

A light ripple of applause stops me from elaborating any further.

'Thank you for joining us,' Harriett says. I notice the mustache man roll his eyes up and to the left, taking in the time. He'll be calculating that I arrived about twenty-two minutes late and then had the audacity to cut his time with Harriett short. I'm sorry. I didn't mean to interrupt their session. I just wanted to... well, I dunno what I wanted to do... I guess I was just trying to join in a group therapy session for my one time this week—just like my doctor told me I should.

'Teaching, must be stressful in the modern age, right?' Harriett says, nudging me along.

'Well, yeah… It is. Teaching is… well, it's chaotic,' I say glancing at all the blank faces staring either at me or through me. Some of them have sat back into their chairs, already bored by another sob story, even though I haven't begun telling it yet. They probably zoned out at 'teacher.' My story isn't new. It isn't innovative. It's far from unique. 'But it's not just the teaching…' I continue, 'it's well… I'm in so much debt. Student debt. One hundred and sixty thousand dollars of student debt. I was in one hundred and eighty-thousand dollars seven years ago, so… I guess it's going in the right direction.' I laugh sarcastically, only for it to be met with an awkward silence. 'I studied media, tried to get a job as a reporter, but… nobody would hire me. I was told twice that I wasn't pretty enough to be a reporter. So, I retrained, to become a college professor. Just so I could try to teach people how to do what I failed to do… to get a job in media.'

'A hundred and sixty K in debt, wow,' the mustached man's hologram says, before whistling through his bristles.

'That's how it is these days if you want to be educated,' I reply, shrugging one shoulder at him. 'The average student graduates college ninety-thousand dollars in debt. I just almost doubled that average. Because, well… I failed at my first audition, didn't I? I wasn't pretty enough.'

I notice two of the heads arced around the semicircle shake.

'Go on…' Harriett encourages me with another roll of her hand.

'Well, now I'm more depressed than ever… so I did something stupid, and I don't know… I already regret it. I think I do anyway.' I suck an ice-cold breath in through the gaps of my teeth and shiver before folding my arms and hugging myself. 'But most of the time I just think, well I had no choice. I had to do it.'

The mustached man leans forward in his chair.

'Do what?' he asks.

'Derek!' Harriett snaps.

'I'm not saying,' I reply, closing my lips tight and shaking my head.

I'd be murdered if I said I had a bid accepted in the Dark Web. They say if you enter the Dark Web you should never talk about the Dark Web. So, I don't. And I won't. Damn right I won't. I'm only here to say I'm depressed. To admit to my depression. That's what they recommend in these therapy rooms. That you face up to your depression before you can fight it.

I managed to vomit all my bile into the wastebasket. None of it splashed the college's light-gray carpet. The Blynq message was short and simple.

'Your bid has been accepted. Your untraceable Sia band has been delivered'.

When I got home that evening it was lying in my hallway; pushed through my letterbox.

I only know about the Dark Web because I know pretty much everything there is to know about the web in general. I've spent my adult life either studying media or teaching it. You learn more when you teach than you do when you study. As soon as I started to learn about the Dark Web, I navigated my way down there. Off grid. To where everybody is anonymous. It's scandalous that anybody can be anonymous online. But that scandal is about to earn me a pretty penny. The prettiest penny I'll ever earn in my life. I placed a bid for two hundred and fifty K. More than enough to pay off my student debt. If I get my hands on two hundred and fifty K, I'll be in credit for the first time since my Momma used to give me a five dollar note as pocket money back when I was a teenager. That's when we used to have notes. And not just a credit score that reads like a list of random numbers every time I check my accounts on Sia.

I'm pretty certain that if I get back into credit, then my depression will just float away. That's why I took three months to think it through, before I placed a bid on the Dark Web. I might have to kill somebody to earn that two hundred thousand. But that's the conundrum I figured out of the past three months. It's either kill, or kill myself. That's how low my life has sunk. Dog eat dog is where I've been led to. All because I got into a financial mess when all I was looking for was an education.

'Of course you don't have to say,' Harriett says, turning back to me. 'All we want you to know is that we are here for you, Madison. To listen to and support you through whatever it is you feel a need to share with us.'

'I'm not sharing everything,' I say. 'I just… you know…'

'Madison, listen to me,' Harriett says softly, her big brown eyes holding my usually shy gaze. 'Don't do anything you'll regret.'

'I won't. I'm not stupid,' I say, shrugging.

'Of course you're not stupid,' she says. 'You're a teacher. So… what is it you teach?'

I notice two attendees on the end of the semicircle have zoned out, their eyes flicking away, lost inside their Sia.

'Media,' I say, tuning back to face Harriett's big brown eyes.

She raises one of her unkempt eyebrows, then uncrosses her legs and leans forward on the edge of her seat, resting her elbows onto her knees.

'Fascinating subject, right?'

'There is no subject more fascinating,' I reply. 'Never has been.'

My eyes flick upwards as soon as I say it because a yellow light has just begun pulsing in the top corner of my Sia. I immediately tear the band off my forehead, ending the group therapy session, then I race to the kitchen drawer where I had left the anonymous Sia band that was pushed through my letter box.

As soon as I clasp it to my forehead, I see the red button throbbing in the top corner. A new email. I was told I'd be notified by a yellow flashing light on my original Sia when the email came in on my untraceable Sia. If I reply to this email, that's it. I'm in. I'll have entered the Dark Web, for a bid of two hundred and fifty K. I'll do it. I'll do whatever I have to do for that money. I'll even kill somebody if I have to. I've thought this through. Being in credit is the only way I can lift myself out of this misery.

I scan the email quickly. It's asking if I'm interested in a local Yoga class. I was told that would be the case. All I have to do is reply, 'I'm in,' and then, well... I'm in. Inside the Dark Web.

I don't hesitate, because I've thought it through. I've made my decision. I can't go on like this. Nobody should have to go on like this.

I tip-tap my fingers against the holographic keyboard in front of me, then sweep my eyes left, sending off my two-word reply.

I'm in.

BOBBY DE LUCA

Soon as I push through the door I feel as if I'm making a mistake. Maybe it's too soon. I haven't even met her yet. Not in person.

'Can I help you, sir?' a tall guy with sharp cheek bones asks, staring at my six chins from behind the glass counter.

I look back outside the store, then inside the store before taking my hand off the door and allowing it to shut—leaving me in the silence of a square of glass counters with the strange-looking guy with sharp cheekbones.

'I, uh…' I say, a little uneasy as I take three steps toward him, 'I'm hoping to look at some engagement rings.'

'Sure, sir,' he says, nodding. 'Allow me to lead you to our backroom.'

He moves away from me, sweeps a black velvet curtain to one side, and holds it open for me to follow him through. So, I do. I don't know why I feel so unsure. I had been sure of myself all the way over here; especially after the doctor told me I didn't have LiD. I promised myself that if I didn't have LiD I would ask her—ask her to become Mrs. Belinda De Luca.

'May I get you any drinks, a herbal tea? Perhaps a nutrient water?'

'Do you do a cappuccino?' I ask.

'Sorry, sir,' he says, shaking his head.

'Ah, not to worry then,' I say. 'All's I need, I guess, is an engagement ring. I'm gonna ask my girlfriend to marry me.'

'Congratulations, sir,' cheekbones says, nodding again. 'Have you been dating long?'

'A year,' I say.

'Lemme guess,' he says, 'you met online?'

I shrug.

'Uh… yeah,' I say.

'I'm joking… just a jeweler's joke. Every couple meets online.'

He walks away from me, his black satin trousers making a sweeping sound until he has disappeared back out through the velvet curtain, leaving me alone in a small, dark velvet room, sitting on a small, dark velvet stool.

'Mind me asking you a question,' I shout out through the curtain.

'Of course, sir,' he shouts back.

'This…uh… it's been troubling me. But… is it true you're supposed to spend three months' salary on an engagement ring?'

I cock my head to hear his answer. Only to hear silence. Until his satin trousers begin sweeping their way toward me. When his face appears through the gap in the curtains, his teeth are fully showing and his nose is scrunched up, as if his face is trying to apologize to me.

'Three months' salary is the norm,' he says. 'That is how most men who walk in here tend to calculate their budget for an engagement ring.'

I blow a large exhale out through my lips.

'I just… I just find that hard to believe,' I say.

'Well… listen,' he says, 'I can do a quick calculation now for you, if it would help. Like,' he says, 'how much do you earn per month?'

'Well, y'see,' I say shrugging, 'that's my problem. I don't get no wage. I… I run my own business. A successful business. And so, my money is all just turnovers and spends and spreadsheets.'

'Oh, congratulations, sir, what business do you work in?'

'Catering. We provide to high-end hotels, that sorta thing.'

'And how much does your business turnover every month, if you don't mind me asking?'

I look around at nothing but black velvet walls, then down at the black velvet carpet beneath my black polished leather shoes.

'About one point five mill.'

I notice one of his eyebrows is twitching when I glance back up at him.

'So, you wanna spend about four and a half million on a ring?' he says.

'Fuck no. Hell no. I've never had that sort of money my whole life,' I say.

'What about one point five mil?' he says.

'No. Wait. Hold on a minute. I don't have money like that… I have never had one point five mil to my hand ever. My business is rich. I'm just kinda modestly rich. I don't got no wage. Even if I was to sell my business, I probably wouldn't end up with one point five mil in the bank. I uh… listen to me. Maximum I'm spending is one hundred thousand dollars. That's it. Even that amount is… it's kinda… Well, it's kinda making me sweat.'

'One hundred K,' he says, tilting his head to the side and sticking out his bottom lip. Then he spins on the spot, sweeps the curtain open again and then disappears.

Fuck! What am I doing spending a hundred K? She probably won't even say yes. She's probably not thinking the way I'm thinking. But I keep coming back to the fact we're both making a decision to sell our businesses so we can go traveling the world together. We've agreed to spend the rest of our lives together. Literally together. Not through Sia. But beside each other. In real life. Traveling the world with whatever money we can get our hands on for selling our businesses. Why wouldn't she think I was gonna ask her to marry me?

We used to do business together... that's how me and Belinda first met. The two of us came across each other in a holographic conference room when we were looking at repackaging some of the food we make. After a while we evolved those business meetings to just the two of us. Then we started meeting over holographic dinner dates. Then we started having holographic dinner dates that weren't about business at all. We began opening up to each other like I ain't ever opened up to anyone before. We are both sick of the rat race of running our businesses, especially using all this technology we're all being forced to use. This Sia shit is melting everybody's brains. I don't want nothing to do with Sia no more. Belinda feels the exact same way. That's what we really bonded over. So, we're doing it. We're really doing it. We're both selling our businesses. Then we're gonna go to Italy, to France, to Greece. We agreed we'd start in Europe. But we're gonna travel the world. The whole world. Next to each other. Like our bodies will actually be next to each other. For real.

I look down at my huge belly while I wait on cheekbones to get back to me. That's when I notice Jesus glistening at me, as if he is begging for a kiss. So, I oblige. I kiss him. I like kissing him. I've been kissing him ever since my confirmation when I was a little boy. My pops bought me this medal in May 1993 when I was just twelve years old. I haven't taken him off of my neck ever since.

'C'mon, Jesus,' I whisper to him. 'Make her say yes.'

Then I kiss his little gold face.

'Here you go, sir,' cheekbones says, reappearing through the curtain, holding a black velvet tray. I drop Jesus back to my chest. 'I have brought you all of our rings valued from one hundred thousand up to two hundred thousand dollars.'

VIKTORIA POPOV

The men in black suits drove me in their big black car to a big house—bigger than any house I had ever seen. They made me take a shower and then gave me the best food I had in my life. We just stared at each other across a table while I ate. Until the interpreter arrived.

'Viktoria,' the interpreter said, 'these men need to know why you killed Boris Belbovic.'

I told the interpreter everything. I told him about the time I was happy in Ukraine. Then about the day I went to the store for some bread and some milk. I told him I heard the blast of the grenades while I was in that store. I told him I dropped the milk and ran out of the store. I told him I screamed. And cried. And dug my fingernails into the insides of my hands while I was calling out my son and my boy's name over and over and over again. Then I told him about the rickety airplane ride to America. And about the daydreams and dreams that wouldn't leave my head. I told him that one day I was walking around the streets of Dorchester when I saw a man who walked like a Russian. I told him I followed him. Into a store. Where I heard him asking for cigarettes in a Russian accent. Then I told him I followed the Russian to an alleyway where I wrapped my hands around his throat and squeezed and squeezed as hard as I could.

Boris Belbovic was a well-known Russian gangster. A gangster these Boston gangsters who picked me up at the shelter had wanted to kill for years.

They laughed at my story. And then they were hugging me and bringing me even more of their food.

'Could you do it again?' they asked. 'Could you kill again? For money?'

'Yes,' I said, without pausing. 'Yes I can kill again.'

They nicknamed me the Russian Hitwoman. Even though they knew I wasn't Russian. They told me that Ukrainian Hitwoman didn't sound cool enough, that I had to be known in their circles as the Russian Hitwoman.

Over the next seven years I killed twenty men for them. I would make four hundred thousand dollars as a hitwoman for the Boston Mafia. Twenty thousand dollars per hit. I didn't care that I wasn't killing Russians no more. I only cared that I had a new life. I would try to forget about my Ivans; forget that my hometown was bombed; forget that I used to be called Elin Chenko. I was a new person. I was Viktoria Popov. The Russian Hitwoman. Making more money than I ever thought I would ever make.

I learned English by watching television shows on TV. Then I got a job in a local drug store in Somerville. That was my front. My secret life. I would work eight hours a day in the drug store for fifty weeks a year just to earn the same twenty thousand dollars that I could earn with one phone call from the Boston Mafia. Sometimes I had four or five hits in a year. Other times the gangsters wouldn't call on me for a long, long time. Until they stopped calling by the early thirties simply because the men I was working for were either all dead, or in prison. The Mafia was dying out. By 2035, I was no longer a Russian hitwoman. I was just a clerk at a drug store, earning a few cents over minimum wage. I had lived two lives. One as a Ukrainian girl filled with hope who married their first-ever boyfriend and became a mother at twenty-three. The other, a hitwoman in Boston who killed so many people that I would be sentenced to twenty lifetimes in prison if I was ever caught.

I enjoyed both of those lives. But I am not enjoying this one. I have no friends. And no family. That is why I set myself up on the Dark Web. Placing bids. Only very few bids ever get accepted on the Dark Web. But I thought with my history as a Russian hitwoman for the Boston Mafia that I would get more jobs than most. But I didn't get any. Not until yesterday.

That is why I am now sitting on a Greyhound bus, heading for the capital.

I have no idea who I have to kill. Or where I'll have to kill them. All I know is that I had a bid accepted for one hundred thousand dollars. I have been thinking ever since I had my bid accepted that as soon as I kill whoever I have to kill that I will finally go back home to Ukraine. I feel I belong in Ukraine. That I will have a better life in Ukraine than I have in America.

'Hey,' I say, leaning forward on my seat. 'Is that it?' I nudge the woman sitting next to me. 'Is that it?'

'It is,' she says, nodding her head. 'That's it.'

It looks smaller than it does on Sia. In the movies the White House is the size of a giant football stadium. But in real life it is not very big at all. It's small. It's disappointing.

'Small, isn't it?' I say, turning to the woman next to me again.

She shrugs a shoulder at me.

'It's bigger from the inside,' she says.

'What? You've been inside?' I say. 'You've been inside the White House?'

'Sure,' she says. 'I work there.'

TIMMY BUCKETT

I was dreading that dinner. But it turned out to be pretty fun in the end. Well, fun for me, anyway.

I thought Caggie's Dad was going to have a heart attack when I took my red Make America Great Again cap out of my back pocket and plunked it on top of my head. I love my MAGA cap. They're so cool. So retro. It was fun watching him squirm. He didn't say anything over dinner at all. He just sat there, picking his food up with his fingers and throwing it into his fat mouth.

'Give me the nine iron,' I say to my caddie.

When I look down at the ball, I notice the club change in my hands. So, I pause to take a breath, then I swing back before clipping the ball as neatly as I can.

'Ball played one hundred and thirty-seven yards,' Sia tells me. 'Now on the green, nine feet from the hole.'

Cool. A nine-foot putt to finish under par. I think I've only ever managed to finish under par around Augusta once before. A couple of years back when I was playing this game all day every day.

'Play putt,' I say. The green looks like it's sloping left to

right, so I aim ten inches left and subtly swing my grip back…
then forward.

'Spunk bubble!' I shout, as the ball lips out of the hole.

I step forward to tap in the par.

'Seventy-two shot today, Timmy,' Sia says. 'Great round of
golf. Would you like to play another eighteen holes of Augusta?
Or perhaps another course from around the world?'

'No, fuck off, Sia,' I say. Then I fall back onto my couch and
move my eyes up into the top right-hand corner to catch the
time. Nine p.m.

Lonely time I call it. Where it's normally just me and my
thoughts until I fall asleep. I hate this time of the day. Which is
why I'm thinking of asking Caggie to move in with me.

I haven't had company since my old man threw me out of
the house.

It's not like I hadn't had a warning. I had. He had told me
for months leading up to the election that if I voted for Wyatt
then I was no son of his. When I came back from the voting
booth on the morning of November 8, 2044, my bags were
already packed. I actually couldn't believe it. I didn't think he'd
go through with it. That's the thing with these lefty radicals.
They preach that they're all about caring for the people. They
don't even care for their own.

I was only seventeen then. I stayed on my drug dealer's
couch for a few weeks and got involved in shifting some gear
for him. He was working for the biggest crime gang in Baltimore. Scar's gang. Scar's a big bastard. His shoulders are as
wide as he is long. And that scar that runs all the way down
through his eye until it reaches his chin is the scariest thing I
think I've ever seen. That's why I didn't wanna mess with
him. It's why I didn't wanna get involved in the first place.
Because I knew he wouldn't hesitate in ending the life of
anybody who messed with him. But I couldn't help myself.
Not when I was left alone with a hundred grand's worth of
gear. I thought I'd be rich if I stole it. So, I did. All of it. That's

why I came down here. To the capital. Because I was told that they pay more for their powder down here. I sold every grain of it on the streets of Washington within two months. And clocked myself almost all of the hundred K. Seven months later that money was all gone. But here I am, still in the capital two years on, because I've nowhere else to go. I sure as hell can't go back to Baltimore. If Scar ever caught up with me, he'd tear every limb from my body until I begged him to kill me.

I don't hate Washington. Not anymore. Especially now that I've met my girlfriend.

'Hey, Sia,' I say. 'Call Caggie.'

She left two missed calls on my Sia while I was playing golf. It's time I got back to her.

Sia pulses until Caggie blinks in front of me, her arms folded, her jaw swinging.

'Christ sake, Timmy,' she says.

She sounds mad.

'What?' I say, acting all innocent.

'Did you have to be such a dick to my dad?'

'He was a dick to me. He brought up politics. I just wanted a nice dinner.'

'Fuck you!' she says.

'Hey, that's unhealthy language for a seventeen-year-old.'

'No. I mean it. Fuck you, Timmy. I wanted that dinner to mean something. It had to mean something. And there you were with your fucking Donald Trump hat on, smirking.'

'It's not Donald Trump's hat. It's mine. He's been dead for almost twenty years.'

She huffs.

'Y'know… you tell me you're twenty, but you act younger than me. Like a fifteen-year-old. And I… I just can't…'

I roll my eyes. Not to take in the time. But because I hate this kinda drama. Fuckin' chicks always put this shit on me. S'why I can't hold down a girlfriend. S'why I'm already two seconds into this holocall and already thinking of reversing my decision —and not asking Caggie to move in with me.

'You can't what?' I say, tossing my hands into the air.

'I can't... I dunno. I can't be dealing with a boy for a boyfriend. Not now. Not with...'

'Not with what?' I say.

She uncrosses her arms and sighs. More fucking drama incoming, I bet. Fuckin' chicks.

'Look, Timmy. I begged you to come have dinner with my folks because... well, because I need you to get along with them. It was important for me to have them meet you before... well, before...'

'Before what?' I ask.

'Before we tell them... I'm pregnant, Timmy. You're gonna be a daddy.'

A gasp belches out of me as I sit upright on the couch.

'The fuck I am,' I say.

POTUS. SALLY W. CAMPBELL

The hum of Air Force One has always been a welcomed focus director. I've done a lot of my best thinking in the skies, lounging back on this tanned recliner. I couldn't believe the size of this aircraft when I stepped foot on it for the very first time over two years ago as a VP candidate. It's like a grand hotel that can somehow soar forty-five thousand feet above the earth. Jarod Wyatt had arranged for Air Force One to pick me up when he wanted to seduce me onto his ticket. I didn't need seducing. Even though I knew he only wanted me as his VP because the majority of Republican members were proven to agree with my messaging. Wyatt had once labeled me the 'radical center of Republicanism.' Eighteen months later he was wining and dining me in DC because he realized that adding me to his ticket was his guaranteed route to the White House. He knew it. And I knew it. What we didn't know, and couldn't have known back then, was that tumors were beginning to bubble inside his brain. He was dead within three months of his diagnosis. And suddenly 'the radical center of Republicanism' had the keys to the White House.

I don't know if I'm radical. And I don't know if I'm center. I just know that I'm a Republican. I've been an out loud and proud Republican since I was a teenager. I love America. I believe in America. I believe in America First. And I say that as woman whose grandparents were born in different corners of the Black world. Thousands of miles away from this very country I adore. The makeup of my DNA doesn't deter me from believing in conservatism. It doesn't deter me for favoring social conservatism or favoring unlimited economic possibility. I believe in the American people. I believe they are capable of building the greatest economy in the world. The greatest country in the world... It's just these people have been led down the wrong path. That's all. By a dire media. A media that divided them; that enraged them; that consumed them; that deluded them. I saw it all coming from the front row. I watched the news evolve from twenty-four-hour news channels into one hundred-and-forty-character tweets, before it evolved into twenty-four-hour rolling holographic headlines designed to subliminally corrupt the population's mindset. No context to a story was necessary anymore. Just headlines. Whether they were true. Or not true. There's no doubt news has made America bipolar. It made everybody make a big decision for life: red or blue. I decided I was red when I went to college and began studying socio-economic politics. I realized I believed in the conservative system. In putting America first. I understand that sounds insular and narrow-minded and selfish to most who haven't studied politics. But I am a conservative whose heart beats loudly for those all around the world. It's just that I don't think the rest of the world is America's responsibility. How can we think we can look after the rest of the world when we can't even look after ourselves? If we put America first, we can lead by example. That's why I've remained a Republican. I may not look like a Republican. But I am. And I have been since I began studying politics.

I hadn't intended to go straight into politics after I'd gradu-ated. I wanted to enjoy my life; take some time out to travel. To see the wider world. Only I didn't have the money after I graduated. Just heavy debt. And I sure wasn't asking my foster parents to fund my travels. They'd done enough for me. More than enough.

While I was graduating Princeton, the twenty-four news channels I had been brought up on a diet of were evolving into those one-hundred-and-forty-character tweets, and Donald Trump was being catapulted to the White House. I couldn't believe it. The fact that a cheesy reality TV star made it to the White House wasn't the surprise for me. The surprise was more that he won the Republican ticket. That's when I began to watch the political party I believed in sweep itself into a party that had lost the heart of itself; that had lost a grip on the realities of what our country was facing. The day after Trump took the keys to the White House, I signed up on the ticket at the next local elections in Kansas as a proud Republican. As a Republican who wanted to get a grip on the party I loved so I could help pull it back to its sensibilities. We are the party of Abraham Lincoln. Of Teddy Roosevelt. Of Eisenhower. Of Reagan. Of proud democracy. The Republican Party has helped advance the world more than any other global political party throughout the twentieth century. Then, for whatever reason, we dropped the ball into the madness pit at the beginning of the century. I couldn't understand how, right in front of my eyes, the Republicans transitioned from one of the most respected political parties globally into a right-wing farce and a global laughing stock... until one day it all made sense to me. It was in the immediate aftermath of winning the Kansas governorship for the first time back in 2028 that I figured out my truest ideology. I began to understand the politician I needed to be. The politician my mama and my sister would be damn proud of. I wasn't just a Conservative. I was a liberal Conservative. I've been called a walking, breathing oxymoron. But only in America could a liberal Conservative be oxymoronic. I am a progressive Republican because I believe in progress as much as I believe in America. I had learned the hard way that America was being oppressed by its media. So, I made revolutionizing the media we consume my central policy as a politician. I've been advocating for putting a halt to the technology that has been turning American people into robots for decades. All because I managed to figure out that the American people weren't the problem at all. The algorithms were the problem. They were poisoning people's minds. I knew that the day Donald Trump won the keys to the White House. But I could never be sure. Not until I drilled down into the statistics. It's essential we put a stop to it. But we can only do that if Zdanski scribbles her name at the bottom of that Bill.

She didn't give much away when I visited her in New York. But it has to be eating away at her. Every time she looks at Philip Meredith she will know what she has to do. She knows it's what's best for the people of this country. She's always known. She is well aware of all of the statistics, of all of the proof. She just chooses not to broadcast it. Why would she? That'd be like the NFL admitting they're responsible for the deaths of thousands of ex-players from head injuries. Such an admission would wipe the NFL out. It would be business suicide.

'Air Force One ready for landing,' Frank Quilly's voice says, 'Ten minutes out.'

I sigh, before sitting more upright in the tanned recliner, frustrated. The calming hum of Air Force One didn't direct my thoughts in the right direction during this short flight. I got distracted, by my obsession with getting the Release Bill signed. It's not as if I don't have a million and one other things to do. The Democrats in the House are consistently insistent that I spend more time fixing the fact that we are behind our target to meet Net Zero before 2050. They have a right to be insistent on that. We've been a terribly slow country when it comes to Climate Change. Though we're certainly not the only ones. It's not only the Democratic side of the House that is waiting on answers from me. The Republicans are, too. They're on me all the time about my inconsistent approval ratings, almost bullying me to reach out to the more right-wing arm of our supporters. The majority of Republicans were happy for me to take power in the aftermath of Wyatt's death. The polls told us that. But those polls were taken in the midst of a nation numbed by the loss of its president. The more the party members begin to peel back my ideology over the subsequent months, the further away from me they have wanted to get. Which is weird. Because my popularity is growing among the opposition. Fifty-three percent of Democrats feel I am a worthy president. Which isn't too far from my popularity inside my own party. I've learned that's just politics. Everybody and everything in politics is divisive. Because the news media makes sure it's divisive.

'Madam President,' Taylor says, marching into the President's Sky Office with Hooch by his side. They stride in unison, dressed in their perfectly-fitted black suits, toward my desk and when they stop they peer down at me. If they weren't tasked with literally protecting me, I'd be intimidated by them. Taylor is six-foot nine. Hooch a mere six-foot six.

'Yes, gentlemen?' I say.

'Just before we land, we've been tasked with informing you that the threat on your life is a Code Red.'

'Code Red?' I say, siting more upright in the tanned lounger.

'Code Red,' Taylor says. 'It's the highest code to warn of threat on a president's life.'

'Yeah,' I say, nodding. 'I know. Why am I a Code Red?'

'Don't worry, Ma'am,' Hooch says. 'Every president always flits between a Code Orange and a Code Red. It's nothing to worry about. We just need to let you know.'

MADISON MONROE

Ten students. Nine holographs. One real-life attendee. Neve. The only one with her hand up. The only one who ever puts her hand up.

'Why do they call right-wing people 'Sleepers'?' she asks this time.

'Uh… because right-wing people started calling left-wing people 'Woke',' I reply. 'Years ago… back in the twenties.'

'So, when did the left start calling the right 'Sleepers'?'

She doesn't relent. Her hand always up. Her mouth always motoring.

'Not until the late 2030s,' I tell her.

'Why'd it take so long?'

I smile at her. Then nod my head, impressed. I think she smiles back. But it's hard to tell. Because she's always cradling her chin with her hand, and her facial features barely move.

'Any more questions?' I say, clapping my hands together before moving my eyes into the top left hand-corner to take in the time. Two more minutes left until the bell needlessly pierces our ears. I've noticed I've been in a slightly better mood since my bid was accepted in the Dark Web. Princes0032 is my name. It's preposterous that you can be anonymous online.

And when you're off grid, with the GPS not picking you up, you can literally do anything and go anywhere without being tracked. I'm upbeat. But nervous. Kinda like the time I did my auditions for the News networks back in the day. It's a kind of nervousness mixed in with excitement that I haven't felt for years. Because I literally have no idea what's going to happen next.

I squint out into the lecture hall, pausing for any other hand to shoot up, other than Neve's. But nobody's hand rises. Nobody's hand ever rises anymore. The students are here. But they're not literally here.

'It's just you, Neve,' I say, smiling at her again.

She stares over her shoulder, sheepishly and slowly, at the nine holographic peers around her, then faces me and rests her chin into her hand again.

'You said you would answer the question I asked you last week today if we had time… about whether or not you think Sia is causing all of the misery in America?'

'Oh,' I say, pushing an awkward laugh out while I begin to pack the pens I didn't use today back into the satchel I didn't need to bring with me today, just to buy myself some extra seconds.

'Well, Sia brings a whole wealth of value to our lives,' I say. 'Look around you, Neve. Students are here from all corners of the country. We couldn't do this if it wasn't for Sia.'

She leans away from her hand and scrunches her face up at me.

'Well, yes we could,' she says. 'I bet when you went to college there were students from all corners of the country. But they didn't stay at home. They came to the college. To live near the college. And to study at the college.'

I squint back at her. This girl doesn't just have questions. She has answers, too.

'Of course,' I say. 'It's just, Sia allows us to be in contact with anyone from anywhere, right? That's the point I'm trying to make. Sia has progressed technology to a level where we probably just couldn't live without it anymore.'

'But, Professor Monroe, humans survived without it for hundreds of thousands of years.'

It's crazy how much she reminds me of me. It took me into my seventh year of teaching to finally find a mini me. It's such a pity that she's not pretty. She would make a great reporter.

'Well,' I say, 'they say humanity has advanced more in the past five years than in all five hundred years that went before it.'

'But... those advancements are making people miserable,' Neve says.

She's perfect. Or at least she would have been a perfect student. Back when I used to care about students.

'Doesn't that make you a conspiracy theorist?' I say back to her. Nailing her with the exact sentiment she nailed me with last week.

She doesn't smile. She just shakes her curly ginger locks from side to side, her hand still cradling her chin.

'But don't you think Sia is killing humanity, Professor? My neighbor's Grandma has Locked-in Dementia. They say Locked-in Dementia only came about because of Sia. I would just like your own personal opinion on whether you think Sia is making us miserable... that's all.'

'Wow. You don't relent, do you, Neve?' I say, pushing a fake laugh out of my nostrils. 'Listen, I think it's making me miserable, that's all I can tell you.'

Shit! That may have been too much to share. Even if it is my truth. But I'm not supposed to teach my truth. I'm supposed to teach the curriculum.

She's glaring at me, and it makes me feel uncomfortable, so I quickly glance around at the other nine students. A couple of them are tuned in, waiting for me to justify what I've just said. But most of them are flicking their eyes in all directions, lost inside their AI.

With the silence lingering too long, I have to look away from them. So, I spin on my heels and glance behind me at my gun. The gun the college gave me, housed inside a glass box that can only open with the press of my fingertip. There's a gun for every teacher in every room of the college. There's a gun in every room for every teacher in every school throughout the country. Even Elementary schools. I've only ever fired this gun once. When the college brought us to a shooting range a few years back. I didn't know what I was doing. But I fired a bullet through the side of the drawing of a teenager pointing a gun my way, so the authorities told me I was "fine to pass."

The bell pierces, relieving me of the strain of having to follow up on my admission of misery. Without looking back at the classroom, I can bet the nine holographic students have already blinked off. I can hear Neve, all alone, rummaging inside the backpack she didn't need to bring today, probably loading it with the pens she didn't use. But I don't turn around. I keep my eyes firmly on the handgun as though it's calling out to me. In fact, I've been hearing it call out to me ever since my bid was accepted in the Dark Web. That fascinating mix of positivity mixed with nervousness rolls around my stomach again. Then, suddenly, arms wrap tightly around my elbows, pinning them into my ribs. A hug. From behind. Engulfing my body with the warmth only a fellow human being can bring.

'I'm sorry Sia is making you miserable,' she says.

When she releases the hug, I feel the warmth flush away, and by the time I spin back around, Neve is waltzing up the light-gray carpet, swinging the straps of her backpack over her shoulders.

I think about calling after her. To thank her for the hug. But I don't. I hesitate. And then she's gone, out into the hallow hallways of the empty college.

I unclasp the Sia band from my head and immediately swing around to rummage inside my bag to grab at the untraceable Sia band. When I slap it to my forehead, I hold my hands to my hips and sigh loudly into my empty lecture hall. It takes a second for the Sia to blink on, but when it does, a blue holographic light immediately begins to pulse in the top right-hand corner. A Blynq message. Blynq and you'll miss it. I was told a Blynq message would come through today. I'd been counting down all of the seconds of Neve's end-of-session questions just so I could find out what I have to do.

I wink my left eye to accept the blue pulse and a dark figure blinks in front of me, dressed in a black hoodie, his mouth and nose covered by a dark burgundy scarf.

'Listen up, Madison Monroe and listen carefully because Blynq messages delete after they're viewed. You will have three simple tasks to carry out to earn your bid of two hundred and fifty thousand dollars,' he says, mumbling. 'The first task will be carried out tonight. Tasks two and three will be carried out next Thursday evening. Here's task one. Tonight, you will be visiting 1183 Dumbarton Street. Prove to me you can access this property. Walk around it. Scope it out. Tell me what you see.'

'Scope out a premises? That's it? That's all I have to do?' I ask nobody.

'But that's just the beginning,' the holographic figure continues in the Blynq message. 'Tasks two and three are going to be where you truly earn your two hundred and fifty K.'

3

ANNIE BRIGHTWATER'S SLIM FRAME STOOPED OVER THE TABLE AS she ever-so-gingerly dropped chopstick pinches of noodles into her taut, thin, lipless mouth. Annie always stooped. She was tall for a woman; tall and gangly. And thin. Almost stick thin. Although she was six feet tall, she weighed only one hundred and twenty-six pounds. She was so tall and skinny that she developed a slight hump on her back that worsened over the two decades plus she had worked for Zdanski Corp. But only little by little. So little, that those who knew her best hardly noticed her perverting posture. Sarah-Jane certainly hadn't noticed. The last thing Sarah-Jane ever noticed when she was in a room with Annie Brightwater was Annie Brightwater's posture. The only subject on her mind, whenever the Chief Operating Officer of Zdanksi Corp. was in Sarah-Jane's company was, of course, Zdanski Corp. And Zdanski Corp. only.

Since the corporation had been founded, less than a year after the launch of the very first *The Zdanski Show* podcast way back in 2022, Zdanski Corp. had evolved from a news media company run by the country's most-watched TV anchor with one podcast to its name, into the largest, most influential and most powerful media company in America. Zdanski Corp. soared in tandem with the popularity of *The Zdanski Show*, doubling in profits, then quadrupling in profits before it would surpass Comcast as the most influential media company in America, and the fifth biggest company in the country by the turn of the thirties. Two years later, Zdanski Corp. would buy out Comcast for two hundred and fifteen billion dollars. It had already acquired multiple media companies by that stage — both local and national — as well as over a thousand news websites. By 2040, Zdanski Corp. owned almost seventy percent of all media consumed by Americans on a daily basis and most certainly possessed a net value that mirrored its power.

It was the reaction to her debut podcast — in which she exclusively broadcasted the footage of the Benji Wayde killing that birthed such a monumental movement that it almost ignited a civil war back in the early twenties — that gifted Sarah-Jane her real power. Philip Meredith — being the media brains he is — or, rather, was — had the wise foresight to embed *The Zdanski Show* logo onto the footage that shook America. And so any time anybody from anywhere around the world wanted to view the murder of Benji Wayde online, *The Zdanski Show* would receive free publicity. A lot of the time, depending on which media was broadcasting the infamous footage, the logo would be blurred out. But that made it even more satisfying for Phil—for he knew all too well that every-body around the world knew exactly which logo hid behind that blur. *The Zdanski Show* logo—the logo of a family company consisting of a family of three who have never been a family. Just a company. A company worth seven hundred billion dollars. The biggest media company in America. The third biggest company in the whole of America. Behind Meta — now run by Max Zuckerberg. And DragN—the brainchild of Sterling Ziu—whose invention of Sia damned the Smart Phone to redundancy within twelve months. DragN were now reported to be worth one trillion dollars—the richest company to ever exist in America. While Meta — a company founded as the seed of an idea for a website called Facebook back in a Harvard Business School student's dorm room forty-three years ago — was currently worth seven hundred and fifty billion dollars. The second largest company in America. Just ahead of Zdanski Corp.

Annie Brightwater lived to promote Zdanski Corp. over Meta as number two. Zdanski Corp's market value was her infatuation. An infatuation she was well compensated for. Sarah-Jane, however, wasn't as obsessed about the company's market value. The figures were so bloated and hyperbolic in her eyes that she found Annie's specific obsession with being Number Two all rather redundant. Growing the company was never about the money for Sarah-Jane. It was all about the power. The control. It was Annie who was employed to look after the money. Annie had been Sarah-Jane's C.O.O. for almost all twenty-five years of the corporation's existence. She was her best-ever hire—after Philip Meredith, of course. Sarah-Jane had been filling with dread at the thought that Annie might retire soon, especially since she had creeped past the average retirement age of seventy some eighteen months ago. The dread remained, no matter how many times Annie insisted to her boss that the word "retirement" didn't exist in her vocabulary.

'If we can get your own show back up to the audience numbers it used to get, the whole brand will grow with it and we can overtake Meta as number two by the end of this year,' Annie said in her cracked, husky voice, before dropping another chopstick pinch of sushi into her narrow mouth.

'Annie, honestly, I'm really not that interested,' Sarah-Jane returned.

'In what?' Annie replied, 'in getting bigger numbers for your own show? Or for owning the second biggest company in America?'

Sarah-Jane shrugged both shoulders, then looked around the dimly-lit back corner of her favorite restaurant. The surroundings had barely changed in the thirty years she had been dining here.

'I'm not that interested in either, to be frank,' she said looking back at her wiry C.O.O. 'The numbers tuning into *The Zdanski Show* are insignificant in the grand scheme of things. Literally every single American views some form of media from Zdanski Corp. every day. That's where the real power lies.'

'But you're the face and name of Zdanski Corp. If your show is doing well, it benefits the entire brand. The entire corporation.'

'Annie,' Sarah-Jane said, pointing one of her chopsticks across the round table, 'I had the number one podcast for over two decades. The fact that numbers have fallen the past few months doesn't mean much to me. I own a company that's a lot bigger than just *The Zdanski Show*.'

'Phil would vomit if he heard you saying that,' Annie croaked. 'Phil was obsessed with the numbers.'

'Still is,' Sarah-Jane said, pushing a tiny laugh out of her nostrils. 'He's only become lucid twice this week. Both times the first thing he asked was, 'how are the numbers?'

Annie grinned as she chewed, and when she stopped, she tongued the inside of where her lips should be.

'Your show can do much better,' she said. 'You need a big story to start the new season next month. That's all. Get a great story for your show and Zdanski Corp. will soar even more. It could surpass Meta by the end of this summer.'

'Annie,' Sarah-Jane sighed, then tossed a chopstick into her bowl. 'The reason I brought you to Sosa Restaurant today, and didn't hold this meeting over Sia, is because… well, it's because what I've got to say is a lot more important than Zdanski Corp. being the number two company in America. The reason I flew you out to New York to be with me in person… what I'm about to tell you… it's monumental.'

'Holy shit,' Annie said, dropping her chopsticks into the bowl beneath her, causing a clang to echo around the dimly-lit back corner of the restaurant. 'This has got something to do with Ziu meeting Zuckerberg the other day, hasn't it?'

Her voice grew even huskier. In the silence that followed, Annie could tell by the somber features of Sarah-Jane's aging face that something rather shocking was about to come out of her mouth.

'The President has a plan. A radical plan. A plan that would lose Zdanski Corp. billions every year. Our value would drop significantly.'

'What the…' Annie paused to glance around the restaurant —only because she rarely swore, 'actual fuck?'

'The President has drawn up a Release Bill. She mentioned it to me and Phil a few years back when she was first put on Wyatt's ticket as vice president. She said it's imperative that America dramatically cuts down on its usage of Sia. She has all of the data to back up her argument. People are more insular. More depressed. More angry. Humanity's lost itself. She knows it. I know it. You know it… We all know it.'

Annie pursed where her lips should be, and the pupils of her round eyes dilated.

'And…?' she said.

'She wants to cut usage of Sia to one hour a day.'

'The fuck?' Annie shouted. Heads in the main dining room of the restaurant swiveled toward the Zdanski table where Sarah-Jane was leaning toward her guest, subtly hushing her. 'Sorry,' Annie husk-whispered back, 'but did you just say one hour a day?'

Sarah-Jane sat back in her chair and straightened the sleeves of her blouse.

'She wants the Three Zs to sign the Bill. To shut Sia down. To shut down the amount of media everybody's consuming. If the three of us agree to sign this Bill… the artificial intelligence we rely on will shut down for twenty-three hours a day. It'll only turn on between six p.m. and seven p.m. Outside of that hour, everybody will get their lives back.'

'But… Wait… How can? Hold on! You're not gonna sign it. Are you?'

Sarah-Jane shrugged, then picked up her chopsticks and retrieved a pinch of sushi.

'I dunno,' she shrugged.

'What? Hold on. Wait!' Annie said, confusion washing over her. She took the time to wipe the corners of her thin lips with a napkin, then laid it back down, 'tell me… tell me everything. What the hell is this Release Bill?'

Sarah-Jane slapped her hands together before leaning both elbows on to the table and then, slowly, her chin on top of the steeple her fingers had formed.

'It's called the Release Bill because Sally W. Campbell wants to release the American people from the technology. She wants us to get back to being human again…'

'Okay,' Annie said, her dilated eyes now squinting, her mind whirring, her index finger rolling, inviting Sarah-Jane to continue.

'Well,' Sarah-Jane said. 'My biggest problem is that I agree with her. I believe Sia causes Locked-in Dementia. I believe the increasing numbers of those suffering with mental health problems are because of Sia. I believe we are all losing touch with one another. What the President is saying is correct. We all know it. The media just doesn't talk about it because… well, that'd be the media shooting itself in the foot, wouldn't it?'

Annie shook her head, then reached underneath the table toward her North West handbag. Once she had removed her Sia strap, she slapped it to her forehead and her eyes immediately began to twitch and switch and scroll and roll.

'One hour a day, you say?' she muttered to herself, her eyes still darting. 'Jesus Christ, Sarah-Jane, you'd be squandering pretty much everything you control.' She blinked and winked, then tutted again. 'This is just a rough estimate, but Zdanski Corp. would go from being worth seven hundred billion dollars to around ninety billion. Not only would your money dilute, your power would, too. What the hell is President Campbell offering you to sign this bill?'

'Nothing,' Sarah-Jane shrugged.

'Nothing?' Annie husked.

'The saving of humanity, I guess,' Sarah-Jane said.

Annie surveyed the restaurant around her, twisting her head like an owl, then she eyeballed Sarah-Jane and stooped her wiry frame forward.

'Have you even considered what Phil would say to you right now? He wouldn't even entertain such a discussion—'

'Wouldn't he?' Sarah-Jane said, while chewing, her chopstick doing all the pointing again.

'Course he wouldn't,' Annie croaked. Her face was stern, her mouth thinner and tauter than usual. 'You said the President mentioned some sort of Release Bill to you as a radical policy when she was put on Wyatt's ticket a few years back. What was Phil's reaction then?'

'He laughed at the idea. Of course he did. He's Phil. He was obsessed with numbers even more than you are, Annie. But... back then, we never thought the Release Bill would ever become a reality, did we? It was so out there as a concept. As radical as radical gets. We knew Sally W. Campbell was only put on Jarod Wyatt's ticket to appease the growing number of people unhappy with the machines taking over. But never in a million years did we think Zuckerberg and Ziu would go for it. Why would they? They'd lose almost everything they have. None of us ever believed Campbell's radical bill would ever see the light of day. She was only supposed to be a puppet of a vice president. But... who would've thought Wyatt would get a brain tumor two years in... and here we all are now, with a liberal Republican in the White House, and a copy of the real-life Release Bill sitting pretty on the top of my kitchen island.'

Annie repeatedly rubbed her brow with her index finger, trying to massage all Sarah-Jane had revealed into her brain.

'Well, I guess you have your answer,' she finally said. 'If Phil laughed at the first mention of the Release Bill, then you know what he thinks of the Release Bill.'

'That was then,' Sarah-Jane said. 'That was before Phil got locked in. Sia took him from me. It melted his brain. Just like its melting more and more American brains every year. And growing.'

Annie sighed.

'Look,' she said, her head subtly shaking, 'This Bill sounds absurd. I… I don't know what to think. But surely Zuckerberg and Ziu aren't going to agree to this.'

'That's why they met last week,' Sarah-Jane said, before taking a sip of her Chateau Margaux. 'The word is Zuckerberg has persuaded Ziu to sign the Release Bill. Now they wanna meet me. They wanna get the three of us in a room.'

'Jesus, Sarah-Jane,' Annie said, washing a hand over her face. 'This would turn the world back on its head. You'd have to sacrifice almost everything you've ever built. How on earth are you gonna make that decision?'

Sarah-Jane placed her glass of Chateau Margaux back down to the red velvet tablecloth, then swiped a curled thumb across her bottom lip.

'I'm not gonna make the decision,' she said. 'Phil is.'

VIKTORIA POPOV

I got off the Greyhound bus at the next stop and e-scooted round and round the outside fence of the White House for two full hours. I didn't stop the entire time. I just kept scooting.

No matter what way I looked at it, the White House seemed small—smaller than it looks in movies or on TV. Margarite tried to convince me it was big inside. I guess she would know. She works there. As a duster. Her job is to walk around sweeping with different size dusters and brushes, every surface of every room inside the White House. There is a team of three of them. They start in different rooms every morning, then sweep their way through the President's home until their shift has finished.

I asked her about the presidents she had worked for when we got off the bus. She said President William Barkley was polite and would nod and smile at the staff as he walked by. But Jarod Wyatt was obnoxious. Which she told me means rude. It was a new word for me. Even twenty-five years later I am still learning new English words. She said she felt sad when Wyatt died. But she didn't really like him, so she didn't feel too sad. She does like the new president, though. She said Sally W. Campbell is nice, even if she thinks she is a bit radical. Americans use the word radical about politicians all the time. Maybe she is right about President Campbell, though. She is a little crazy. She hates Sia. I think if it was up to her, there would be no Sia no more. She wants us all to go back to the twentieth century. When I watch her in interviews, she is always blaming Sia for all of the problems. Sia did not cause all of the problems. Politicians like her did. They are the ones who have ruined this country. When I first moved to America in 2022, it was so much brighter than what I was used to in Ukraine. Now I can't wait to move back to Ukraine.

After I scooted around and around the outside fence of the White House I put my Sia band onto my forehead and asked it to lead me to the Clifton Motel. It was ten miles away. About seventy-minutes by e-scooter. The motel isn't very nice. But it's only costing me one-hundred and ninety dollars per night. It is the cheapest one I could find. But it will be all worth it. When this hit is done, I'll get much, much more money than that. One hundred thousand is a lot of money to me. Enough to get me back to Ukraine. So I can be Elin Chenko again.

I've been sitting on the toilet in the motel room for thirty minutes now, with my underwear and jeans around my ankles, staring into the top corner of my Sia, waiting on the blue light to pulse. Blynq messages do what they say they will do in their name. As soon as they are watched, the message deletes. Kinda like those old *Mission Impossible* movies Tom Cruise used to do when I was a child. It is crazy that Blynq messages are legal. Because it is a perfect way for anybody planning to do crimes to do their crimes. The message deletes forever. In the blink of an eye. It even says that on the advertisements on Sia—"Gone in the Blynq of an eye."

I was told I would receive a Blynq message when I arrived in Washington. But I've been sitting around my motel room for a long, long time now after walking all the way round and round outside the fence of the White House, and not one light has pulsed in the top of my Sia.

I yawn. Then I look over my shoulder and into the toilet

bowl to see if I've peed while I've been sitting here. I have. So, I yawn again, then I reach down for some toilet paper to wipe myself before I drag my underwear and jeans back up.

'Toilet flush,' I say.

Then I walk to the bed and fall onto it face first, yawning again. I am so, so bored in this tiny room. When I flick my eyes toward the time, I realize it is already tomorrow. I don't think I can stay awake any longer to wait on the blue pulse. I need to close my eyes. When I wake up, the Blynq button will be pulsing. And then I'll know all I need to know.

BOBBY DE LUCA

'Sia, turn the lights on,' I say as soon as I step inside the front door.

When I close it behind me, I let a deep sigh blow out through my lips. Then I remove the red satin box from my coat pocket and walk toward my desk to toss it on top of it.

I can't believe I just spent one hundred and seventy K on a tiny platinum ring that weighs about as much as a feather. It may have three pear diamonds on it, but the ring feels weightless. Worthless. It was originally marked at one-ninety, but cheekbones back at the jewelers told me he could knock twenty grand off this particular ring. So, I thought I was getting a bargain, until he popped the red box he had wedged the ring in into the palm of my hand and it barely felt like anything was in my hand at all, let alone a one hundred and seventy K gift.

When the box lands on top of my desk, I look around, my eyes squinting. I've done it again. Walked into my office and not known why I've walked in there. I keep doing this; walking into different rooms in my house, then forgetting why I walked into them in the first place. That's why I thought I was getting LiD; it's why I spent the morning in the doctor's examination room having my brain scanned.

Maybe the doctor's right. Maybe I'm just suffering the placebo effects of LiD, because we keep hearing about it all the time. They tell me LiD has doubled in the past twelve months, and that it's likely to triple over the next twelve months. No wonder we're all so fuckin' scared; all petrified we might be getting it, too. I need to forget about all the statistics, all of the noise that all of the news is spewing out through Sia. I just need to chill the fuck out. Take each day as it comes. I need to stop stressing about things I have no control over. I gotta get myself a life without Sia. Without noise. I gotta get to Europe. With the only person who thinks the same way I do. My girlfriend. My soon-to-be fiancée.

I waddle my heavy frame toward my kitchen, looking around; my paranoia still nagging at me, even though the doctor said I didn't have no LiD.

'Hey, Sia,' I say as I punch the buttons on my coffee machine to make myself an authentic cappuccino. I drink about eight of these a day. I can't get enough of them. 'Call Belinda.'

A glow of silver pulses around the edges of my kitchen, then it turns green before Belinda blinks in front of me, curvaceous and beautiful, even if I am probably alone in thinking she's beautiful. Belinda is heavy. Not as heavy as me. But heavy. And she has allowed her hair to turn its natural white color instead of dying it like most woman in their sixties do. Which is fine by me. I love Belinda because she has no airs or graces or any pretentiousness at all. She is who she is. Belinda Gascoigne. My girlfriend. My soon-to-be fiancée.

'How ya doin'?' she asks me in her cute Canadian accent.

I didn't tell Belinda I was seeing the doctor today. I don't want her worrying about me. I don't want her questioning the plans we have made.

'Good,' I say, smiling at her. 'How 'bout you?'

'Good, too,' she says. 'I uh... I can't stop thinking about Lake Como and Lake Garda and Venice and the Amalfi Coast.'

'Oh, me too,' I say. 'I swear, the best years of our lives are gonna be our final years,' I say.

She grins at me, then reaches out her two arms, so I do too, before we hug the air in front of us. We always do this. We've done it on every holocall every day for the past eight months; ever since our work meetings turned into dates.

'I can't wait to hug you for real,' she says.

'I'm gonna squeeze you until your eyes pop out,' I tell her.

She laughs that cute little chuckle and my heart flips itself over cos I am so in love. I have to be doing the right thing by asking her to marry me. I have to be. She won't say no. She loves me as much as I love her. Besides, we've already agreed we're gonna spend the rest of our lives together. She has to be expecting this; she has to be expecting me to get down on one knee…

She's been married before, though. Maybe one marriage through her life is enough. Her husband died young. When he was forty-one. She's been single the past twenty-four years. Which sounds like a long time to a normal person. But not to me. Cos I've been single my whole life. Not by choice. But because of my weight. I've been obese since I was eight years old. The mirror made me believe no woman would ever find me attractive. Not until about ten months ago when I started to think Belinda Gascoigne was staring at me through our work meetings as much as I was staring at her.

'I wish I could come see you,' I say.

'Soon,' she says, still hugging air.

I'm desperate to get to Vancouver for a hug. A real hug. A body-to-body hug. But work is too busy at the moment. In a few weeks, when my busy time is all over, I'll plan something. I'll catch a flight. I'll get to her house. Then I'll squeeze her so hard that the eyes pop out of her head, before stepping back, just so I can get down on one knee with the red satin box held in my hand. I can't ask her to marry me over a holocall. I know the world has moved on, and folks like to live inside their Sia, but some traditions should remain sacrosanct; like actually meeting your partner in person before asking them to marry you.

'Soooo,' she says, grinning at me as she lifts her head up from her air hug. 'I've got some news. My lawyer says that if I put my business up for sale, then it should sell within a month. So, I'm thinking of doing it next month, which means by June, we can set off.'

My heart flips the way only Belinda has ever made my heart flip. I can't believe I'm getting this lottery win so late in my life. Maybe I deserve it, for all my hard work at making De Luca's a legitimate company, and not just a front for my pop's Mafia ways.

'I can't wait…' I say, sniffling because I can feel a sob coming on. 'I can't wait to travel the world with you. I can't wait to toss these fucking Sia bands in one of those Italian lakes so we can just live in the real world. The actual world. I love you, Belinda Gascoigne.'

She holds a finger to her eye, pressing a tear back inside.

'I love you too, Bobby De Luca,' she says in her cute Canadian accent.

TIMMY BUCKETT

All she's doing is sobbing. I don't see why she needs to do that on a holocall. Can't she just fucking hang up the call, go cry in the corner of her bedroom and when she's ready to talk, just call me back?

I've been sitting watching her shoulders shake up and down for the past ten minutes. I'm bored. But I'm also fucking furious.

How did she let this happen?

She shouted at me when I told her she had to get rid of it. I don't wanna be a dad. I can barely look after myself.

'You can't just get an abortion,' she yelled.

'Yeah, you can. In California. It's legal in California,' I told her.

And then she sat in the corner of her bedroom, put her hands on her face and started to cry. Ten fucking minutes ago.

I don't know what else I can say. I've said it all. She's not keeping that baby. She can't keep that baby. I'll make sure of it.

While she continues sobbing into her hands like a kid, I scroll my eyes through my socials, blinking my left eye twice, to mute it in case Caggie realizes that I'm reading the news rather than watching her shoulders shake.

We'll Find Proof Campbell Gave Wyatt Cancer, insists QAnon leader.

I sweep my eyes to the next headline.

Black and Latino Crime Rates Rise by 15%

I fuckin' knew it. Immigrant crime rates are always rising. Sweep.

10 Reasons Women Are Inferior To Men.

I wink at that one. Only because I don't mind reading articles if they're top ten lists or some shit like that. They're easy to read. They're just a headline followed by ten other headlines.

10. Jesus didn't choose any woman to be an apostle. Twelve men. Zero women. That tells us all we need to know…

I grunt a laugh out of my nose. Funny cos it's true.

9. Women are physically weaker than men.

'Are you… are you fucking scrolling through the news while I'm crying?' she says.

I wink out of my socials.

'No,' I say.

'You were. I could see your eyes, rolling and scrolling. You're such an A-hole, Timmy. I can't… I can't even begin…'

'Listen,' I say, trying to end her amateur dramatics. 'I'll pay for it. I'll pay for it all. The abortion. I'll get your flights. I'll pay for the surgery or whatever an abortion is…'

She sighs. A deep sigh. Her eyes look really heavy. And baggy. As if the pregnancy is already making her uglier.

'Timmy you work packing boxes for Markt. You don't have the money it would take to get me to California.'

'I do… I mean, I will. I'll get it.'

'You earn fourteen dollars an hour, Timmy. Minimum wage.'

'I'll get the fucking money. Trust me. Trust me, Caggie. I'll do it. I'll do it for you.'

'I don't wanna be that girl, Timmy,' she says, sucking snot up her nose. 'I don't wanna be the girl who had an abortion when she was seventeen.'

'What you wanna be instead…' I say, shrugging. 'The girl who became a mommy at seventeen? Look…' I say before pausing. Because I don't know what I want to say, other than she needs to get her ass on a fucking flight to California pronto. 'Me and you, I see a future for us together. I was going to ask you to move in with me soon. But… we can't enjoy our lives if we have a little shit running around our ankles, can we? How am I supposed to get a better job than packing boxes for drones if we are tied down to a baby? How are we going to have fun together if we are tied down to a baby, huh? Come on. I wanna have fun with you, Cag. I want us to enjoy being together. Not arguing. Not fighting. If we have a baby, hell, we'd be arguing all the damn time.'

She wipes her face with her sleeve. And suddenly the knot in my stomach begins to loosen. Because I can tell I'm winning her over. She's melting.

'But you're a Republican,' she says. 'You don't believe in abortion.'

'I ain't never said that.'

'Yes you have. You told me you stand for everything the Republicans stand for. They abolished abortions in all states but one.'

'Well,' I say, scratching at my hair. 'I mean, I am against abortions in general, but for desperate situations like this…'

'Every abortion is a desperate situation, you dumb ass,' she shouts at me.

The knot in my stomach tightens as I watch her face wrinkling, ready to sob again.

'Listen,' I say. 'Cag, I want to be with you. And you wanna be with me, right?'

She sniffs again, then nods her head.

'Yeah, of course I do,' she sobs.

'Well, there you have it,' I say. 'You can have me. Or that growing mutation inside your belly. Surely that's not a difficult decision for you, is it, Cag?'

MADISON MONROE

I was convinced I had remembered the address. But now that I'm in here, I'm not entirely sure that I do have the right place. There's nothing unusual in here... it's too... well, it's too *nothing*. Too boring. Too ordinary. I don't even know what I'm here to do. Though the hoodie in the Blynq message didn't say I was to do anything. I just had to prove that I could get in here. And I have. Sia helped me to get in here. Sia teaches anything and everything. Legal or illegal. The darkest, black corners of the Dark Web have an answer for any question. Even the sickest answers to the sickest of questions. That's where anonymity has led us to. Breaking into a home is an easy answer to find. I bet I have to prove I can get into this home as task one because I'll probably have to end up killing whoever owns this place. I know I'll have to kill somebody. That's what you have to do to earn a paycheck of two hundred and fifty thousand in the Dark Web. I wasn't being naïve when I bid that much. I knew I'd have to carry out something pretty dark. For me, it was kill, or kill myself. So, I chose this option. I chose to kill.

It's weird in here. Lots of dark-wood furnishings; a chunky dark-wood desk with a widescreen computer on it, and a huge arch-shaped dark-wood cabinet standing tall in the far corner.

It's pretty clean. And neat. Except for the pile of paperwork next to the wide computer screen. I don't want to touch any of it. Because the hoodie just said I had to make sure I could access this office and that I was to "scope it out." So that's all I'm doing. I'm scoping it out. I can read the top sheet on the pile. It's an invoice. From the Heart Hotel. For thirty-six thousand dollars. Wow. Just one invoice is thirty-six grand. I bet whoever owns this office is super rich. It makes me wonder who wants him killed. Maybe a jealous business rival. Maybe a bitter employee. Or his wife. Looking for the insurance payout. Though I could be wrong. Maybe this is a woman's home. The office is probably a little too neat to be a man's office. Though there are those framed photographs on the wall. Of men. All lined up with their arms around each other, smiling at the lens of the camera.

It looks kinda homely, I guess. That's what I'd call it. A homely office. I don't know what else to report back to the hoodie. Other than to say it is a homely and kinda neat office. I accessed it. Just like I was asked to. I "scoped" it out. There's not much else for me to do. Other than to look at those boring, old-fashioned photos on the wall, studying the faces of grinning men. So, I decide it's time to leave. I climb back out the way I came in, leaving not a trace that I was here, and as soon as I'm outside, I place my hands in the pockets of my dark bomber jacket, keep my head low, and begin walking at a slightly rushed pace. When I cross the street, I jog the length of the side-walk until I turn down the narrow lane that leads to the Potomac River. As I race across the cobblestone bridge, my heart skips with fright. I feel more frightened racing away, than I did breaking into that home. As soon as I have crossed the bridge, I skip onto one of the many narrow sidewalks that move away from the river. I don't know if it's the jogging or the adrenaline that is making me feel breathless. So, I stop, take my hands out of my pockets and stoop to press them to my knees so I can begin to steady my breath.

When I lift my head, I let out a soft, silent sigh, before pivoting like an owl, peering up and down the length of the desolate sidewalk.

'Sia, record a Blynq message,' I say when I realize all is clear.

A pulsating of silver waves web away from me and then a small red light blinks on, starting the recording.

'I did it,' I whisper. 'I accessed the office of that home. I got in no problem. Walked around for a few minutes. Scoped it out. It's uhh… it's homely,' I shrug. 'That's all I can say. It's a homely office. But, uh… that's it… that is task one done.'

I wink, to stop the recording, before sweeping my eyes to the left, sending the Blynq reply to the hoodie. When I put my hands back into my pockets, I dip my head down and begin walking for home.

POTUS. SALLY W. CAMPBELL

'We've six thousand soldiers stationed on the outskirts of Tehran,' General Tunstead says in his purposely gruff voice. 'We are ready to move.'

I look around the Situation Room. Kyle Borrowland is the only one here with me in body. The other eight are calling in from different corners of America. Different corners of the world, in fact. Tunstead is hollocalling from the outskirts of Tehran—his trigger finger, as ever, irritatingly itchy.

'Madam President,' my security of state says in the pretentious manner she usually addresses me.

'Yes, Vivian?' I say.

'General Tunstead says America is ready to move in. We just need your word...'

I slap my hands to my face. To stop myself from saying what I want to say: That America shouldn't be moving in anywhere. But I can't say that. Not out loud. Not in front of a war cabinet Jarod Wyatt handpicked specifically to assert our authority as a military force around the world. Vivian is right to be squinting at me and pretentiously calling out my hesitancy. I'm aware I've been hesitating on this issue. I've been daydreaming. I've spent my life daydreaming. Daydreaming about better days.

Daydreaming about a healthy, wealthy, happy America. So… with my daydreams on the edge of becoming a reality, why would I be bothered about America going to war in Iran again, when America has its own self-inflicted war to win.

'This conflict with Iran has been going on for nearly half a century,' I say through my hands. 'How has it gotten this far?'

Through the cracks in my fingers I see Vivian shrug. So, does Kyle Borrowland. When I remove my hands and glance at the General's hologram opposite me, he doesn't even bother to shrug. He opts to sit still, breathing heavily through his hairy nostrils. I would love to tell him that I feel our foreign policies have been a joke throughout my lifetime. That America is way too obsessed with being viewed as the biggest guy in the gym. Who has ever been impressed by the biggest guy in the gym? Everyone thinks the biggest guy in the gym is the most insecure guy in the gym.

'When do you need a final decision, General Tunstead?' I ask.

'Ideally in forty-eight seconds, but forty-eight hours would be our limit,' he says. 'We'd have to pull our soldiers back by then. The earlier you give me a decision, the better, Madam President.'

'Earlier the better,' I say, subtly smiling at him. 'I hear you, General. I will be in touch as early as I can… certainly within forty-eight hours.'

He lifts his bulbous chin as a response. He despises me. Of course he despises me. He's a Wyatt guy. The biggest, brutest, brutalist kind of Wyatt guy.

'Any other business?' Borrowland asks for me.

The General coughs loudly while he raises his hand.

'I have,' he says. 'Madam President. I don't wish to alarm you, but the threat on your life is in Red.'

'I've heard. The Secret Service have already informed me,' I say. 'But, uh… isn't every president's life threat a Code Red?'

'Well,' General Tunstead pinches his bulbous nose. 'Mostly

Orange. I just need to tell you through protocol that you have tipped into Red over the past few days. We're monitoring it. Everybody who needs to know knows. Rest assured.'

'I trust my life in your hands, and the hands of the Secret Service,' I say.

'Madam President,' the General says, nodding.

'Okay… dismissed,' I say.

The eight holograms blink away as soon as they can, and when they've all disappeared, I spin in my chair to face Borrowland. He is, as he usually is, almost slumped in his chair, as if he is screaming with his body language that he takes everything in his stride.

'What should I do about Iran?' I ask him.

He may be a Wyatt pick as Communications Director. But he's a good pick. He serves the office of the President. Not the individual. That's why I have kept him close.

'Why would you give Iran any of your head space,' he says, sitting more upright, 'when you have more important things to do?'

I love that Borrowland gets it. He knows America is in no state to tell the rest of the world what to do.

'You haven't heard anything from the Zdanski camp, have you?' I ask.

'Nothing,' he says. 'In truth, Madam President, my sources aren't aware of the Release Bill… the net is so tight. Only you and I, and the Three Zs know anything about this. When word eventually comes from Zdanski, it won't come through my sources. It will come direct from her… I'll know when you know.'

I slap my hands to my face again. I'm aware it's a rather rude act of body language, but I need to do it in order to think… to *really* think. I tap my fingertips against the strap stuck to my forehead to rid it of all of the noise.

'Come on, Borrowland,' I say through my hands. 'You're the

Communications Director. Your job is to know Zdanski... what's your gut telling you? You think she'll sign it?'

'I've no idea,' he says, sitting more upright. 'Nobody's ever been able to second-guess Zdanski. All we know about Zdanski is what Zdanksi wants us to know about Zdanski.'

I remove my hands from my face and slap them onto the conference table in front of me.

'Sia,' I say, relenting. 'Call Max Zuckerberg.'

4

THE IRONY WAS NEVER LOST ON DR. CLASSEN THAT HE HAD TO USE Sia to examine patients for LiD.

The doctor, overweight with a gruff brown-ginger beard, was standing in front of a slumped Phil, his eyes moving and scrolling as he studied a live 3D holographic X-ray of his patient's brain. Dr. Adler Classen — Austrian before he was American — was the neurosurgeon specialist at DC's George Washington University Hospital—a specialist on the ever-advancing evolutions of Alzheimer's and dementia. He had named, in a medical paper, a form of LiD as an "inevitability" six years before LiD was first diagnosed. He argued as far back as 2038 that some extreme marriage of ADHD and dementia would make itself known due to the unique and unfamiliar ways the human brain was consuming information on a daily basis. It was no surprise to him when a new strain of Lewy Body Dementia, where people began to get locked further inside themselves, began to multiply in diagnoses by the mid-forties and was given the sobering yet basic title of Locked-in Dementia. Sarah-Jane was as aware as most that not one of the almost ten billion humans on the planet quite understood how the mutation of LiD from Lewy Body Dementia occurred. But she also knew that very few, if any, out of the ten billion, understood more about this phenomenon than Dr. Adler Classen. Which is why she had paid, on six separate occasions since Phil's first diagnosis six months prior, Dr. Classen two hundred thousand dollars to fly into New York from Washington, DC. This time, however, she, and Erica and Phil, flew to him in DC on their private jet. It was worth it to disturb Phil, Sarah-Jane argued, to get him to Dr. Classen's facility—to an environment that might hold a fractional advantage to sustaining Phil's rare lucid moments. Dr. Classen's fee for this one-hour consultation wasn't shy of the two hundred thousand she usually paid him to fly to New York. Money bought the best healthcare practices in America. That had been the way since the birth of the American healthcare system almost three centuries prior. But this amount of money usually bought more than the vacant shrugs and shakes of the head Dr. Classen seemed to produce every time he examined Phil's brain.

'I'm afraid it's the typical shutting down most patients of Philip's age range experience when they are first diagnosed with LiD,' Dr. Classen said, his Austrian upbringing still evident in the pacing, if not the tone, of his accent. 'Philip's case is like hundreds of other patients of similar age that I've assessed over the years. Younger patients, they can stay lucid for longer periods. But patients of Philip's age, in their mid-eighties, they get locked in more easily, and they tend to stay locked in for longer periods of the day. By about a half a year after first diagnosis, we find that people in their eighties are normally locked inside for good, I'm afraid. Miss Zdanski, opportunities for Philip to become lucid are really few and far between. Maybe one or two times a day. For only seconds. Maybe a minute at most. I am so sorry.'

Sarah-Jane sighed as she glanced across the plush suite toward her daughter, as she sat with her ass perched on the edge of the red-suede covered bed Dr. Classen usually examined his patients on. He, meanwhile, was still moving and scrolling his eyes to study, further, the unusual patterns bubbling inside Phil's brain.

'There is unfamiliar activity,' he said. 'Two out of the three units of Philip's brain are working perfectly. As perfectly as a man twenty years his junior. But the temporal lobe, where the hippocampus is, is producing unusual stimuli. Unknown activity. But this is the problem we neurosurgeons face with this new strain of dementia. It is all so new, even for somebody like me. LiD is still in its infancy. Philip's hippocampus… it is sizzling as if it is burning. But why it is burning… I do not know. All I know is that when the hippocampus is producing the kind of stimuli Philip's is, then it is a sure sign of developed Locked-in Dementia.'

Sarah-Jane and Erica exchanged somber glances across the length of the suite.

'But what can we do, Doc?' Erica said, still perched on the edge of the red-suede bed. 'You say Phil can come back to us, for seconds, once or twice a day, but what can we do to get him back for longer?'

Dr. Classen blinked his eyes away from the 3D brain hologram to stare over his shoulder through his hanging brow at Erica.

'The usual,' he said. 'Try to get Philip's focus back to familiar territories. Read him his favorite books. Sit him in front of his favorite movies. His favorite TV shows. Have him listen to his favorite music from times gone by…'

'That's it?' Sarah-Jane said, dismissively. 'That's the expertise you're giving us? The same expertise I can get by asking Sia? Is this what I've paid you a hundred and eighty thousand dollars for, Doc? To tell me the same information I can find online?'

'Miss Zdanski,' Dr. Classen said, pressing a hand against the beat of his heart, 'LiD, I'm afraid, as I've previously mentioned, is still in its infancy. We need much more analysis and scientific research on brains just like Philip's to fully understand it. We need to learn why this lobe,' he stepped toward Phil and held his fingers to Phil's forehead, 'where the hippocampus is, is producing unusual and inconsistent stimuli—the type of stimuli we had never seen in a human brain prior to late 2044. We are probably, I'm afraid, two, maybe even three years away from having any purposeful research on this strain. I'm sorry, Miss Zdanski. But no evolution of dementia has ever multiplied so quickly. Neuroscientists are usually given much more advanced notice of evolutions in diseases like dementia. We get to analyze and research and test before the disease multiplies too quickly. But LiD... it's a brand-new disease for a brand-new generation of humans whose brains are evolving from the processing of way too much information.'

Erica stood up from the red-suede bed and took two steps forward in the silence that followed the doctor's morbid monologue.

'Dr. Classen, let me ask you,' she said, whipping her Sia band from her forehead, then holding it out; the band hanging like a slug from the pinch of her fingers, 'In your unbiased, expert opinion, is Sia the root cause of LiD?'

Dr. Classen nodded his head once, then touched, with the top of his index finger, his own Sia band clasped to his hanging brow.

'I am afraid we are still some years from knowing that as a fact, too,' he said. 'But... in my opinion, there is no doubt. The birth of Sia and the birth of LiD is almost the sequence... as if they are twins. Humans get locked into a machine almost every hour of their waking day and then suddenly a new aggressive form of Lewy Body Dementia — that locks its patients inside their own minds — just happens to evolve. That is no coincidence. Not when we learn cases of ADHD are up one-hundred and eighty percent over the past five years. Dementia is up two hundred and twenty percent in the same period. Depression is growing so exponentially that researchers can't put a figure on it, because a figure they put on it today, will have increased by tomorrow. Different strains of Alzheimer's are at an all-time high, also. Many mental health issues are evolving and multiplying. These mental health problems simply wouldn't multiply at this rate, not without the consumption of technology. Ever since the evolution of the smartphone some forty years ago, humans began using their brains differently. And you know what they teach us on the first day of neuroscience school, ladies? It doesn't take long for the brain to learn new habits.'

'If Sia was causing so many mental health issues, why doesn't the world know all about it?' Erica asked, her hands on her hips.

'Well,' Dr. Classen said, before producing a subtle, throaty laugh while turning to Sarah-Jane, 'you, Miss Zdanski, would know the answer to that more than I would.'

The plush suite fell silent again, save for a gurgle in the patient's throat. But when all three heads snapped their necks to face Phil, his chin was still tucked into his neck, and his eyes looked dead, as if they were staring not *at* the tiles beneath their feet, but *through* them.

When Dr. Classen turned back to face Sarah-Jane, her knuckles were rolling against her temples—something he had observed her doing on no fewer than six occasions in his company recently, but something he had never witnessed her do in all fifty years he had watched her on his television or on YouTube before she began to enter his home for the first time via live 3D hologram to deliver her show four years ago.

'What I must say is, I preferred watching you, Miss Zdanski, on TV, than I do in hologram,' he said. 'They were more innocent days. This…' he stabbed a chubby index finger against his Sia band again, 'is a magnificent humanitarian achievement. But it is killing humanity. Killing great people like Philip. Not many are more aware how many wonders Sia has done for science than I am. Right now, for example, Miss Zdanski, I am staring at a 3D model of your brain. It is just as beautiful as you are.' He laughed from his throat again. Then received, as a reward, a smile from Sarah-Jane. It was the first time he had seen that beautiful smile in person. But that was to be expected. Friends and family of his patients rarely smiled. Why would they when he was constantly delivering devastating news to them? 'But the simple fact is, despite all of this wonderful technology, humanity is better for not having it…' He smiled back at Sarah-Jane. Subtly. As though he were soaking in a moment he had fantasized about since he was a teenage boy.

'Who's he?' Phil grumbled.

Suddenly Sarah-Jane and Erica were on one knee, by his side, clutching at each of Phil's shoulders. Dr. Classen turned slowly to the patient, then rolled and scrolled his eyeballs, glaring at the 3D holographic image of the brain in front of him.

'Phil, Phil,' Sarah-Jane said, shaking his shoulder. 'Phil, it's me. It's me. Tell me, Phil. The Release Bill. Sally W. Campbell's in power. She wants me to sign it. What do you think?'

'No, no, no,' Dr. Classen said, his Austrian accent coming through. 'This is not how we greet a patient of LiD when they become lucid.'

Phil's eyes zoned out, and his chin tucked back into his neck —as if he were a toy whose off switched had just been flicked.

'But we only get him back for seconds,' Sarah-Jane said.

'This is why,' Dr. Classen said. 'Because you are asking him too much, too soon. He has barely become lucid before you are asking his brain to work. Give him time when he becomes lucid. Touch him. Smile at him. Play his favorite music… Then begin by asking him very simple questions. 'How are you?' What is your name?' Questions like that.'

Sarah-Jane and Erica stared at each other as they stood back up in unison.

'But… but will we get him back for longer, if we ask easy questions and play his music or whatever?' Erica asked, somberly.

Dr. Classen sighed through his nose, causing the tip of his thick ginger-brown mustache to sway.

'We have seen minor results that way,' he said, 'but in most cases, especially for those of Philip's age demographic, the patient may come back for just a few seconds, maybe a minute at most, then they just…'

'Get locked in again,' Erica said, finishing his point for him.

'Come on, Doctor,' Sarah-Jane said, her knuckle rolling against her temple again. 'You're the leading practitioner in the entire United States on this subject… Tell us. Tell me. What can we do to get Phil back for longer? There has to be something… something Sia doesn't yet know.'

'Honestly, Miss Zdanski, there is nothing. Not really.'

'Not really?' Erica said, one eyebrow lifting.

'Well, there is the Ripple Stimulus, but again, it works in very few patients, very, *very* few… less than four percent. And those four percent are usually a lot younger than Philip. The Ripple Stimulus is still in trial stages. And hasn't been fully worked through proper channels to--'

'Ripple Stimulus?' Sarah-Jane said, squinting.

'It is a tiny machine still in its infancy,' the doctor said. 'It stimulates the brain. But it costs a lot of money. Two million dollars just for one tiny hand-held machine. And there is a long waiting lists of hospitals and universities waiting to get the funding for one for further study—including right here at George Washington.'

'Get me one!' Sarah-Jane spat.

'I'm sorry?' Dr. Classen asked, scratching at his ginger-brown beard.

'Get me a Ripple Stimulus machine, I want to buy one.'

'No,' the doctor said, awkwardly laughing, 'they are not for the public market. Just for upcoming trials.'

'Doctor,' Sarah-Jane said, 'make a phone call to whoever Mister or Mrs. Ripple Stimulus is and tell them Sarah-Jane Zdanski wants to buy one of their machines right now. Erica and I… we'll wait outside.'

Sarah-Jane held a hand to the back of her daughter's lower

back and led her out the suite's sliding doors and into a bright-white lit squared empty waiting room decorated by rows of bright, glossy red-and-white striped painted chairs. When the doors slid closed behind them, Sarah-Jane tugged at the collar of her silk blouse.

'I need to fucking breathe,' she said. 'I just... Erica... let's talk about anything. Anything other than Phil. And Li —fucking—D.'

'We could talk about work,' Erica suggested, shrugging.

'Work?' Sarah-Jane sighed.

'Yeah, you're launching a new season in three weeks. We don't even have a launch show.'

'I thought you finalized the Timothée Chalamet interview?'

'Yeah, well. Yeah. We have Timothée lined up. He's a green light. But we're not launching with him, right?'

Sarah-Jane eyeballed Erica, staring into the beady round brown eyes she had inherited from her father.

'Is a five-time Oscar winner not a good enough launch?' she asked.

'Has it ever been?' Erica replied.

'There's never been a five-time Oscar-winning actor before, Erica. That's the point.'

Erica arched an eyebrow.

'Isn't a Hollywood star more a second show kinda guest?'

'Really?'

'Isn't that what Phil would say?' Erica posed.

Sarah-Jane scoffed, not because she was reminded of the one subject she didn't want to talk about, but from the pinch of guilt that was infiltrating her thoughts simply because she knew damn well that what Erica was saying was true. Phil would never have opened a series with a celebrity interview—whether the guest was considered the greatest screen actor of all time or not. Sarah-Jane knew she was sailing into the new Zdanski season blind—without the eyes, the ears, and the nose of her right-hand man. Nobody knew news like Philip Meredith.

Without his nose for a story, Sarah-Jane had, in the latter half of her most recent season, sunken into the tired category of a late-night celebrity interviewer. Her show had always been better than that. It was no coincidence that the audience numbers at the tail end of last season ran parallel in decline with Phil's diagnosis. For the final three months, *The Zdanski Show* hadn't been doing much of anything different than the other late night shows weren't doing: interviewing celebrities, attempting to create a moment that could fly viral across Sia.

It had become evident to Erica that Sarah-Jane scoffed more these days than she smiled. Her star had no doubt dimmed. She was grief-stricken. Her partner in business, in bed, in life, and in crime had been slipping away in front of her famous light-green eyes.

Sarah-Jane shook her head, trying to rid it of the stark image of Phil with his chin tucked into his neck and a string of saliva hanging from his beard.

'Maybe the Release Bill could be the story?' Erica posed. 'Imagine announcing the Release Bill on the first show back? It'd be the biggest story of all time.'

'Announce that I am giving up all of my power… all of my money?' Sarah-Jane pivoted to face her daughter, then crossed her arms under her breasts. 'Is that what you think I should do, Erica? Sign the Release Bill?'

The doors behind them swept open before Erica could respond and Dr. Classen strode out from between them, his brow even more sunken, his eyes blinking and winking.

'Miss Zdanski, can you please put your Sia band on, I just want to AirDrop you into this conversation?'

Sarah-Jane glared at her daughter, then slapped her Sia band to her forehead before a 3D holographic of a handsome, overly-tanned middle-aged man with a thick headful of salt-and-pepper hair appeared in front of her, grinning with blinding white veneers.

'Miss Zdanski, I am such a huge fan,' the tanned man said. 'I have been following your career since I was a little boy. I remember watching your very first show on CSN way back when.'

'Oh, gee,' Sarah-Jane said, batting away the compliment with a faux smile.

'Miss Zdanski,' Dr. Classen said, interrupting the tanned man's flirtations, 'this is Michael Guarguito, he is the C.E.O. of Knetickle—the company who own the rights to the Ripple Stimulus.'

'Dr. Classen tells me you want a Ripple Machine, yes?' Guarguito asked.

'Please,' Sarah-Jane said, a pitiful look plastered across her face.

'No problem,' Guarguito said.

'Really?' Sarah-Jane said, her mouth dropping open, her green eyes almost catching light again. 'I could have the money transferred right away-'

'No, no, you can have one for free, Miss Zdanski. Of course you can. You are Sarah-Jane Zdanski. I am such a big fan. Let me ship one out to you right away.'

VIKTORIA POPOV

I toss. And turn. And toss and turn again. Then I groan. And stretch. And yawn.

When I sit upright and bang my head against the wooden rail, I realize where I am… and why I'm here.

The Sia band I have strapped to my forehead awakens a split second after I sit up, and after a little pause, the blue light begins to pulse in the top right corner.

The Blynq message has arrived. My next step on the road to one hundred thousand credits. My next step on the road to becoming Elin Chenko again.

I wink at the pulsing blue light and as soon as I do, a dark figure appears in front of me, standing at the end of my bed.

'Viktoria,' he says. His voice is soft. Soft like you wouldn't think a man paying a hitwoman one hundred thousand credits would sound. 'This is a huge hit. But given that you are a very experienced assassin, we see this as a stroll in the park for you. We trust that you are in Washington, DC by now. You sure as hell better be. Because that is where your target lives. This coming Thursday, we need you to take out this target. We will let you know soon just who that target is.'

The figure blinks away. And so does the message. Never to be seen again.

I rub at my eyes because they are stinging me a little. They do that sometimes in the morning.

'Sia,' I say, 'what is the population of Washington, DC?'

'Washington, DC,' Sia replies, before pausing, 'has a population of nine hundred and ten thousand, five hundred and two people.'

Almost a million in the capital. I could be killing any of them. It could be Margarite, the feather duster from the White House. She's the only person I know out here. She was really nice to me when we got off the bus together. My target could be any of the crowd of people who were walking or scooting around the White House just like I was yesterday.

I scroll my eyes to my calendar. Today's Monday. Three more days until the assassination. Three more days until I kill the twenty-first person I will have ever killed. It is still crazy to think I have killed so many people. That's why I try not to think about it. The same way I tried for years to not think about my life in Ukraine. I am good at blocking out the past. Perhaps you have to be good at blocking out the past when your past is so full of tragedy.

I have allowed myself to think about my Ukraine again. But only recently. I try to remember baby Ivan's face. And my husband Ivan's, too. The harder I try, the blurrier their faces get in my mind. But I prefer thinking about them that way rather than look at my old photographs. I have never looked at my photographs. It always seems too difficult to look at them. But the more my mind tries to picture their faces, the blurrier they get. And now, with me moving back to Ukraine after this hit is done, I think I might look at their old photographs. It might be time for me to embrace my past.

I sweep my feet out of the bed and grab the kettle before walking into the small shower to turn it on. That's when the blue light blinks in the top corner of my Sia again.

I wink at it as quickly as I can, and the dark figure appears again, standing beside the toilet I sat on for over an hour yesterday.

'Viktoria,' he says. 'I know you are awake, because I know you've just viewed the Blynq message I sent during the night. Here is your mission. We need you to kill this person, and we need you to do it how a professional would do it. This needs to be the most precise hit you've ever carried out.'

He rolls his right eye upward, and an image of a smiling face appears in front of me.

'Holy shit,' I say, before slapping a hand to my mouth, making a pop sound. 'You want me to kill… her… *her*? How the hell am I gonna do that?' I ask nobody as I squint at her glistening brown skin in the photograph. I have never killed a woman before. I have never killed a Black person before.

The image blinks off and so does the message. Lost forever.

And I slap my hand to my mouth again.

BOBBY DE LUCA

I don't know why I pat down my pockets as if the box had suddenly leapt from wherever I left it and made it into my trousers. I am certain I tossed it onto my desk when I came home. But it's not there now. What was I thinking? Leaving a one hundred and seventy K box outta my sight?

I look under the cushions on my sofa again, then I begin spinning around the center of my living room.

C'mon, Bobby. Think. Think!

Fuck! I'm losing my God-damn mind. I really am.

I pick up gold Jesus from my chest and kiss his face again.

'C'mon, Jesus, lead me... lead me to where I left that fuckin' ring.'

I hear a creak... I'm sure it's a creak. Like floorboards. Or the door, maybe? I dunno. Or maybe I'm just going fuckin' nuts.

I walk out of my living room, and down the hallway toward the kitchen where I'm sure I heard the creak come from. And I look around, cocking my ear into the silence. Nothing.

Where the fuck did I put that box?

I try to play my afternoon back in my mind. And I remember I took the box off my desk after I had been on a call to Belinda... I pulled the ribbon, to open the box, then my secretary Janet holocalled me. We spoke. For about ten minutes about next Saturday's dinner. When the call ended, I sat on the couch for a few minutes, just to take the weight off. Then… when I thought about looking in the box again, it was gone… one hundred and seventy K gone in the blink of an eye…

I should be getting back to work, not walking around looking for a red satin box. It's not as if it isn't one of the busiest two weeks of the whole year. I have begun to step back from all of the pressures of work over the past few months, eager to realize that the business can survive without me before I finally sell it. But I need to get some work done. I need to get this busy season out of the way, then I can chill out with my fiancée… if I can find that fuckin' box.

I pat down my pockets again. I don't know why. Then I stand still in the room, squinting all around. I'm sure I hear another creak. Definitely from the kitchen. So, I walk back down the hallway, until I set foot on my kitchen tiles again. I don't know what's going on. I just know I'm sick of feeling this way; as if I don't really know what's going on; as if my mind is playing tricks on me. This is supposed to be the happiest time of my life. I'm about to get engaged. I'm about to sell this business that drives me crazy. I'm about to travel the world. With the most perfect woman I've ever met. So why am I always feeling paranoid? It's these fucking things. These Sia bands… shouting noise at me every time I strap it to my forehead. That's why I try to run my business the old-school way; away from Sia. But it's not easy. Too many people want to meet on holocalls; too many people want to order their products through Sia. It's tough for people like me… people who grew up without a phone stuck to their hands. Heck, my pop didn't even have a computer when he first set up De Luca Catering as a front for his Mafia ways. He just dealt in paperwork. I wish we could just go back to that. I don't remember ever being stressed before smartphones. I don't remember ever feeling as if I had to live up to anybody else's standards other than my pops. I peel the Sia band from my forehead and toss it down to the sofa. Because I despise it. I despise everything it stands for... And that's when I notice it. In the corner of the sofa, tucked away as if it's trying to hide from me. The red satin box.

A rush of relief flushes through me. And I remember that pretty soon I won't need Sia. It's just gonna be me and Belinda... Me and my soon-to-be fiancée.

POTUS. SALLY W. CAMPBELL

Max smiles his thin lips at me, then tilts his ear toward his shoulder like a puppy dog, desperate to reassure me.

'President Campbell,' his hologram says, 'I promise. Ziu is one hundred percent on board. He's ready to sign the Bill. Sia's hurt him, too. He gets it. Totally.' I put my face in my hands again, and begin to tap my fingers against my forehead, to think it through… I can't believe we may be on the periphery of making America happy again. 'If Philip Meredith is suffering as bad as you tell me he is, Zdanski will sign it, too. She has to…'

'I don't know…' I say, shaking my head, then allowing my hands to open on either side of my face. It's a habit I've had since I was eleven years old. 'With Zdanski, I'm not sure. Who's ever been able to tell what Zdanski is thinking?'

'I wanna talk to her,' Zuckerberg says. 'Get me, her, and Ziu in the same room and we'll close her, President Campbell. We'll win her over… we'll be able to help her to understand that it's now or never…'

I breathe out through my bright-red lips. I hate that I have to wear lipstick every day. 'Lipstick, or plummeting approvals,' a senior member of the Republican Party told me when I was a junior member. He was as right as he was rude. I ran the data.

And as a result of that data, I wear makeup every damn day. Not wearing it would tumble my ratings more than crashing the economy.

'I can't imagine Sarah-Jane accepting a meeting with you two...' I say, dropping my hands to my sides. 'She's...'

I pause. To shake my head.

'She's what?'

'Elusive. You know that. She runs the whole of America from that penthouse in downtown Manhattan. She has all four hundred and five million Americans dancing to her tune from that penthouse.'

'I thought you were a fan,' Zuckerberg says.

'I am a fan... Personally. I like her personally. What can I say, she's a Kansas girl. And she's always been nice to me. She gave me my first platform way back when... If it wasn't for her, I would have never gotten myself on the map. She likes me, too. Personally. I know she does. We have a connection. But politically. Well, I guess we've always been icebergs to each other's Titanics.'

'Listen,' Borrowland interjects. It's the first time he's spoken since we holocalled Zuckerberg inside the Situation Room. 'Why don't you, with all due respect to Sarah-Jane, pose the question to Zdanski about meeting with Zuckerberg and Ziu. She might see it from their point of view. They do have multi-billionaireism in common. They could win her over.'

'There is no winning Sarah-Jane Zdanski over,' I say, holding the palms of my hands up. 'She makes her own decisions. Always has.'

'Not true,' Borrowland says.

'Sorry?' I say, squinting.

'That's not true. Zdanski doesn't make her own decisions. Phil Meredith makes her decisions. Always has. From as far back as her days as a roving reporter on the streets of Northern Kansas. Phil is the decision-maker. He's the one who can't be won over. But with him out of the game... it's worth it for

Zuckerberg and Ziu to speak with her… to see if they can break down her wall.'

I mull over the thought, tapping my fingernails against the Situation Room's conference table as if it were a grand piano.

'I'll ask,' I say. 'It's all I can do… but in truth, I wanna give her some space. Some time. Last thing we want to do is scare her off.'

'S'all I ask,' Zuckerberg says.

A purple light blinks in the top corner of my Sia.

'Sorry, Max, gotta go,' I say.

He salutes me, as he always does, then he blinks away, before I wink my right eye at the purple pulsing light.

'Will you be much longer in the Situation Room, Madam President?' Sofia, my Chief of Staff's hologram asks. 'Your two o'clock, Mr. Pete Davidson is here.'

'Yes!' I reply, remembering. 'Of course.'

They call the American presidency the impossible job. Once in office, it takes forty-eight hours to realize why. The president spends more time dealing with insignificant matters than we do significant matters. We're pulled from pillar to post on a schedule that is so tight, it's incredible that presidents haven't been dragged out of the White House by doctors in white coats.

'Gotta go, Borrowland,' I say, swiveling on my chair before getting to my feet. 'Gotta go meet the King of Late Night.'

'Hey, you tell Davidson,' Borrowland yells as I'm dragging open the heavy glass door of the Situation Room, 'that he hasn't been funny since the thirties.'

TIMMY BUCKETT

'Fuck!' I shout.

I stick my thumb into my mouth and suck on it as hard as I can.

That's the third cut I've had in the past two weeks packing these boxes.

It's a shitty job. The shittiest of all the shitty jobs I've had since I ran out of money. But it's all I've got. It's all I could get.

It's not easy to get a job when your main work experience is selling stolen drugs on street corners.

I pop my thumb out of my mouth and stare at it. It's a tiny cut. Not too bad. I'll live. Unlike that fucking baby growing inside Caggie's belly.

I think I won her over. She stopped crying eventually and said if I can find a way for her to get to California then she would get rid of whatever it is that's growing inside of her. But that's only because I told her I'd be a better boyfriend in the future. That I'd try to get a better job. That I'd stop spending so much of my time on my socials—reading and listening to right-wing news. Caggie thinks she's right wing, too. But she doesn't put a lot of thought into politics. She says it's boring. I don't know why anyone can say it's boring. War is never boring. The reds against the blues could never be boring. Not to me. Not when my red team keeps beating the blue team all the darn time. We've won all but one presidential race since I was born in 2027. And to think the lefty libtards keep calling us the "sleepers," when we're the ones who keep finishing ahead of them all the time. That's the thing with lefties. They think they're so clever, that they've no idea how stupid they are.

'Yo, Timmy,' the boss shouts. 'Do I pay you to stand around sucking your thumb?'

'Sorry, boss,' I say. 'Just cut it off the edge of the cardboard box. S'all good now.'

'Well hurry up… there's a queue of drones outside waiting on these packages. You're falling behind. Again.'

'Actually, boss,' I say, pressing my throbbing thumb against my jeans, 'I wanted to ask you… is uh… is there any chance of some overtime coming up? I really need the cash, boss.'

'You?' he says, surprised. Probably because I usually clock in as late as I can, then clock out as soon as I can. 'Now, why would I pay you more money just to stand around sucking your thumb, huh?'

'Sorry, boss… it's just, I really need the cash right now. It's an emergency.'

He scratches at the side of his head.

'We do got some extra hours available… but not for you, Timmy. You're just too darn slow, kid. You quicken up, who knows how many hours I can get you in the summer.'

Oh, fuck off. Summer would be way too late. Caggie will be six months pregnant by then.

'Okay, maybe in the summer,' I say.

'Get your ass back to work, Buckett.'

I turn back to my workstation and grab a pair of fake Ray Ban sunglasses.

I blink my eyes twice while I stuff the sunglasses into a small brown Markt box, ready for a drone to come collect it, and I wait until the circle in the middle pulses.

'Yes, Timmy?' Sia says.

'Hey, Sia,' I whisper, 'how can I earn more money on the side?'

MADISON MONROE

I haven't been able to stop my adrenaline from pumping.

I've been on my couch all night. Sometimes sleeping. Sometimes staring at the blown lightbulb hanging above my head. I've been walking around that homely office over and over again in my mind. I haven't gone near the lesson I was supposed to plan. But I'll have to get to it. Because I've got to give that lesson in just three hours' time.

I shut my eyes tight with guilt, and my belly drops. What if I get addicted? Addicted to bidding in the Dark Web? This is why I haven't slept. My mind keeps jumping from one thought to another. I guess that's where the Dark Web leads you. I guess I just gotta keep focused. Take one task at a time. I've already completed task one. I'm almost in credit for the first time in my life. I gotta stop my head from thinking; thinking so much that I can't sleep. I'd take another CBD pill, if I hadn't taken three throughout the night already. I've just got to focus. Focus on my reality. Two more tasks. Then I'm done. Then I'm in credit. And the gray cloud I've been living under can go get lost somewhere else.

Clause jumps onto my lap, digging her nails into my arm. I almost bat her away with the annoyance of the pain; as if it's her fault her nails haven't been clipped in I-dunno-how-long. It's not as if I don't have anything better to do. I don't. But I too often choose lying on this couch, getting lost inside Sia than I do caring for my cat. Which says it all. Cause my cat is all I've fucking got.

'I named you right, girl, huh?' I say, opting to tickle the top of her head, rather than bat her away. She purrs into my armpit, and I squeeze her tight, apologizing for being such a miserable roommate. I guess Clause waking up for the day means I've woken up for the day. With only small amounts of sleep to get me through it.

I sit up on the sofa, and stare at the two Sia bands I purposely left draped over one of the cushions, wondering which one to slap to my forehead first.

'Fuck it,' I say to Clause, before stretching over her and reaching for the untraceable Sia band. As soon as I slap it onto my head, I glance into the top left corner to check the time. 5:05 a.m. Jesus. It's earlier than I thought. Then I glance to the top right… at nothing. No blue light. No new Blynq message. I guess he'll have been asleep since I left him that Blynq message telling him I scoped out the house. It's way too early for him to get back to me. So, I unclasp the untraceable band and reach for my own one. A yellow light in the top corner blinks as soon as I clasp it to my head. A holocall message left at 4:33 a.m. Jesus. *Somebody's* up before me.

I blink at the yellow light and a green light pulses for a split second before a pudgy twenty-something brunette woman appears in front of me.

'Hi, Madison Monroe… great name by the way. I'm Laura Trailing. I am a researcher at DCNews.' *DCNews…* 'I got your contact details on Careerz. You're Head of the Media Faculty at Washington Liberal Arts College, right?' *Well… I'm the only one in the media faculty.* 'We were wondering if you would like to appear as a guest on *Good Morning DC* later this week?' *Holy fucking shit.* 'Thursday morning. We're doing a discussion on the Three Zs allegedly meeting up, and we want two expert guests on media to join Marley and Dom on the couch. You know Marley and Dom, right? *Good Morning DC?*' *Of course I know Marley and Dom!* 'Well, we would like you on the show for your expert opinion, so reply to this holocall as soon as you can. And... I guess I'll talk to you then.'

I immediately wink my left eye to reply. And by the time the pulsating silver fades to red to begin my recording, I convince myself that I shouldn't sound too desperate. Too enthusiastic. I should just be breezy. Grateful, but breezy.

'Hi, Laura Trailing, great name by the way,' I say as soon as the red light signals the recording has begun. 'I'm Madison Monroe and I *am* free on Thursday morning and would *love* to be on the couch with Marley and Dom. It would be my pleasure.'

Then I blink my left eye, ending the recording, before sweeping my eyes to the left, responding to the best invite I've ever had in my entire life.

I clap my hands twice. I've learned through group therapy that my clapping is a tic; a tic for any time I get too excited. I get big highs and big lows. Which sounds fun. But it's not. It's torturous. Life is best lived in the balance. I've never been able to find that balance. I get excited. And I get deflated. Which is a horrible way to live. Because even when I'm excited, I'm anxious about the inevitable deflation. So, that's why I clap when I'm excited about something. It's a tic that reminds me I might be getting too high... and that I should take a little slice of comedown.

'Sia, show me clips of *Good Morning DC* with Marley and Dom,' I say.

A holographic rolling scroll of 3D clip options sweep slowly by me.

Eight hundred thousand views. Seven hundred thousand views. Six hundred and fifty thousand views. One million views! Wow. Marley and Dom bring in big numbers for a State network. Well, I guess it used to be a State network. But there's no such thing anymore. Not really. Anybody can access any news network they want from any place in the world they want. I pause… to think. How will I wear my hair for the show? I'll have to… I'll have to buy something new to wear. I haven't bought anything new in… I dunno. What am I gonna say on the show? They want me to talk about the Three Zs meeting up. Hmmm… I tickle Clause's neck, my mind navigating through the excitement. I'm about to be on TV. It's all I ever wanted. Then… without any warning, my excitement dramatically drops—a weight punching my gut. The Dark Web screams out; reminding me of my guilt. *Uugh.* It's such a horrible feeling when the low plummets me from such a high.

I push myself off the couch with a deep sigh and walk toward my kitchen cabinet to reach for my CBD pills. They're the only pills that can level me out; the reason I've managed to stay sane while shivering in a cold, dated college, teaching holographic students even though I hate it. What's saddest about that is teaching at the college is the highlight of my day. When I come home… I come home to nothing. To nobody. Just Clause. The only time I get to see my family is the odd time I can afford the five hundred dollars it costs for me to fly back to Williamsburg. Which is pretty much about two times a year. My folks still live there. So does my brother. It's where my best friend used to live, until she moved to Dallas to marry her asshole of a husband. Now we only see each other in hologram. Which I get. It's fine. But it's also pathetic. I'm married to a Liberal Arts College in a city a five-hundred-dollar flight away from home while Kira is married to a guy who keeps promising her they'll be rich one day but who continues to come up disappointingly short. We try not to sound too depressed about where our lives have led us to when we do holocall each other. But it's hard to not sound depressed when you are depressed. Which is probably why we don't holocall each other that often anymore. Maybe once every three or four months. That is why the whole thing is pathetic. It's like we accepted our miserable lives without putting up a fight. Kira is my best friend. I see her three times a year. As a hologram. The only people I see in person are the students who pass in and out of my lecture room from semester to semester. When I started teaching I used to see a new wave of students every six months... Now it's more like a trickle of students. Last semester I had two students turn up regularly in person which was by far the worst turnout I'd ever had. For this semester, I've just got one. Neve. Neve who reminds me of a ginger, white me. Neve who gave me the first hug I've had in I dunno how long.

I drop three CBD pills into my mouth, then stretch to turn the faucet on in the kitchen to fill my palm with enough water that will help me gulp them down. I don't usually do three pills. Not at once. But I need them. The crash from that high was too much. I can't let myself fall that far down again. I need to keep my head above water. I need to concentrate. I've got two more tasks to carry out. On Thursday. Then it'll all be over. And I'll be out of debt for the first time in my adult life.

'Oh shit!' I shout out loud, remembering.

Thursday. That's the same day I might be appearing on *Good Morning DC* with Marley and Dom.

POTUS. SALLY W. CAMPBELL

'How about this one?' Davidson says, glancing down at me so he can watch my reaction to his roast, 'How do we know the President thinks she's ugly?' I shrug and smile at the same time... awaiting his punchline. Surely it can't be as cruel as his setup. ''Cause she hides her face about twenty times a day.'

I laugh my best fake laugh again, as he puts his hands to his face, to play peekaboo, mocking me.

'Yes. Good one,' I say. 'Include it.'

Davidson winks his eye, loading his new joke into his Sia cannon, ready to fire it out at me on the night of the White House Correspondents' Dinner.

'What about this one?' Davidson says, scratching his silver hair. 'Campbell hates the media so much that she wants us all to lose our jobs. She thinks she's the next Abraham Lincoln, but really she's just the next Donald Trump. You're fired. You're fired. You're fired.'

Davidson squints at my silence.

'A bit dated?' he asks.

'It's not that it's dated, it's just... look, Pete, roast the fact that I'm a woman in office, roast that I'm a Black woman in office, roast me for being a single, Black woman in office, roast that I play peekaboo with my hands all the time, but please, don't make fun of my plans to regulate the media. Not on this night.'

'What?' he says, the bags under his stoned eyes tightening as he squints at me.

I sigh inside because I know nobody says "you can't" to Pete Davidson. He's been the king of late night for almost two decades. I, personally, preferred the good old days. At least Fallon and Kimmel didn't make it personal.

'I, uh…' I say, sitting more upright, 'I'm planning on making the regulation of media the main focus of my speech on the night, so it'd be an awkward situation for me to be in to give the media a serious lecture about regulation, only for you to roast me about it before I've even begun.'

He grins his wide mouth, showing me all of his teeth and all of his gums.

'Well now you know that's all I'm gonna do,' he says. 'Sia,' he shouts, 'set reminder to write more jokes about media regulation.'

He winks. Maybe at me. Maybe inside his holographics. I don't know.

I hate this. Not the being roasted part. That's all part and parcel of being in public life. I just hate how much of a time waste it is. Mean joke after mean joke after mean joke. For no benefit to anyone, or anything. Maybe that's just me… the lack of humor of a middle-aged woman who has only known tragedy her whole life.

'How are you gonna make that funny?' Davidson says, shrugging his bony shoulders. 'Giving the journalists a lecture on media?'

I cough into a balled fist, clearing the awkwardness from my throat.

'I'm, uh…' I say, 'I'm not doing comedy… no. I'm purposely going to use my speech to deliver a message to the media. Off the record, Pete, my speech is going to be a speech for the ages.'

'No jokes?' Davidson says, the bags under his stoned eyes tightening even firmer.

'No jokes,' I say.

'You're a joke,' he says.

Then he grins, showing all his teeth and gums at me again before spinning on his heels and walking away. I really don't get why we have to have comedians at the dinner. It erodes the biggest opportunity the President has to hold the most powerful industry in the country to account. But I guess that's why they hire comedians. So they can laugh their accountability away.

'Hey,' Davidson calls out, spinning back and pointing at me. 'I know America is miserable as much as you do, presidito. I just choose to remedy that miserableness by making 'em laugh.'

Then he spins again and walks off, down one of the long corridors of the White House.

'Hey,' I shout after him, 'how does Pete Davidson fill Madison Square Garden every time he performs there…? Because he invites all of his exes.'

'Ha. Good one,' he shouts back without turning around. And then he's gone… around the corner and out of sight.

'Sia,' I say in the silence of the East Room, 'call Sarah-Jane Zdanski again.'

The red light pulses at the side of my holographics… Unlikely to turn green. This'll be the fourth missed call I've left her. My intuition is starting to wane. I really thought she'd go for it. I've always felt she agreed with me on media regulation, even though she never admitted it out loud. I could see it in how she embraced my arguments… how much she admired my position. She knows America is miserable. She knows, more than anyone, why. And now she can see it right inside her own home. With Phil fading away in front of her, she has to admit the truth to herself. Sarah-Jane Zdanski has a pulsing heart. I know she does. I felt it press against me.

The red pulsing stops, and I sigh in disappointment at

another unanswered call, before glancing into the top right corner of my holographics and winking at the purple light.

'What's next, Sofia?' I ask my Chief of Staff.

'You have a school performance to attend that you are twenty-minutes late for,' Sofia says. 'But… General Tunstead is also awaiting your appearance in the Situation Room for an emergency meeting. He is adamant that his holograph is not gonna move from there until you join him, Madam President.'

5

PHIL APPEARED EVEN MORE GAUNT WITH THE TINY BLACK, EGG-shaped blob hanging from his left temple, his head tilted to one side, his eyes heavily glazed over, and a bubble of drool clinging on to the bottom of his wispy, gray beard. Nobody had moved to protect his modesty, not until Michael Guarguito, having stuck the black egg to Phil's temple, stood back. Only then did Sarah-Jane motion to the nurse to get to work.

While the nurse was wiping at Phil's mouth, Guarguito nestled himself as close to Sarah-Jane as he possibly could, holding on to the bottom of her hand while pressing, into that hand, the trigger for the Ripple Stimulus—a squared, black handheld pad that had a touch-sensitive sky-blue button pulsating in the center of it. Guarguito had volunteered to personally show Sarah-Jane how to use the machine. In fact, he had insisted on it; flying over from Silicon Valley to tutor her in person.

'So, as I have already said, Miss Zdanski,' Guarguito whispered, grinning his white veneers, 'each shot is two triggers. Two pushes of this blue pulse. One, two. You can offer this double shot just once per day. That is the legal permission for trials as we stand. We, as you know, are awaiting more funding and approval, but we have given you permission, granted under the licence offered to George Washington University, to loan you this machine for trial purposes.'

Sarah-Jane nodded as she took hold of the trigger, then she stepped toward Phil whose slumping body was being lit by the low-light lamp sitting prominently on the side table next to the plush velvet orange sofa he was slouched on. Despite the anticipation of using the Ripple Stimulus to coax Phil back to life, Sarah-Jane's light was still largely dimmed. Her eyes weren't so green. Not anymore. The sight of Phil slumped in a slumbering mess in front of her sure was a heavy burden to bear. Equally so, was the pulsating purple button in the top corner of Sarah-Jane's holographics. Usually, her Sia would flash a yellow alert sign to remind Sarah-Jane of a missed attempted contact. But for one specific person it flashed purple. And it had been pulsating purple for pretty much the entirety of the morning.

'What are the chances of a wake up from first-time use?' Erica asked Guarguito as Sarah-Jane ominously palmed the black handheld pad.

'We have had first-time wake ups, yes, absolutely,' Guarguito answered, before laughing a little, 'but, uh… in men of Phil's age, not so much, of course. The problem with LiD is that everybody is at a different stage. It's like a fingerprint. Every person's dementia is different, always has been—dementia is unique to each and every individual. With LiD, individuals who are young and who only get locked in infrequently, the Ripple Stimulus can hold off their diagnosis. We've seen proof of that in early testing over the past seven months. But for those truly locked in, and older in age, it's, uh… well, it's very difficult.'

'Phil has a young brain,' Erica said, causing Sarah-Jane's shoulders to shuffle with a hint of laughter, even though she had been somberly staring at the black egg-shaped blob stuck to the side of Phil's left temple. The Sia band on his forehead — showing a holographic 3D version of what Sarah-Jane believed was his favorite-ever movie — *Goodfellas* — was crooked, but that was nothing new for Phil. Even in his most lucid days, Phil's translucent band was always slapped to his forehead at a slant. He didn't care what he looked like. Never did.

'I'm ready,' Sarah-Jane said to nobody.

Erica and Guarguito stepped forward in unison while the nurse remained in the shadows of the living room.

'One, two,' Sarah-Jane said as she stabbed her finger twice to the sky-blue pulsing circle in the center of the touch pad.

A crack of sound sizzled in the black egg on the side of Phil's head, and there was a pause before his left arm vibrated. After another pause, he slapped his left hand against his left knee. Then his hand fell back down to the sofa…

That was it. They were the only movements the Ripple Stimulus forced Phil into, aside from his chin tucking back into his neck.

'Phil,' Sarah-Jane called out. 'Look, it's *Goodfellas*. Remember this scene, Phil? You used to laugh at this scene.'

A sober silence swept through the penthouse—from the infamous marble-topped kitchen island all the way through to the open-planned living room they were all currently standing in, staring at Phil who was vacantly staring at the plush carpet beneath their feet.

'Not to worry,' Guarguito said, rubbing his hands together. 'Maybe next time. Let's see how on-going treatment with the Ripple Stimulus works for Phil. Like I said, no more triggers for at least twenty-four hours.'

'I've heard you say that a hundred times,' Sarah-Jane said dismissively as she stared vacantly at Phil.

'Thank you, Mr. Guarguito,' Erica said. 'If you can see yourself out…'

'Oh,' Guarguito said, a criss-cross of wrinkles meshing on his tanned forehead, 'I assumed I could stay around for the first rounds of the trial, to help Miss Zdanski out. Maybe we could all have lunch together and—'

'No,' Sarah-Jane said, spinning around, the trigger slapped

between her two hands like a sandwich. 'We will be in touch as soon as there is any response.'

Guarguito looked down at his shiny black shoes before glancing back up at a woman he'd been lusting after since tenth grade, his fingers fidgeting with discomfort. Then his mouth disappointingly popped open, and he bowed, slightly, before swiveling on his heels and pacing down the long hallway of Sarah-Jane's plush penthouse. When the front door closed with a thud and a clunk behind him, Sarah-Jane turned to the nurse and flicked her head—to shake his presence from the shadows of the room.

'Fuck, shit, bitch!' she spat, throwing the handheld pad onto the sofa next to Phil.

Erica reached out to squeeze her mother's shoulder. But Sarah-Jane didn't feel her touch, even though it was highly unusual for her daughter to ever touch her voluntarily.

'I'm staying off this fucking thing,' Sarah-Jane groaned, swiping the Sia band from her forehead. 'I don't wanna turn into… what is it you call 'em, Erica? Zombies.'

Erica glared at the liver spots on the top of Phil's balding head and sighed at the sight of them before turning back to her mother.

'I'm afraid you're gonna have to put that band back on,' she said. 'We've gotta call the President. She's left at least six missed calls this morning.'

Sarah-Jane held her heavy green eyes closed, then roared her frustration from the back of her throat.

'Fuck my life,' she said. Then she slapped the band back on to her forehead and held both hands to her hips.

'Sia, call the President!' she ordered.

After two pulsing tones, Kyle Borrowland popped up in front of her, dressed impeccably in a three-piece green-and-navy tartan suit.

'Miss Zdanski,' the President's Director of Communications said, nodding. 'Miss Murphy.'

Both Sarah-Jane and Erica nodded back at Borrowland, faux smiles creased on the edges of their lips.

'The President's been looking for me,' Sarah-Jane said.

'She has indeed,' Kyle replied, 'but right now she is in a meeting. She did, however, instruct me to interrupt her should you ring back, so if you don't mind waiting, I'll let her know…'

'Sure…' Sarah-Jane said.

Borrowland's holograph blinked away, and as soon as it did, Sarah-Jane glanced at her daughter.

'What the fuck am I gonna say to the President?' she whispered. Erica blew out her cheeks, then looked over at her father's elongated liver spots again, but she didn't say anything. Simply because she didn't know what to say. 'Has there ever existed a bigger moral dilemma for any one human being?' Sarah-Jane asked. When Erica squinted at her mother, she noticed her green eyes were losing their glow. 'Oh, come on, Erica,' Sarah-Jane spat, even though all Erica had done was squint at her, 'would you give up hundreds of billions of dollars to save the people?'

Erica tilted her head, and then coughed lightly into the back of her hand, just to clear her throat before answering.

'I don't know what I'd do…'

'Yes, you do,' Sarah-Jane said. 'I asked you a few days ago when we were in DC whether or not you would sign the Release Bill, and just before you answered we were interrupted by Dr. Classen. But I could tell… I could tell you had an answer… Erica, you have an answer for everything.'

Erica coughed into her hand again. A forced cough. To buy herself an extra second to think.

'Well, if you're asking what I would do, I'd sign the Bill,' she finally admitted. 'But asking me what I would do in your situation and asking me what you should say to the President right now are two entirely different questions. For two entirely different days.'

'You would sign it?' Sarah-Jane said, squinting at her daughter. 'Bullshit!'

'Yeah… I would.'

'Erica,' Sarah-Jane sighed, a hint of a sarcastic laugh forcing its way out of the side of her mouth, 'let's not forget that when Phil found you, you were pretending to be a child suffering with cancer just so people would give you a few extra dollars.'

Erica almost replicated her mother by squeezing a sarcastic laugh out of the side of her mouth.

'That was a quarter of a century ago,' she said. Sarah-Jane shook her head, not to disagree with her daughter, but specifically to rid her mind of her growing grief. 'Listen,' Erica continued, 'if it makes you feel any better, I think you're doing the right thing. Phil should make this decision. He's always made the decisions.'

Suddenly, the President appeared in front of them, glowing, once again, in a microsilk purple dress suit. It had become her staple palette as soon as she was afforded a wardrobe consultant when she was surprisingly added to Wyatt's ticket ahead of the 2044 presidential election. The purple was supposed to represent the coming together of the two political parties. The amalgamation of blue and red. It worked. A growing majority of Americans genuinely saw her as the great glowing hope for the country. Nobody had united the Republicans and the Democrats like this before. It was as if nobody had even entertained the idea that the two parties could work in harmony.

'Sarah-Jane,' the President said, breathless. 'They want to meet you. Ziu and Zuckerberg. They said they'll visit you in person wherever suits you best.'

Sarah-Jane rolled her tongue against the inside of her cheek.

'O-kay,' she said, slowly.

'As soon as possible,' the President said.

'I have, uh… things to do, Madam President…'

Sarah-Jane was still talking slowly, really slowly; her eyes focused through the President's holograph and at Phil slumped numbly on their orange sofa behind her.

'Listen to me, Sarah-Jane, and listen good,' the President continued. 'At the White House Correspondents' dinner in two weeks' time, I'm going to call out the amount of media we consume and officially label it an addiction. I'm going to tell America that they are inside Sia way too much; that mental health problems are soaring, and that scientists are openly attributing LiD to the amount of media we consume.'

'Wait,' Sarah-Jane said, holding a finger up, 'you promised you wouldn't allow the Release Bill to become public knowledge. That it was just between you, me, Zuckerberg and Ziu until it was signed.'

'I won't mention the Release Bill,' the President said. 'But I will be mentioning all the damning statistics and facts we have collated that link Sia to the growing misery in America. Our intelligence tells us that not only do the American public wish they could cut down on Sia, but that they actively want us to help them cut down on Sia.'

Sarah-Jane dug a curled knuckle into her temple and held her heavy eyes firmly closed again. She adored Sally W. Campbell. Hugely respected her. Yet despite that adoration and respect, the new President of the United States was proving to be a painful thorn in the media mogul's ass cheek. At this point in the discussion with anyone else, Sarah-Jane would respond that, 'The media haven't reported any statistics that prove Americans want less Sia,' but she knew the President was too savvy on this specific subject and understood all too well that Sarah-Jane held the power on exactly what the media did and, in this case, did not report. The media were hardly ever going to divulge news that suggested in any way that they, themselves, were responsible for all of this misery.

'This is insane, Sally… if you don't mind me calling you Sally.'

'Course not,' the President said. 'We go back way before I had an official title.'

'Sally, when you were given the VP ticket and you came to me with the radical notion of the Release Bill, you never could have thought in a million years it would ever see the light of day.'

The President clasped her hands across the naval of her purple dress suit.

'Sarah-Jane, I've always believed in the Release Bill. And I've always believed in it because I've always believed in doing what's right for everybody, not just some bodies. Listen, Sarah-Jane, I know we go way back. I've always respected you. Looked up to you. And you've helped me so much... you've had me on your show lots of times, even though I was preaching things media folk didn't want to hear. I'll bet what you can't believe, Sarah-Jane, is that I got this far. That I got into a position where I can draw up an emergency Bill and have it passed.'

Sarah-Jane shook her head.

'That's not true, Sally. I always believed in you. I just... y'know, I never thought it would get to the position where all of the power would essentially be in three people's hands. And even then that those three people could possibly agree to give it all up.'

'The time is now, Sarah-Jane,' the President said nodding, her hologram taking one step closer to the media mogul. She stared into Sarah-Jane's heavy-green eyes, then slowly curled her fist into a ball to drive home what she was saying. 'We can do this,' she said, shaking that wrist. 'We can relieve the American people of their misery. Humanity is consuming too much information. It is literally driving us crazy. It is making people hateful. It is making them resentful. It is making them mad. And sad.'

Sarah-Jane dug her knuckle further into her temple while

she squinted through the President's hologram to take in Phil slumped into the orange sofa again.

'The timing is wrong,' Erica said, filling the silence by speaking for the first time, causing the President's hologram to pivot toward her.

'It's now or never, Erica,' the President said.

'Not with Phil like this,' Erica replied.

'No,' the President responded, shaking her balled fist. 'It's exactly *because* Phil is like this. I would never have pursued you to sign a Release Bill that dilutes about eighty percent of your power. Not until it hit home. Not until Phil got locked in. Now you know exactly what America is going through...'

Sarah-Jane sucked her teeth.

'I can't buy that Ziu has been won over. That guy breathes for money. His ego's way too fragile to give up everything he's built.'

'Max Zuckerberg has assured me Ziu has been won over,' the President said. 'That's why they want to meet you...' The President glanced over her shoulder and nodded, then looked back at Sarah-Jane. 'Listen, I've got to go. But Sarah-Jane, please, if you've ever listened to anyone in your whole life, listen to me right now for these next two minutes. The speech I make at the Correspondents' Dinner next week, it's going to be one for the ages. It's a call for a radicalized overview of the media we consume. For the welfare of humanity. To stop us from allowing the machines to control us; to stop humans becoming slaves to the algorithms. We either do something about it now, or we live with these machines controlling us for the rest of human existence. Sign it, Sarah-Jane. Sign it for Phil. Let him watch you sign this Bill. Let him witness his own legacy while part of him is still alive.' The President pursed her lips at Sarah-Jane. 'My speech is going to be called "Roll the Clock Back." That's what humanity needs to do—roll the clock back. One hour a day of technology. That's it! That's more than enough. Heck, humanity lived for two hundred thousand years without any technology. If people wanna play basketball, they can go to a basketball court. There's a deserted court in every neighborhood in America. If people wanna play golf, they can go to an actual golf course. If they want to exercise, go outside and exercise for crying out loud. If they want to meet their friends, let them go out and meet their friends at a restaurant, or a cafe. Not by sitting at home on their sofas talking to holographs with a tray of fast food on their laps. Humans need humans, Sarah-Jane. We need the human touch to return. We need to roll the clock back. I am begging you, for the sake of humanity, meet with Zucker-berg and Ziu, listen to what they have to say…'

A silence filled the penthouse, save for the subtle motorized sizzle from the black egg stuck to Phil's left temple.

'Okay, I will,' Sarah-Jane said, ending the silence. 'I'll meet with them. If you arrange it, I'll meet with them.'

MADISON MONROE

The CBD pills have leveled me out a little. I'm trying to not get too high thinking about being on *Good Morning DC*, while also trying to not get too low thinking about everything else. I eyeballed the top right corner of my Sia all the way over here, waiting on that producer to send another yellow pulse my way. But she hasn't. Not yet anyway. I rewatched, over and over again, the holomessage I sent back to her. I sounded cool. Cool and calm. And breezy. And polite. I was definitely polite. I'm always polite. She'll get back to me… she will… Just like the hoodie will on the untraceable Sia. They'll both get back to me before Thursday. Before D-Day.

I swing the door open to see the back of her thick ginger curls in the front row. The young me, drowning in the silence of a dozen empty rows of empty desks.

'Morning,' I say as I make my way up the center aisle between those rows of desks.

'Hope you're feeling better, Professor Monroe,' she says as I pass her. I wait until I'm at my desk, then I spin around and offer her my smiliest eyes. But I say nothing. Only because I don't really know what to say to that. 'You look tired, Professor Monroe,' she says, squinting at me.

My yawn answers for me, just as I was about to lie to the only student who bothers to turn up to my lessons. I think she laughs at my yawn. But I'm not sure, because my eyes watered as I yawned.

When I sit, without saying anything back to Neve, I blink my eyes twice, until the pulsating starts.

'Sia, bring in my students,' I say.

Six pop up in front of me, dotted around different desks in the lecture hall. Another one or two might arrive late. They usually do. Seven students in by nine a.m. is actually a regular starting number for me these days.

'Okay,' I begin. 'Good morning, everybody, last lesson we were discussing the mechanics of a news story, today we're moving on to 'feature reporting.' Can anyone tell me the difference between news reporting and feature reporting?'

Neve's hand shoots up.

'Anybody?' I say.

She looks over her shoulder, peering through the curls of her ginger hair at the six holographic students dotted around different rows behind her.

'Hey, you, blond boy at the back, what's your name again?' I shout.

'Huh, me?' he says, sitting more forward. Suddenly, a glow of yellow pulses against the wall of my lecture hall and my stomach rolls over with a twinge, just as I hold a flat hand to the blond boy. 'My name is Stephen Dal—'

'Hold on,' I say. 'Sorry. Stop! Give me a few minutes. Sia, turn off my students and open the incoming holocall.'

My students blink away. And I turn to the side, before winking my left eye once; to be met by the pudgy researcher who left me the most exciting holomessage I've ever received in my life this morning.

'Hey, it's Laura. Laura Trailing,' she says.

'Great name,' I reply.

She kinda smiles at me. But it's almost like she didn't get the joke. Or perhaps that joke's already run its course with her. I need to play it cool. She needs to like me.

'Sorry for the delay in getting back to you,' she says. 'Today's show has just ended and... I... where was I? Yes! You are Madison Monroe... Yes! We need you as a guest on Thursday's show. Marley and Dom are due to discuss the rumors that the Three Zs have met up...'

'Uh-huh,' I say, nodding my head like a lap dog.

'Have you got strong opinions on that subject matter?'

'Uh-huh, definitely,' I say. 'I doubt many people have stronger opinions than me.'

'Wow. Great. Well, we're going to have you in conversation with Marley and Dom on the couch, opposite another panelist, Una Ferrelly—the author. She'll be arguing that Sia is causing mental damage to our kids, and you'll be...' she pauses as somebody squeezes by her in whatever narrow corridor at the back of the studio she is holocalling me from. 'Sorry, it's distracting here right after a show,' she says. 'Where was I? Yes... you'll be on the couch with Una Ferrelly for a ten-minute slot on the Three Zs. We pay one thousand dollars for a ten-minute segment. You good with that?'

'Sure... yes, sure. More than good,' I say. *Holy shit. A grand? A grand for ten minutes?* 'Excuse me, Laura, if you don't mind me asking... I don't mean to be too forward but all I've been thinking about since you left that first holomessage for me in the small hours of this morning is whether or not this could be a regular gig for me? If I could be someone who appears time and time again with Marley and Dom talking about media because, you know, there just isn't a bigger topic to tackle right now...'

'We were only talking about this in our post-production meeting yesterday,' she says, smiling at me. 'Sia is the growing trend in what people want to talk about, so we have a feeling it's going to come up time and time again... certainly with Campbell in the White House. She has the entire nation talking about Sia. We need Sia, though, right? Media can't work if we don't have Sia. So, us media types, we gotta defend ourselves, right? Would you be up for that? More regular appearances on the couch with Marley and Dom?'

'Absolutely,' I say without hesitation.

'Great… well in truth, it's a blessing you're Black. I was looking for a Black media teacher all around DC yesterday… we must've called every college in the state till I came across you.'

'Cool,' I say, masking the weight that's just landed in my gut.

'Okay, and so, yes… where was I? Una Ferrelly will be putting an argument forward that too much media is causing mental illnesses, and you will be arguing the opposite.'

'The opposite?' I say.

'Yeah… you're comfortable with that, right? You just have to come back with all the statistics that say media can't be at fault and that Sia brings us all closer together and doesn't drive us further apart, and that, y'know, Sia does so much great for humanity. That sorta thing. You know the argument, right?'

A breath I was holding pours out of my mouth as another punch lands heavy in my gut.

'Sure,' I say, swallowing my guilt. 'Sure… I can do that.'

'Great… well, I need you to holocall to this account on Thursday morning before seven a.m. You are going on air at seven-twenty and will stay on air until our commercial break at seven-thirty a.m.'

'Oh, we do it through Sia?' I ask.

'Yeah,' she says, squinting back at me. 'Small guest debates, yeah, we just do them through Sia. When we have big-named guests, we like to get them on the couch in person with Marley and Dom. But you and Una will holocall in.'

'Okay,' I say, looking down at my dirty trainers, nodding my head, my gut swinging low, my pride deflating.

'You sure you got it?' she says. 'Holocall to this account before seven a.m. You will be arguing why it's ridiculous to blame Sia for the nation's mental health problems… okay? Tell you what, I'll give you a call later this evening and we'll talk through what you need to say.'

I nod my head. Slowly at first. Then more quickly.

'Great,' I say.

She winks her left eye once, then blinks away; disappearing from the side of my lecture hall, leaving me enveloped in a depressing silence, my pride continuing to deflate.

'Oh my God, Miss,' Neve says, her voice echoing around the hollow room. 'Are you going to be on *Good Morning DC with Marley and Dom*?'

BOBBY DE LUCA

I grip the side rail of my bed to crouch down. It creaks. And the creaking makes me panic a little. Because when I have to do this in real life, there won't be a bed next to me to lean on for support.

When my left knee reaches the bedroom carpet, I release my grip on the bed rail and steady myself. Then I gulp, before looking up at my reflection in the mirror.

'I have been struck by you since the moment our companies first started doing business together,' I say. 'Now I am proud to say I am in love with you. And I love you so much that I don't think I can ever live without you, Belinda. Will you please do me the biggest honor of my life and become my wife?'

I pop the box open with a flick of my thumb and stare at the gleam of platinum in the reflection of the mirror.

At least the ring looks good, even if I don't. I've never looked good. I came to terms with that a long time ago. Besides, Belinda doesn't want to travel the world with me because I look like Zac Efron. She loves me because we want the same things. A better life. A life without being tied to our businesses. A life without being tied to Sia.

I hold my eyes closed in hope, then, when I open them, I pick Jesus up from my chest and kiss his tiny face.

'Please, Jesus,' I whisper, 'make Belinda say yes.'

I kiss Jesus's face again, then drop him back down to my chest. I like to leave Jesus by my heart; to come with me everywhere I go. My pop was the same. He carried Jesus with him everywhere he went, too. Which was kinda weird; because my pop did some fucked-up shit. He prolly even shot guys in the head while his gold-plated Jesus was laying against his heart.

They say pop was the last of the made guys. A true Italian who rose to the top of the mob in Brooklyn. He only opened *De Luca's Catering* as a front for his Mafia ways… A route to launder the dirty money he used to collect. But by the time the nineteen hundreds turned into the two-thousands, the Mafia was dying out… so the catering company had to become a legitimate business around about the same time I was becoming an adult. It meant that instead of using a gun for work which is what I always thought I'd have to do, I was using a wooden spoon—helping in the kitchen before finally inheriting the whole damn business when pop passed away. The business was all I was left, but I made it work. Especially when I moved it out of Brooklyn to Washington, DC. Only now it doesn't work for me. Because I gotta be on Sia all the time to make it work. And I sure as hell don't wanna be on Sia all the damn time. I hate Sia. Which is why I'm giving it all up. So I can spend time with the only woman I've ever loved apart from my Momma. I only got my Momma for my first five years. I'm gonna have Belinda for a lot longer than that. I better have her a lot longer than that. Hopefully another thirty years… maybe thirty-four if I can make it all the way to a hundred like I keep promising her I will. At least I'll have something to live for, other than a business that causes me more stress than it makes me happy. All I need is me and Belinda… the two of us traveling around the world; relaxed, calm, chilled, happy, without any need for any holographics ever again.

I take another sip of my cappuccino and as it's warming my throat I wonder just how much better this stuff is gonna taste in Italy. But I shouldn't let thoughts of Italy distract me from work. It's too busy. I really need to get back to it.

I pat down the pockets of my trousers.

'Fuck,' I whisper to myself. 'Where did I leave that Sia band?'

I pick up the corner of the duvet from my bed. It's not under there. So, I lean on the bed to get back to my feet so I can go looking for it somewhere else. I swear I spend most of my time looking for stuff I've lost. That's why I was convinced I was starting to get LiD. My memory just ain't what it used to be. I used to run my business though memory. Now I can't remember where I left something I had in my hand just ten minutes ago...

I laugh to myself. Cos I remember. I left my Sia band on the cabinet next to the toilet. I took it off to have a dump earlier... so I could have a dump in peace, without reading about President Campbell or Max fucking Zuckerberg. It's a relief that I remembered that. Because it shows I'm not losing my mind. I just forget for seconds... That's all. I just forgot for a few seconds. I'm not suffering from LiD. I'm just suffering the placebo effects of LiD.

When I walk into the bathroom, I have to look around until I see it lying flat on the edge of my bath. I pick it up, and slap it to my forehead.

'Sia,' I say, before sighing with frustration. Because I really want all of this to work out in my life. 'Play me my holomessages.'

VIKTORIA POPOV

This one will be different. Definitely different. Why wouldn't it be? This isn't a mob hit like I am used to. This is a Dark Web hit. And Dark Web hits are different.

Some of the Mafia guys I worked for on the streets of Boston turned me on to the Dark Web back when the Dark Web was on cell phones. As technology grew, the Dark Web grew with it. To a place where everyday people can place bids to do something illegal. It could a be a bid for a hundred dollars to do a quick drug exchange, or a bid for a hundred thousand, or even hundreds of thousands, to carry out a hit. The more random everything is on the Dark Web, the better the Dark Web runs. It means the police can't keep up. The police have never really been able to keep up with the Dark Web. It is almost impossible when everyone operating in the Dark Web is anonymous.

The Dark Web isn't run by gangs. It's run by everyday ordinary people. The worst kinds of everyday ordinary people. The ones who want people dead. Maybe a husband who wants his wife killed so he can claim her insurance. Maybe a wife who found out her husband is cheating. Maybe a rival for a position in work. Or, a neighbor who pissed you off. If you want a murder carried out, all you got to do is accept a bid on the Dark

Web. And reply as an anonymous account on an untraceable Sia using Blynq message. That way, nobody has any chance of catching you. It is as if this technology was set up just to help people organize murders.

I tried to think long and hard last night about my Ivans' faces. I think I saw both of them for a split second. But most of the time their faces were just a blur. I know I have the shape of their heads right in my mind. And their hair. It's just the features on their faces that stay blurry.

I decided last night that I'm definitely going to return home when I get this one hundred thousand. Not to Shyskove. Because that's part of Russia now. But maybe I'll go to somewhere on the outskirts of Kyiv. To see if I can fit in. I don't know. I don't know where I belong anymore. Maybe nobody will think I fit in. Because I am a little crazy, perhaps. Though everybody is a little crazy these days. They say it's because of Sia. But it's not. It's because of the politicians.

'Sia,' I say, thinking of politicians, 'what is the square footage of the White House?'

Even though there are hundreds of people e-scooting around the fence with me, not one of them looks at me when I talk to Sia. We've all gotten used to it. People talking to themselves; people acting crazy.

'The White House is five thousand, one hundred squared feet,' Sia tells me.

So, it is bigger than it looks from out here.

'Can you show me inside?' I say.

My holographs blink, then, rolling out in front of me is a long bright red carpet with clean white walls and pillars standing tall on each side of it. I blink to refocus ahead of me, to see the people e-scooting alongside me around the outside fence of the White House, and when I see my path is clear, I refocus my eyes back into the hologram, to the inside of the White House.

'Sia,' I say. 'Take me to the Oval Office.'

POTUS. SALLY W. CAMPBELL

I don't mind spending time in the Situation Room. At least it's not another school play or comedy performance I'm forced to sit through with a fake smile plastered on my face as if people aren't dying of misery on the streets of the country I'm sworn to protect. But right now, listening to the General spew his hatred, I believe deep down in my soul that all he is spewing is redundant. None of what he says matters. Not one word of it.

'So, we're ready to green light as soon as you nod your head, Madam President,' he finishes with.

I glance at the other faces dotted around the conference table; four here in person, eight calling in from who-knows-where.

'Tell them to stand down, General,' I say.

'What?' he snarls.

'I said, tell your soldiers to stand down. America's focus right now is not Iran. We are not entangling ourselves in more warfare in the Middle East. Not when we've our own wars to tackle right here.'

'But this mission has been eight years in the—'

'The length of the planned mission is of no concern to my judgment, General,' I tell him. 'Your soldiers will stand down.

That is the last word on the matter. Now, have you any other business to raise in this meeting?'

He folds his arms across the chest of his impressive uniform and purposely sighs heavily out of his disgusting nostrils, so that everybody around the conference table can hear his disdain.

'All else I have to report, Madam President,' he says, dismissively, 'is that the threat to your life is still a Code Red.'

'Great,' I say, grinning sarcastically at everyone.

Only my Vice President, Raya Vasquez, smiles back at me. The others can't hide their resentment. As if they think I personally injected cancer tumors into their hero Jarod Wyatt's brain.

'Any other business from anybody else?' I ask around the table.

Vasquez raises her left hand. Like she always does. I like Vasquez. She reminds me of a young me. It's why I handpicked her from the streets of Tampa to be my vice president. She impressed me more than any young politician I've ever come across when she was Mayor of her hometown. She, like me, has spent her entire political career attempting to drag the Republican party back to its senses.

'Madam President, I have had a conversation with Professor Wickle about the latest findings on the effects of Sia,' she says. 'He would like to brief you as a matter of urgency.'

'Yes… Yes. Definitely. Now that's an important meeting,' I say, glancing up at General Tunstead's hairy nostrils. 'Please, Vice President Vasquez, set that meeting up as a matter of urgency.'

'Will do,' Vasquez says.

'Okay, if that's it, I gotta get out of here,' I say before standing and blinking my left eye twice, ending the holocall. I nod at the four people left in the Situation Room in person while reaching to pull open the heavy glass door.

As soon as the door swishes closed behind me, and in the

silence of the corridor, I allow the weight of the decision I just made on Iran whistle out from between my lips.

'Madam President,' a voice calls out.

'Yes?' I say to nobody. Until I see Kyle Borrowland speed-walking toward me, his satin pink suit swishing.

'Zdanski has turned up. She's sitting down right now with Zuckerberg and Ziu.'

'Holy cow,' I say. 'It's really happening… How long has she been there?'

Borrowland rolls his eyes upward to catch the time.

'Our intel says she sat down twenty-minutes ago,' he says.

TIMMY BUCKETT

I applied for the only two cool jobs Sia presented. But they're cool jobs because they're above my station. TYSports are looking for a gamer on one hundred K a year. It said experience essential. Well, I have the experience of seven years of playing games every darn day. It's hard to have more experience than that. Though I bet I have no chance at that job. Cos they're looking for professional experience. Not stoner experience. I dunno how a guy like me is gonna catch a break if I need experience to get a proper job. How are you supposed to get experience if you need experience to get experience? There was another job—for an administrator on the team of Rex Henshaw Junior. He's a Republican senator candidate out in Connecticut. I'd love to work for a guy like him. But so would thousands of others, all with social proof that that they have experience in politics. My socials may prove I'm a die-hard Republican, but they don't exactly scream anything professional, other than the fact that I've worked packing boxes at Markt for the past couple years… ever since I sold the last stash of drugs I stole from Scar.

When I daydreamed of landing the one hundred K a year job as a gamer, I pictured me and Caggie living in a nice apartment. With an en-suite attached to our bedroom. It looked like a nice life. Then I heard a baby crying and I sat upright, blinking myself awake from the nightmare.

'Sia,' I say, before she begins pulsing at the side.

'Yes, Timmy,' Sia says.

'Where is the cheapest place to get an abortion?'

Sia pulses… and pulses…

'The only state abortion is legal in the United States of America is California. Prices are dependent on your health insurance policy.'

'And if I don't have health insurance?' I ask.

'Private abortions begin at nine thousand nine hundred and ninety-nine dollars,' Sia says.

I slap my hand to my forehead. Flights to and from California will cost another five grand. That's fifteen K in total.

'Sia,' how much do I have in my bank account?'

Sia pulses again as she goes in search of the answer.

'You have two hundred and eleven dollars in your current account and…' she pulses again… 'zero dollars in your savings account.'

'Just the fourteen thousand eight-hundred short then,' I say.

'Sorry?' Sia asks.

'Shut up, Sia,' I say. Then I blink her away.

I tried to call Caggie earlier. But Sia honked back at me. She wasn't wearing her band. She was probably lying in bed, sobbing again. I'll win her over. I always win her over. I'm just not traveling to her house to win her over. When she puts her Sia back on she'll see my missed calls. Then she'll call me. She always does. I hope she calls me soon though. Cos I'm bored. Bored of being inside Sia, trying to work out how we can get that baby out of Caggie. I even thought about reaching out to my dad. To tell him I got myself in trouble and that I need fifteen K to get myself out of it. See what he says. I'm not even sure if he'd be able to get his hands on that kind of money even if he did wanna help his own kid.

A thud at my door causes me to sit upright on the couch.

That must be Caggie. It has to be. She's come to talk. She's come to her senses.

'Who is it?' I shout.

'Timmy, open the door!'

A man's voice. Not Caggie's old man, is it? Fuck! Has she told him? Has she fucking told him she's pregnant?

I open the lock from my door and pull it open a little, just to peer out the tiny gap. But the door slams toward me. And suddenly the back of my head is crashing off my floorboards.

'Hey, Timmy,' a man says, standing over me. 'I hear you're looking for a job.'

I shake myself awake. Because that was some blow to the back of the head. Then, I slowly rub my fingers through the back of my hair, before staring at them. No blood.

'Who-who-who are you?' I say.

'Like I said, I've got a job for you.'

'Whatcha mean you gotta job for me? Who are you?'

He grins down at me, and then nods his head toward my sofa. So, I scramble back up onto my feet, still pressing my hand against the back of my hair before I walk slowly back to the same sofa I've spent the entire morning on, lost inside Sia.

When he sits beside me, I notice he's dressed in all-black leather; leather gloves, leather shoes, leather pants. He even has a leather shirt on. I can see the collar of it under his leather jacket.

'Isn't it shitty that we all gotta go to California anytime we want some bitch to get rid of a mistake?' he says, grinning at me.

'Huh?'

'Your bitch got pregnant, didn't she? Now you need the cash to… y'know, eliminate that mistake.'

I hold my eyes closed, and then try to blink them open again, only because this blow to the back of my head is making me hear some pretty crazy shit.

'How the fuck do you know about that?' I say to him.

He leans forward, making his leather pants squeak.

This is odd. Very odd. He must be mid-forties. Salt-and-pepper hair. And I guess he's kinda normal looking. He doesn't look like someone who would threaten someone. He looks just like a regular guy off the street. Except for that weird-ass leather suit.

'Let's just say, I know everything,' he says. 'Last night you were asking Sia how to get abortions. This morning you've been looking for jobs to get you the money to afford that abortion, am I right?'

'T'fuck? You're tracking my Sia?'

'It's easy to track Sia,' he says, squeaking his shoulders. 'That doesn't take no genius.'

'And?' I say, rubbing at the back of my hair again.

'Well, I've been looking for the best person I can find who will carry out a job for me.'

'What kind of job?'

'A big job,' he says.

'How much?'

He grins at me. As if he's trying to scare me.

'Fifteen K,' he says.

6

THE THREE OF THEM HAD BEEN SITTING IN THE DIMLY-LIT BACK corner of Sosa Restaurant for just over twenty-minutes, yet the subject they had arranged this meeting to discuss had not once been mentioned. Mainly because Max Zuckerberg and Sterling Ziu had spent fifteen of those twenty-minutes struggling through the menu before awkwardly ordering from the handsome waiter. They then spent the next five minutes ordering their tipple after forgetting to look at the drinks menu. Sarah-Jane didn't have to look at the drinks menu, of course. She nodded to the handsome waiter to short-hand order her usual glass of Chateau Margaux. Sterling Ziu eventually opted for a Whisky Sour with Scottish bourbon while Zuckerberg asked, overly politely, for a glass of cold tap water—with crushed ice and a lime slice.

'It's nice here,' Zuckerberg said when the waiter walked off with their orders, before shuffling his chair closer to the red-velvet draped circular table.

'It's my favorite restaurant in the world,' Sarah-Jane said.

Her face was muted, unanimated.

Ziu looked around, his dimpled chin jutting out, his head nodding.

'Pity they don't do a steak,' he said, a hint of a smile on the corner of his lips.

The quip was met with silence, causing the atmosphere between them to stretch even more awkwardly. Within the awkwardness, Sarah-Jane looked down at her clasped hands on top of the red tablecloth, then quickly hid them underneath that table. She hated her hands. Had hated them since they first began to wrinkle some twenty-five years ago. She glanced around the restaurant, as if she hadn't taken in this view a thousand times before, and as she did, she realized why she loved dining here. It wasn't just the familiar nut-free food. Or the staff. Or the ambience. It was the nostalgia. In the quarter-of-a-century she had been dining at Sosa Restaurant, it had barely changed. She lived for the red-velvet tablecloths and the blood-orange lighting. And the waiters bringing you your food instead of a drone. Sosa Restaurant reminded her of a time gone by, of a life less depressing—before technology consumed humanity, stretching and stressing them into zombies.

'I, uh…' Zuckerberg said, breaking the silence, 'hear that your legendary producer Philip Meredith is not well. I'm so sorry, Sarah-Jane.'

Zuckerberg's voice sounded squeaky and monotone. A little like a cartoon character. A lot like this late father. He had also inherited his father's high hairline, but, thankfully, his mother's flawless, sallow skin—making him almost handsome, if a little awkward. Certainly handsome enough to marry Saskia Brekken —one of America's hottest influencers. It was Saskia who introduced Max to Sally W. Campbell. As far back as the early thirties when he was just the heir to Meta, and not it's CEO. If it wasn't for that introduction, the very notion of a Release Bill simply wouldn't exist. And most certainly the three most powerful people in America wouldn't be sitting around a table in the dimly-lit back corner of Sosa Restaurant.

'Thank you,' Sarah-Jane said, draping her red napkin to her lap before hiding her hands back under the table again.

'He's literally a legend, right?' Ziu said. 'What's the stat? He won like eighteen Emmy awards and never once turned up to collect one? People will be talking about him long after he's gone. I'm not sure you can define a legend with a better anecdote.'

Sarah-Jane smiled. But just with her lips. Her green eyes remained heavy. Neutral. Non-plussed.

'I'll tell him Sterling Ziu called him a legend,' she said, nodding. 'Now... Gentlemen,' she sighed, 'why don't we talk business?'

'Sarah-Jane,' Zuckerberg said, before clearing his throat with a light cough. 'Sterling and I have met twice over this past month. I came to him with the concept of a Release Bill that then Vice President Campbell had in her arsenal as far back as when she was running for governor of Kansas. That was when we only had the Smart Phone Holographics. Back in 2038.'

'I don't need a history lesson,' Sarah-Jane said. 'Let's get to the point. You've got my ear for as long as this dinner lasts, and you both spent the first twenty minutes complaining that there was only sushi on the menu—in a fucking sushi restaurant.'

Ziu snorted an impressed laugh out of his nose, then leaned both elbows on to the table.

'We need to sign the Release Bill, Sarah-Jane,' he said. 'All of the science, all of the forecasts, all of the data tells us we need to sign this Bill. And we need to sign it now.'

'Jesus Christ, Ziu,' Sarah-Jane exclaimed. 'I'm a woman who deals in details. Don't come to sit with me at this table and tell me '*all* of the science, and *all* of the data,' it's not *all* is it?'

Ziu tilted his head, then pursed his lips while holding the stare of Sarah-Jane's heavy green eyes.

'Of course not *all*,' he said, 'but the majority of... yes?'

'And?' she said, shaking her lop-sided bob.

'*And* the majority of the science, the majority of the forecasts, *and* the majority of the data tells us that the machines have taken over. Listen, I don't like losing billions like you won't like losing billions, but the truth is, if we sign this Bill we'll still be in control of the consumption… just on lesser terms. We owe it to the people.'

'Oh, so the playboy is all heart to humanity, is he? All grown up and a man of the people?' Sarah-Jane said, sitting straighter before placing her wrinkled hands square under her chin. 'After sucking up their billions, huh? Well,' Sarah-Jane offered a small applause, before resting her hands back under her chin. 'You're all heart, Sterling Ziu.'

'Can we talk about the Release Bill?' Zuckerberg said, dryly.

'Wait, Zucker punch,' Ziu said, interrupting, 'Sarah-Jane says I'm all heart. I'll give you my heart, Sarah-Jane. You've got the closest person you've ever known lost inside himself. So, I can't top your story. But I'll tell you where my heart is at. And it's probably where most American hearts are. I work my ass off. Just like you. I always have. So, when I go home, I like to… hang out with my wife. It's my favorite thing to do. Always has been. But the past few years… when I get home? Jeez, I don't even watch TV with my wife anymore, even when we're actually watching TV together. She's inside her Sia watching *Baby At First Sight* or some shit like that while I'm watching *Davidson*. That's us watching TV together. It's bullshit. I spend sixteen hours a day inside Sia. You know how much I spend with my sons? Forty-five minutes. My son Zeke, for his fifth birthday last year, I had to attend as a hologram. A fucking hologram at my kid's birthday party for crying out loud.'

Sarah-Jane's brow sunk.

'Why?' she asked.

'Cos…' Ziu shook his head, 'cos I was outta town.'

'See,' Sarah-Jane pointed at him, 'that's why Sia is great. Without Sia, if you're outta town, then you miss your kid's party.'

'Fuck sake.' Ziu flicked the words from his lips with a frustrated whisper. 'Look, Sarah-Jane, forty years ago they put a device in people's pockets that delivered equal parts truth as it delivered lies. And now we wear this maze of information and misinformation on our foreheads, like a third fucking eye. It's consuming humanity. It's killing us.'

Ziu glanced away from Sarah-Jane at Zuckerberg because she was offering him nothing, then he produced an exhale that sounded like exhaustion. He was already frustrated. And drinks hadn't even arrived.

Sterling Ziu was the autistic-nerd turned handsome playboy CEO of DragN—the biggest company in America. He was known more for dating a string of Hollywood's hottest women than he was for creating the lens in which everybody viewed the world through. But that's because that was exactly how he wanted everybody to view him. As a playboy. He figured that being known as a playboy was better than being known as a bloodsucker who controlled the population on puppet strings. Before his thirtieth birthday, Sterling Ziu's power was as unparalleled as his net worth was. He was richer than any person that had ever existed in America. And it was all because of a throwaway line his mother muttered to him when he was just fourteen years old.

'You know,' she said. Sterling was chewing on his iPen at the time. She was holding her iPhone 20 up. The first-ever 3D version. 'They're gonna be holograms next, aren't they?' His mother winked as she said that. She often winked away her throwaway lines. She purposely used throwaway lines on Sterling. Only because she had by then learned to love how different he was. And she knew that one of her throwaway lines would motivate him to be great, if he found the right lane. That just so happened to be the one lane that became his livelihood. Holographic technology. Three years later Sterling had built the very first version of Sia, under a company he called DragN—a reference to his father's Chinese heritage. He quite literally built the biggest company in the history of America inside his own bedroom in Huron—one of the most poverty-stricken neighborhoods of California. Within eighteen months of launch, Sia

would push the smart phone into insignificance. Nobody
wanted an iPhone anymore. They wanted a Sia band. People
engrossed themselves in Sia; from getting their news fix; to
streaming TV shows and movies; to experiencing their favorite
live sports; to hanging out with friends and everything and
anything in between. It had become apparent by the mid-forties
that life was experienced inside Sia. And as a result, just eighteen months ago, DragN, became the first trillion-dollar
company to ever exist in America. The apps, however, developed to deliver those news feeds; or to stream TV shows or
movies; or to experience live sports games; or to allow folks to
hang out with their holographic friends — they were pretty
much owned by the guy sitting across from Ziu at the red-
velvet draped circular table. Max Zuckerberg was the inheritor
of Silicon Valley's biggest success story—Meta. Max's father
created the world's most used social media website, Facebook,
when websites were pretty much the new kid on the block in
the early 2000s. In the throes of Facebook's success, Max's father
Mark raised enough funds to snap up a slew of his social media
rivals, including WhatsApp and Instagram before buying out its
biggest rival Twitter from a humiliated Elon Musk in 2029. By
the mid-thirties, Meta pretty much held a monopoly on social
media platforms. But that was no surprise. Because that was
how capitalism worked in America. It's how capitalism has
always worked in America. The bigger fish eat up all of the
smaller fish… until one percent of the fish own more of the
ocean than the other ninety-nine percent of the fish added
together. But these three — these three sat around this round
table right now in the back corner of Sosa Restaurant — these
weren't just three of the one percent. These were in a different
league entirely. These three controlled almost everything everybody in the country consumed. In the early twenties, six companies owned ninety percent of the media Americans consumed.
By the mid-forties, that ninety percent was owned by only three
companies. The three companies owned by the three people

now sat in an awkward triangle around a circular, red-clothed table in the dimly-lit back corner of Sosa Restaurant. Despite their individual power, these three people needed each other. The radical idea they were meeting to discuss, but hadn't yet brought up, couldn't possibly work without all three signatures. Ziu controlled Sia. Zuckerberg controlled the apps. And Zdanski controlled the messaging on those apps. All three had to agree. If just Ziu and Zuckerberg agreed to the Release Bill, Zdanski would still own the messaging whenever Sia was turned on for that one hour a day. There would be a vast difference in the public perception to a Release Bill that came with the message "they are trying to steal your human rights," compared to a Release Bill that came with the message, "this is what's best for our human rights."

Although Sarah-Jane was dining with two of the most successful men to ever exist in the history of America, she was well aware that she still held the ace card, just like she held in every meeting she'd ever been in. She controlled the most powerful industry of them all. She controlled the news media. The messaging.

'Miss Zdanski,' Zuckerberg said, before clearing his throat with a light cough again. 'This opportunity will never present itself again. When are we ever going to have three people in our positions come to a table like this who are in control of all we control? And when are we ever going to have such a sane President? When's the last time America had a sane President?' Zuckerberg's face had blushed pink as a rush of rage raced through him. 'The stars have aligned now. We need to sign this Bill. We need to release the people. We need to free them...' he clenched his fist and dropped it, hard, to the table, 'of the bullshit we serve up to them every fucking day—'

'Miss Zdanski,' the handsome waiter interrupted, suddenly appearing with a young waitress by his side. 'Here are your drinks,' he clicked his finger, and the waitress stepped forward to push a Madeira wine glass in front of Sarah-Jane before placing a crystal lowball tumbler in front of Ziu, and a tall, frosted glass in front of Zuckerberg.

'Uh, Miss Zdanski, your Inarizushi.'

He placed the bowl of Sarah-Jane's favorite meal in front of her with a subtle spin, then turned to the young waitress again.

'And, uh... who ordered the salmon rolls?' the waiter posed.

'Yeah, that's me,' Ziu said, holding his hand up as if he were an elementary school student.

The handsome waiter placed his bowl in front of him with another spin, then turned back.

'And the plain noodles for you, sir, yes?'

He slid a beige bowl under Zuckerberg's chin, bowing at the table before turning on his heels, rushing the waitress away and then following her into the shadows of the restaurant.

'Well, dinner arrived quick,' Sarah-Jane said, picking up her chopsticks. 'Which I guess means you two don't have so long to win me over. Time's ticking, gentlemen. I don't need lessons, with all due respect, Mr. Zuckerberg, on the uniqueness of us three coming together. I'm aware of that. What you need to do before I finish this bowl of Inarizushi is convince me why I should give up most of my power... almost everything I'm worth.'

Zuckerberg lightly cleared his throat again, then took a sip of his water, the crushed ice jangling as he lifted the tall glass to his thin lips. After placing the glass back down, he leaned toward Sarah-Jane.

'Miss Zdanski,' he said. 'There are lots of reasons to sign the Release Bill. First, we are going to eliminate the anonymous. In the Release Bill, it is imperative that anyone setting up an online account sign up by using official identification like a passport or a driver's license. Nobody can sign up pretending to be some-body else. No profile will ever be anonymous again. We elimi-nate the bots and the fake accounts infiltrating the system and with it we eliminate most of the misinformation and hate being spread online. It would even eliminate the Dark Web. If you want to be an asshole online, you gotta own being an asshole. Let's see how many assholes are left when they have to be an asshole under their own name and face. Intel projects that eliminating the anonymous will remove over eighty percent of misinformation being spread online. It's an imperative function of the Bill. Second,' Zuckerberg said, without pausing, feeling as if he was hitting his stride, even though Sarah-Jane had begun to shovel sushi into her mouth while he spoke, 'we do not only have President Campbell heavily involved in this. She has made such a motion to all major leaders around the world clear and has been assured of their backing. Lejeune in France. Chancellor Schreier in Germany. Prime Minister Whittome in England. Prime Minister Koizumi in Japan. They're all in firm agreement of a minimalizing of media in some form. This just happens to be an American issue, because, well, each of us are Americans, aren't we? America won the race, didn't it? Silicon Valley took over the tech world. And while my father and Ziu were winning Silicon Valley, you were getting busy on the East Coast —evolving into America's shiniest ever TV star. You had the eyes and the ears of America from day one. But jeez, when you went digital and exploded with that Benji Wayde footage, you hit a different stratosphere. When Zdanski Corp. bought out Spotify, you quite literally placed your voice inside the ears of the entire United States. You are the voice. We are the facilitators of your voice. The three of us control Sia and almost everything that goes on inside of Sia. Us three, with this President... we can end this, we can end people's misery.'

'There'll be riots on the streets if you take away people's rights to Sia,' Sarah-Jane said through a chew.

'The intelligence doesn't say that,' Zuckerberg shot back across the table. 'All of the polls say the people want regulation. The people are suffering. And if they're not suffering, somebody close to them is suffering. As you well know, Miss Zdanski. Third,' Zuckerberg said, before pausing, 'I know you don't like to hear this, Miss Zdanski, but the vast majority of the science throws a dark cloud on Sia. Cases of ADHD are up one hundred and eighty percent over the past five years. Dementia, up two hundred and twenty percent. New forms of dementia are evolving, such as LiD.' He paused after saying that, then cleared his throat with that annoying light cough again. 'Depression was a disease that affected one in twenty people in 2007 before the introduction of the first ever smart phone, but that has risen to now being a disease that *one in two* people will suffer at some point in their lives.'

Sarah-Jane shook her head. But she didn't say anything. She didn't use the usual argument her news anchors frequently used when posed with such damning data, by retorting something along the lines of "Cases of these diseases are only rising because we are testing for them much more than we ever did before," simply because she knew such an argument was futile in company of this level.

'Look, Sarah-Jane,' Ziu said, picking up his chopsticks for the first time, 'Zucker punch are aware that all we are losing is data. Data is king, right? We're gonna lose data. But you, you're not just losing data. You're losing the ear of the nation. We understand that is a bigger hit to take than the hit Zucker punch and I are gonna take. We get to control how America consumes its news. But you… you get to control the news. We know you'll be giving up more than us. But we know you're a woman with values. Of class. Of legend. And we expect you to be the classiest, most legendary woman to ever exist, Sarah-Jane. Give up your power to save humanity. Let that be your legacy.'

Sarah-Jane shifted in her chair.

'One hour a day is excessive,' she said.

'It needs to be excessive. We have to roll the clock back. We're gonna strip it right back to its minimum, except on weekend days. We'll obviously open to tender in order to distribute access to Sia more frequently where needed: into industry, into education, into science… But on a personal level, on a human level, we need to live outside of Sia. Sia will be just for necessity. Not to live inside. It's all in the Release Bill; it's a fascinating read if you care to comb through it.'

'I've read the Bill, Ziu, thank you very much,' Sarah-Jane said, lying. She hadn't. Not fully. She'd read parts. And understood the highlights. But she knew what was in it, because she had followed the growth of what was initially a radical theory through her decades of supporting the rise of Sally W. Campbell. Sarah-Jane didn't just support Campbell because they shared a human moment some fifty years ago—she championed her for the same reason she championed anyone. Because she knew they made a good story. Or at least Phil did. He was the one who had the nose for news. He saw the story inside of Sally W. Campbell decades ago. That's why *The Zdanski Show* championed her. But *The Zdanski Show* could never have predicted that Sally's radical ideas would get her this far. To the White House. To where she could make her radical idea became a reality.

'Look, Miss Zdanski,' Ziu said, leaning his forearms onto the table. 'We're the good guys here. We're on the side of humanity. The question you need to ask yourself is, are you?'

Sarah-Jane squinted.

'That was corny,' she hissed.

Then she reached for her glass of Chateau Margaux.

'Listen,' Zuckerberg said, taking up the baton. 'When Sterling set up DragN back in the day from his own bedroom he was just trying to improve video calling. That's all. That's all he wanted to do. Create holographic video calling. When my father set up Facebook back in 2003, he was just trying to find out who the hottest chicks in college were. That's all. He could never have thought it would get to this. Nobody could have predicted this misery. This isn't right.' Zuckerberg's voice lowered. 'I want you to think about the young woman who went to journalism college just so she could get a job as a news reporter. That young woman, Sarah-Jane, would never have wanted it to come to this. Would she?'

Sarah-Jane scoffed, then reached for her glass to down large gulps of her favorite wine.

'I feel faint from the amount of corny,' she said, before placing her glass down and then picking her chopsticks back up. As she was pinching those chopsticks at her sushi, she glanced toward Ziu.

'Have you anything cornier to say to me than that? Other than crying that your wife watches *Baby At First Sight* while you're watching *Davidson*?'

Ziu held his eyes closed and inhaled deeply before opening them again.

'I'm watching my fucking kids grow up inside this shit,' Ziu said. 'And I hate it. I can't stand it anymore.'

'Y'know,' Sarah-Jane said, placing her chopsticks into her empty bowl and then nodding toward the handsome waiter. 'For somebody who says they're all for the people, you sure do you use the word 'I' a lot, Sterling.' The handsome waiter suddenly appeared by their table; Sarah-Jane's light lavender bomber jacket laid neatly over his arm. 'Gentlemen,' she said, before she downed the very last drops of red from her glass. When she stood, Ziu's hand shot up to block her, but he removed it just as she was passing him.

'Sarah-Jane,' he called after her. 'You have to make a decision: are you with the humans… or the machines?'

The media mogul paused, and then nodded the waiter away before turning and stepping back into the glow of the blood-orange bulbs. She gingerly placed her fingers onto the red velvet tablecloth and eyeballed Zuckerberg, then Ziu with intensity.

'I'm gonna need time,' she said. 'That's all I can tell you right now.'

'We don't have time,' Zuckerberg said. 'C'mon, Sarah-Jane, how much longer is Campbell gonna be in the White House? She's so radical she has the elites spitting dust. If news of the

Release Bill gets out, the one percent will have the other ninety-nine percent up in arms.'

'I control the messaging,' Sarah-Jane said. 'I always control the messaging.'

'Exactly,' Ziu said, placing his hand on top of her fingers. 'Which is why you need to be on the right side of this.'

Sarah-Jane swept her wrinkled hand from underneath Ziu's, then nodded at him before winking at Zuckerberg.

'Like I said, I'm gonna need some time. I'll be in touch, gentleman.'

She paced away, sweeping her bomber jacket from the arm of the handsome waiter, then disappeared into the shadows of her favorite restaurant in the world.

MADISON MONROE

'Sitting to our left,' Dom says, his trademark eyebrow raised in its branded arc, 'former journalist with the *New York Times*, now author of the radical book *Sia is Killing Us*, Miss Una Ferrelly... welcome, Una.'

Una nods her strawberry-blonde bob toward the applauding audience, even though she's in a quiet hotel room in San Diego, likely nodding at a curtained window.

'And to our right,' Marley picks up the autocue, twisting her perfectly sculptured face my way, 'Expert on the evolution of Media and Head of the Media faculty at the well-renowned Washington Liberal Arts College, Miss Madison Monroe. Welcome, Madison.'

I nod toward Clause lying on the back of my sofa, trying to not squint my brow in bewilderment at the revelation that the falling-apart Washington Liberal Arts College is "well-renowned."

'Let me start with you, Miss Monroe,' Marley says, smiling at me. She sure is beautiful. She glows in hologram. 'We haven't had any confirmation from anybody involved, but rumors are only getting stronger that the Three Zs met in a New York City restaurant recently. There are suggestions, although not confirmed, that President Campbell put them up to it to discuss her radical proposals for Sia. What do you make of this theory, Miss Monroe? It surely can't be true, can it?'

'It's not happening,' I say without pause. 'It can't be happening. Limiting Sia would be unconstitutional. It would go against the basic human rights of every living person in our wonderful country. Each and every one of us should be up in arms at the very notion that these rumors may indeed be true.'

"Up in arms" is a line I was given by Laura Trailing. She said I should say "up in arms" because it has a strong possibility of being clipped to fly viral. She informed me that phrase has a tendency to hit home with the DCNews audience. *Good Morning DC with Marley and Dom* is the flagship DCNews morning show—a 24-hour rolling news network under the Zdanski Corp. umbrella. Though what network isn't under the Zdanski umbrella these days? Zdanski's been the single most clever media mogul of them all through news history. Unlike the rest of them, she's never cared about right or left, or red or blue. She's only ever cared about dividing the red and blue, making her grasp on the nation firmer than those who have gone before her. Some of her networks are right-leaning, some are left-leaning. Some of her podcasts are blue, some are red. She doesn't care what side of the argument wins. She only cares that there is an argument. That's how she became the most powerful media mogul of all time. Through a very clever and conscious route of divide and conquer. DCNews happens to be one of Zdanski's right-leaning news divisions. And that's why I've been hired for this show today. To give credence to the right-wing view, even though I've always been a leftie; always been a Democrat. I don't love the Democrats. I just hate them a lot less than I hate the Republicans. That's why Marley and Dom gave me my fancy intro as "Head of Media Faculty" at the "well-renowned Washington Liberal Arts College." Even though nothing in that sentence is true. They just want their right-leaning guest to sound as clever and as worthy as they possibly can.

Marley nods at me, as if I did a good job with my opening gambit, then twists her face over her other shoulder, to the far side of the couch where Una Ferrelly's hologram is sitting.

'And you, Miss Ferrelly, your book suggests otherwise right? You believe Sia should be limited?'

While Una Ferrelly presents the argument I usually have inside my own mind, I allow a guilty sigh to seep slowly and silently out of my nostrils. I can handle the guilt of preaching the opposite of what I believe. For one thousand dollars for a ten-minute lie, I can most definitely handle the guilt. I'll be whoever they want me to be. Certainly if it gets me on TV. It's a business. That's all it is. That's what most people don't get. News is a business. Everyone working in news is just doing the job their employers hired them to do.

Besides, lying about how news effects our mental health on a state-wide network has nothing on whatever it is I'll be doing later today. Tasks two and three. Part of me can't wait to find out what I have to do to land that two hundred and fifty thousand dollars; the other part of me is totally shitting bricks. Trying to balance the excitement of getting out of debt with the deep lows of guilt kept me awake again for most of the night. Which is why I probably don't look as great as I should right now. Not for a debut appearance on *Marley and Dom*. But this was the best I could do. I ordered a pretty summer dress from Markt, but it's not an ideal fit. And my hair is a little messy. I should have practiced ironing it out before I attempted it for the first time this morning. Laura Trailing said Black people with straight hair rate a lot higher with their audience compared to those with a natural 'fro. So I did it. I ironed my hair out. As if I didn't have enough guilt to be dealing with.

All three of them stare at me, their expressions blank; Dom's trademark eyebrow arced sharply.

'Sorry,' I say. 'What was the question again?'

I was miles away, daydreaming about what tasks two and three will be later; daydreaming about ironing my hair out to look as appealing to white people as I possibly can.

'I said,' Marley repeats, her soft features creasing, 'what is your rebuttal to what Miss Ferrelly has just said, that Sia is causing new strains of dementia and is causing a multitude of brain diseases to soar.'

'Well,' I say, sitting more upright, readjusting my ass cheeks on my kitchen stool. 'Miss Ferrelly doesn't have great justification for these claims, does she? Three scientists hired by a President who we all know has an agenda against the media and against Sia in particular is not proof of anything, is it? It's just an agenda. Here's the truth,' I say, beginning the monologue of lies I practiced over and over again last night. 'Sia brings people together. It doesn't cause them to drift apart. Last week for example, I had dinner with my best friend. She lives a fifteen hundred miles away in Dallas, Texas. Yet we sat and talked as if we were right next to each other.'

'Okay, well, thank you for that, Miss Monroe and Miss Ferrelly. Right now, we're going to Robyn with the weather.'

'Wait, that's it?' I say to Marley, but she doesn't answer me. She's staring down the lens of the camera, waiting on the director to switch the live shot to Robyn standing in front of her green screen. As soon as the camera switches, Marley and Dom blink away from me and I'm no longer in their studio, but in some cramped, concrete corridor. 'Hello. Hello,' I shout.

'Oh, hey, Madison, listen, you did really well,' a familiar voice says before Laura Trailing appears in front of me.

'Was that ten minutes?' I ask her.

'Just six minutes,' she says. 'The segment wasn't performing well on our live numbers. Maybe people don't want to talk about Sia after all.'

'But I, uh…' I say, before pausing… because I can't find the words. 'I didn't even get to finish my monologue. I had a whole monologue I wanted to—'

'You did well,' Laura says. 'Really well. You adopted the attitude we discussed, and you certainly covered your bases in the time that you did get to talk.'

'Really? I did well?' I ask.

'Yeah, sure,' she shrugs.

'Good enough to, y'know… come on again? You said if I nailed the attitude and the sound bites we practiced then I could probably become a regular guest…'

'Oh,' she says, as if she had forgotten the most important part of the conversation we shared last night after she had coached me on my monologue.

'Lemme… lemme see,' she says. She blinks away, taking the cramped corridor with her, leaving me sitting on my uncomfortable stool in the middle of my tiny kitchen. I hold my eyes closed, trying to replay what I said during the live interview. I was only asked two questions. And I didn't even get to finish my second answer.

'Oh hey,' Laura Trailing says, blinking back in front of me again.

'Hey,' I say, giving her my biggest grin.

'I'm sorry, Madison,' she says, 'but Marley and Dom didn't think you popped in hologram.'

TIMMY BUCKETT

'You used to work for the gangs back in Baltimore, right?' he says.

'The fuck?' I say, rubbing at the back of my hair again; my stomach turning over. 'Did Scar send you? Please don't tell me Scar sent you!'

He scratches at his chin, making his leather armpits squeak.

'Relax,' he says. 'I'm only here to offer you a job cos I know how desperate you are.'

I stare down at the floorboards of my flat, then back up at him.

'Who the fuck are you?'

He grins, showing his yellow teeth.

'You don't need to know that.'

I look him up and down. Maybe I could take him. If I got the first blow in, I think I could take him.

'What is stopping me from knocking your lights out? You're no bigger than me. And what... you're wearing a leather suit. You some fucking insecure homo? Aren't insecure homos more of a twentieth century kinda thing?'

'Now, why would you wanna get violent?' he says. 'I'm offering you a job. That's all. If you want to send Caggie Harlow off for her abortion, then thumping my lights out is of no benefit to you. Timmy, I am a hacker. I hack people and when I see they're desperate, I offer them a job to get them out of their desperation.'

'What's the job?' I ask.

He reaches into the back pocket of his leather trousers, squeezing and squeaking. When he lifts his hand out, he shows me a tiny, silver gun. The size of his hand.

'I want you to fire this into the back of somebody's head.'

'What? Get the fuck outta here,' I say.

'An eye for an eye. You kill this guy for me. I'll pay for you to have your mistake killed.'

'Listen,' I say, rubbing at the back of my hair again. 'You've got the wrong idea. If you hacked me and saw that I used to be in gangs back in Baltimore… yes. That's true. But I'm no killer. I've never been a killer. I was a fuckin' drug runner. That's all.'

'But you are a killer. S'why I'm here.'

'What?' I say, laughing in his face. 'You think I'm a killer cos I want my bitch to have an abortion?'

He sighs. Then pinches his nose, as if he's bored by me.

'I do,' he says. 'Now, I'm offering you this job. Do you want it or not?'

'You want me to shoot somebody in the head?'

'Yep,' he says, nodding.

'And I'll get fifteen K?'

'Yep,' he says, again.

'Okay… I'll do it,' I say. 'I'll do it for fifteen K.'

POTUS. SALLY W. CAMPBELL

I sit, as I usually do on the hard sofas of the Oval Office, clasping both hands around my crossed knee.

It makes such a difference to the tone of a meeting when everybody attends in person. Vice President Vazquez and I are sitting on the east-side sofa, with Kyle Borrowland and Professor Wickle opposite us. I guess this is my inner circle. If inner circles are actually a thing. They are the only people who know about the Release Bill. Aside from the Three Zs, of course. Which is why we really need to get it signed as quickly as we can. Before word leaks out and is met with a surge of resistance before anyone even understands why the Bill is so necessary for the future of humanity.

'Madam President,' the professor says, 'I, of course, bring dismal updates.'

I turn my lips down, with dissatisfaction. But in truth, this will be good news. It's ammunition for my war. Proof that the Release Bill has to be signed.

'All the numbers are up?' I ask.

'They are. All of them,' the professor says, his aged face creasing with concern. 'All mental health ailments are rising.'

'They always have risen,' Borrowland interjects.

'Well,' the professor says, almost laughing 'At what stage does it sound silly to say 'mental illnesses always rise'? Yes we know they do! I know that more than anyone. I've spent my adult life measuring mental health illnesses. Right now, people in America are as likely to be as miserable as they are happy. Is that not the time to say, 'whoa, hold on here, we need to do something about this?'

'We are doing something about it, Professor,' I say.

'It's just… with him,' he points his whole hand at Borrowland. 'With this 'mental health always rises' nonsense.'

'No, no, no,' Borrowland says. 'You are misinterpreting my argument. I am not questioning you. I'm just saying what the opposition to this Bill will inevitably say. We know they'll say: 'Poor mental health is always on the rise.'

'That's why Zdanski is imperative. She has to deliver the message the right way,' I say.

'Have you heard from her?'

'Not yet, Professor.'

'Is it true that she met with Zuckerberg and Ziu the other night?'

I release my knee from my grasp, allowing my purple stilettoes to fall to the blue carpet.

'It is true. She left the dinner inconclusive on signing the Bill, but we're all hopeful. I feel like a lovestruck teenager, to be honest. Waiting on a call from someone I'm desperate to hear from. Only, when I was a teenager my hand was gripped to a Nokia handheld phone… waiting on it to trill. Now I'm waiting on the red light in the top of my holographics to blink. Then I'll know. Then I'll know if I'm seriously going to be able to take America out of this mess.' I grimace at the professor. 'Why don't you fill me in, so I have more ammunition to pass to Miss Zdanski when she finally calls me back.'

The professor coughs into his balled fist, then rolls his eyes and winks twice, calling up his data.

'You say her partner is locked in, right?' the professor says. 'Well, I can tell you that Locked-in Dementia cases are growing at a rate of one hundred and twenty percent state to state. We had forecast that three hundred thousand Americans will be diagnosed with Locked-in Dementia next year. We now believe that will be four hundred thousand. And then the following year, in 2049, almost nine hundred thousand will be locked in. It's the fastest growing strain of dementia we've ever measured.'

I hold my two hands to my face, playing peekaboo, as Pete Davidson calls it, my fingers tapping against my forehead.

'What else?' I say.

'ADHD among children is the second biggest headline,' the professor says. 'It's growing at a rate of one hundred and fifty percent. One in three primary children are likely to be somewhere on the spectrum of ADHD.'

'Why wouldn't children have attention disorders?' Vice President Vasquez says, shrugging her shoulders. She's always had a sharp thorn in her side about children's access to technology. It's why I made her my VP. 'This generation of children has never had to wait for anything. They can change their mind on whatever they are looking at in Sia with the blink of an eye. Literally, with the blink of an eye... Their whole lives they've had access to whatever it is they want... on demand. They're the on-demand generation.'

I nod in agreement with my vice president, and then turn to the professor again to hear more negative data I can include in my arsenal.

'Suicide is the next biggest headline,' he tells me. 'It's up in all demographics. The highest rise is in males and females in their twenties. Ten years ago, twenty in ten thousand people ended their own lives. Five years ago that was twenty-five people in ten thousand. This year, it will be fifty people per ten thousand.'

'Jesus Christ,' Borrowland says, leaning forward, taking the

Lord's name in vain inside the Oval Office. 'Suicide has doubled in the past five years?'

'Yep,' the professor replies. 'The incline on the graph is pointing straight up. That graph is pretty much parallel with the rate of depression. That's doubled in the past five years, too.'

'Still no concrete link to Sia?' I ask.

'Nothing concrete,' he says. 'Other than to be able to prove that we have had different activity in the human brain ever since the dawn of the technological revolution at the start of the century. We can align the data with the technology. We just can't say for sure that this is the reason the brain acts this way.'

'Isn't it obvious?' Vasquez says. 'The brain can't handle the amount of information we are feeding it.'

'Well,' the professor says, pursing his lips at the Vice President. 'Knowing is entirely different from proving.' He turns to me, his jowly face heavy with despair. 'Madam President. We desperately need to do something. Quick. Humanity is at stake. And it's only going to get worse.'

I hold my hands to my face again, tapping my fingers against my thick skull.

'Don't worry,' I say to him when I remove my hands, 'I'm going to change everything. With the stroke of three pens, we'll take America out of its misery.'

'Oh, holy Jesus Christ,' Borrowland says, pressing his hand to his heart before standing up to bless himself because he had blasphemed inside the Oval Office again. 'It's Zdanski. Zdanski is holocalling.'

VIKTORIA POPOV

I spent the whole morning e-scooting around the inside of the White House, while I was actually e-scooting outside the White House.

I went to the Oval Office. To the press room. To the Situation Room. The Treaty Room. Even into the President's bedroom. It's all on there. On Sia. A 3D holographic walk around of the White House. Just like there's a holographic walk around of anything and any place. I used to enjoy walking around Jamaican beaches on Sia when the holographics first came out. But the feeling just isn't the same as real life. And it makes me feel down. Every time you have to blink away from virtual reality it is painful; the realization that the world isn't like that in real life can make you feel miserable. It's sad to look at a pile of ironing on the kitchen counter as soon you blink away from a Jamaican beach. Yet, there are people who live in their virtual reality as much as they can. One man who used to work in the drug store with me always vacationed inside his Sia. He never visited anywhere in person. He would go to different cities around the world for a few days when he took time off work, but in reality he was only walking around the same small square room in his own one-bedroom apartment. No wonder everybody is crazy.

I collapse on to the bed in the motel room and close my eyes. Just so my Sia can shut itself down and I can relax a little. Sia needs a rest as much as I need a rest. I've spent the whole day inside it. And yet no yellow light has blinked on.

I need to know how I'm going to kill her. And where I'm going to kill her.

Killing Mafia guys was easy. And straightforward. I'd be handed a hot gun. I'd find a time the target was alone and then I'd just shoot him behind the ear. Bang. Job over. None of them ever expected me. I looked nothing like the men that usually carried out those kinds of hits. I was able to get in. Fire. And get out. The police always assumed the hits were gangland related. Which they were. But they were looking for gangland guys. Not a tall blonde Eastern European woman.

This is no Mafia killing. But I know I can do it. I'll do what I've always done. I'll get in. Then I'll get out. Out of DC. Out of America. And finally out of this life. Out of this mess of a life.

POTUS. SALLY W. CAMPBELL

As soon as Kyle Borrowland AirDrops the call into my Sia, I hold a hand up in apology toward him, Professor Wickle and my VP who are all sitting on the uncomfortable sofas inside the Oval Office, before I glide toward the hidden door so I can move my way down the hallway and into the brightly lit, airy and silent Cabinet Room.

'How are you, Sarah-Jane?' I ask as soon as I sit in one of the leather-bound chairs dotted around the conference table, trying to sound composed and not desperate to hear what she has to say.

'Madam President,' she says, 'I've missed some calls from you again, it seems.'

I smile using my eyes at her, portraying a patience I really don't possess.

'I was intrigued to hear how you got on meeting with Zuckerberg and Ziu the other night,' I pose.

She pauses. For way too long. So long, my stomach tenses in anticipation of disappointment.

'The sushi was great,' she says.

I smile with my eyes again, huffing out a fake laugh, straight into her holographic face. Then I find myself squinting at her as she pauses again, noticing her green eyes look heavier than usual.

'What about the topic you guys met up to discuss? Was that as appetizing as the sushi?' I ask.

She stares through my hologram. I bet she's focusing on Phil, likely in a slump behind me, drool hanging like a string from his bottom lip. I know what it's like to focus on that sight. I don't know how many times I had to mop up my foster father's hanging saliva.

'Zuckerberg and Ziu couldn't teach me anything I didn't already know,' she tells me.

My lungs deflate as a disappointing exhale shoots out of my nose. She hasn't made her decision. Not yet. All that time I gave her to think it over... and she still hasn't made a decision.

'It really doesn't matter what Zuckerberg or Ziu or even what I say to you, Sarah-Jane,' I say. 'Because you know the truth. You know exactly why the Release Bill must be signed. You do. You've always known. You knew before anyone else. The decision you need to come to does not come down to what *I* can say to you, or what Zuckerberg or Ziu can say to you. This decision is all about you convincing you. You convincing yourself to do what you believe is the right thing to do.' I lean toward her hologram, maintaining the glare of those famous heavy green eyes. 'Do it, Sarah-Jane. Sign the Release Bill. Allow it to define your legacy.'

'My legacy doesn't need the Release Bill,' she says, almost dismissively. She doesn't look like herself. She doesn't even sound like herself. She has never used that tone with me before. 'My legacy is already secured, Sally. I have been the most powerful voice in this country for fifty years. Nobody's ever been more powerful than me. Kids will be learning about me in their history books for centuries to come... with or without the Release Bill.'

'Of course,' I say, holding out a hand to fake squeeze her holographic shoulder. 'You're right. Trying to sell the Release

Bill to you as your legacy is the wrong way for me to approach this. I owe you much more respect than that.'

'I just need more time,' she says.

She purses her lips at me. I've never seen Sarah-Jane Zdanski look so deflated. She's normally the brightest of lights. But, today, she looks as if her bulb has blown.

'The time is now, Sarah-Jane,' I whisper softly. 'Another player could enter the game any day. Somebody will invent a new Sia, a new device that takes over... Somebody else will invent the next big social media platform. Technology evolves. It evolves quickly. You know that more than anyone. That's how we've gotten to the stage where you, Zuckerberg and Ziu own pretty much the entire output Americans receive. But none of you own the thing that hasn't been invented yet. Before somebody else enters the game — the next big multibillionaire — we have to sign this Bill, Sarah-Jane. We need to do it now; while the owner of the media, the owner of the apps and the owner of the device are all in agreement. Then we can write this into legislation forevermore. If we sign this Bill now, all new players into the game will have to abide by the legalities of the Bill we sign. Now is the time, Sarah-Jane. You. Me. Zuckerberg. Ziu. We are in a position where we can put an end to AI overtaking humans.'

She drops the gaze of her heavy green eyes from my face, and from Phil slumped behind my holographic chest, to begin studying the carpet beneath my purple fleck stilettos.

'You continue to misunderstand me, Madam President,' she says, somberly. 'I don't need time to decide what's right or wrong. Of course I know what's right and what's wrong. What I'm simply saying to you is: I. Need. Time. Because I literally can't make this decision right now. I'm not signing away almost everything Phil and I built. Not without his say.'

I bring both hands slowly to my face and immediately begin tapping my fingertips against my Sia band.

'Sarah-Jane,' I say through my hands, 'Phil will not be

making any more decisions. I know he won't. I've been where you are. I've been in the exact position you're in right now. On an important holocall, but staring through the holograph talking to you at the man behind it instead, watching him drool…' I leave what I've said hanging in the air between our holograms for an uncomfortable moment… but she doesn't react. She just continues to study the carpet beneath my purple stilettos. 'This is your decision to make,' I whisper. 'It's your face America tunes in to see. It's your voice they hear in their ear. You are the one whose name has always been up in neon lights. This is the decision of Zdanski… Not the decision of Philip Meredith.'

She nods, and then almost awakens from her slumber, shaking her head before her big, green eyes dart upward to meet my face.

'I remember the very first time I met you,' she says to me. 'How old were you then?'

I puff out a subtle laugh.

'Eleven.'

'Eleven? And yet you walked up to me; you must have been the saddest little girl in the whole country at the time, and yet you walked right up to me with a big, beaming smile and you said, 'Wow, you are so pretty'.'

'You blew me away. You still blow me away,' I say.

'I just wanted to give you a big hug,' she says.

'You did give me a big hug. You squeezed me tight. So tight I could feel that heartbeat of yours thudding against mine.'

'Jeez,' she says. 'Doesn't life move in mysterious ways? If it wasn't for that school shooting… where would I be? Where would we both be right now if a maniac student hadn't decided to shoot his classroom up some fifty years ago?'

I hold my eyes closed, to take a silent moment to remember my beautiful sister, before finally releasing my hands from my face and reopening my eyes.

'You'd have been exactly who you are, Sarah-Jane, regardless. You're not America's biggest influence because Meric Miller woke up one morning and decided to bring a firearm into his classroom. You are who you are and what you are because you are you.'

'You're wrong, Madam President,' she says, shaking her silky, slanted golden bob at me. 'I am who I am because of Phil Meredith.'

I purse my lips at her hologram.

'Okay,' I say, 'I get it. This is a decision for you *and* Phil. But… I want you to know this, Sarah-Jane… LiD is growing exponentially. It's happening. Locked-in Dementia is real. So real it's staring you in the face right now. By next year, another four hundred thousand families will be experiencing what you are experiencing. And that number will only continue to grow, as long as humans are consumed by technology, as long as the machines are controlling the people. We have the latest statistics Sarah-Jane… and they are shocking. I feel I need to inform you that I am going to use the White House Correspondents' dinner next week to address America and to reveal these damning statistics. Depression — on the rise! ADHD — on the rise! Suicide rates — on the rise! Locked-in Dementia… on the rise!'

She holds those heavy, green eyes closed for a moment and inhales deeply.

'You're going to preach to me at a comedy event?' she says.

'It's not a comedy event,' I say. 'The White House Correspondents' Dinner is an opportunity for the President to address the media. And I will be addressing the media the way the media needs to be addressed, Sarah-Jane. I'll be telling them that they are responsible for all of these damning statistics. I'll be equipped with all of the evidence. I won't be preaching to you, Sarah-Jane,' I say. 'I will be preaching to the four hundred and five million people in this country. You may be the one sitting right in front of me while I speak. But I will be addressing the people you control. The Correspondents' Dinner, you see, it's live. It's delivered straight to the American people on the night. Zdanski Corp. won't have time to stitch and edit the show together to align with whatever narrative they want to run with. It'll go out live… to be watched by Americans who can hear exactly what I have to say. It will be a speech for the ages. Aimed directly at the public to bring awareness through facts that the technology we're consuming is killing us. They already know it. They can see it on their own streets… in their own neighborhoods. Inside their own homes. But they need to hear it though the media, don't they? America has always needed the media to tell them how to think. Listen,' I say, reaching my hand toward her holographic shoulder again and softening my voice. 'Please be the same woman who hugged me fifty years ago, the one with the beating heart. I know she would despise what America's become…'

'Madam President,' she says. 'You don't know what that young reporter with the beating heart was capable of.'

'Yes, I do,' I say. 'I know she was capable of becoming the most powerful woman in America. And she did. She really did it.'

'Sally,' she says. 'I love you. I do. I've always thought very fondly of you. I am so proud of who you are. Of the icon you've become. But I need you to understand this. You will not be able to seduce me into signing this Bill. The only person who gets to decide if I sign that Bill is Phil Meredith. And he will decide for me. I know he will.'

BOBBY DE LUCA

This paranoia is gonna kill me. I'm sure of it. No wonder I feel like I'm getting LiD. That was another creak. I know it was. I heard it with my own two ears. And I know my ears are working just fine.

I try to walk as light as I can down my hallway. But that ain't an easy thing to do when you weigh over two hundred and thirty pounds. Another creak. Then the noise of feet sweeping across my carpet. Holy shit! I haven't been imagining this. This is real. Somebody's in my fuckin' house!

I hold my hand against my beating heart as I lean against the wall just outside my living room, and I try to breathe steadily before turning inside, my two fists raised.

'Holy fucking shit,' I say, panting the words out of my mouth.

She grins at me.
It's her.
Really her.
Not hologram her.
But her.
In person.
In flesh and bones.

'Thought I'd surprise you,' she says. 'Now, how about that hug we've been dreaming about for the past eight months?'

I want to sob. To properly cry. Tears and snot and everything that comes with it. But I don't got time for that. I want that hug as much as she does. So, I waddle toward her, my arms outstretched, and when her body leans into mine, I wrap my arms around her back as tightly as I can, until I can feel her heart beating just below mine.

I sniff her white hair as she nestles her cheek onto my shoulder, and I swear my heart is beating heavier than it has ever beaten before. Probably because I can feel two hearts beating.

'I love you so much,' I whisper, just as a tear drops out of my eye.

'I love you, too,' she muffles into my shoulder. I can tell she's crying too.

She squeezes me as hard as she can, even though her arms can't reach all the way around, but I can feel her grip; the palms of her hands digging into the fat of my back.

When we eventually release, I stare into her face. I think she's beautiful. She doesn't agree. She thinks the decades of sucking on vape pens gave her all of her wrinkles. But I love every single crease on that beaming face.

She wipes a curled finger into both eyes, then smiles at me. I can't believe I'm staring at that grin in real life. It's much more beautiful in real life than it is in holograph.

'I'm not here for long,' she says. 'I know this is one of the busiest weeks of the year for you, but… I had a window and I thought all I wanna do is go see Bobby.'

'Thank you, thank you,' I say, leaning in to kiss her forehead.

'I fly out at nine a.m. tomorrow, so I gotta be leaving here about six a.m.'

'What time's it now?' I ask.

Her eyeballs roll up.

'Just past four p.m.,' she says.

'Great,' I say, 'then we got fourteen hours together. Let's just squeeze each other for all fourteen hours.'

I reach my arms around her again and squeeze her even tighter this time, sniffing in her hair. It's only when we fall to my couch that we kinda separate, though I keep one arm wrapped around her shoulders, holding her face close to mine.

Her eyes are still watery. Mine are too.

'I wanted to tell you in person, rather than over Sia,' she says, 'but I, uh… I found a buyer for my business. I'm selling up. May thirtieth is my final day as owner of Cling Packaging. We accepted a bid of four point two million.'

'Wow,' I say.

'At the end of it all, I'll end up with one point four million in my pocket…'

'Same,' I say grinning at her. 'That's what my accountant projected I'd get in my pocket when I sell. We're likely to sell for six million, but because of the dilution, I'll end up with somewhere between one point two and one point five.'

'Amazing,' she says in her cute Canadian accent, 'we'll both be entering into this new life on equal footing.'

'And it's more than enough to see us through the next thirty years,' I say.

'Thirty-four years,' she says, stabbing a pointed finger to my fat belly.

We've often talked about me living until I'm a hundred.

'Oh, wait there,' I say to her, gently pulling my arm from behind her neck before heaving myself up from the sofa, leaving her draped there, her legs touching the carpet beneath her, but her body leaning to one side. She looks beautiful on my sofa. I can't believe she's here. In flesh and bones. I can't believe she is literally draped on my sofa.

'I thought you said we were gonna hug each other for all fourteen hours?' she shouts after me as I disappear out of the room.

I don't answer her. Instead, I walk to my office, before my

eyes start dancing around the place. I didn't leave it in here, did I? Why've I come in here? I spin on my heels, and then waddle up the stairs toward my bedroom. I know where it is. It's in the cabinet by my bedside. I left in there after I practiced my proposal in the mirror once again this morning.

A rush of excitement races through my big belly as I open the top drawer of the cabinet and reach for the red satin box. When I slam the drawer shut and begin skipping down the stairs I feel as if I am a skinny seven-year-old boy all over again —my whole life ahead of me.

As soon as I step foot onto my living-room carpet, I notice she is now sitting upright in my sofa, her eyes squinting at me, the corners of her lips turned up like mine—the two of us grinning like naughty school kids. Only, she doesn't know what's about to happen... I do...

I gently squeeze the arm of the sofa for support as I crouch down to one knee. But as soon as I'm down there, the words vanish from my memory. I can't recall what I had planned to say. Which is weird. Because I practiced it over and over again.

Instead of using words, I hold up the red satin box and flick it open with my thumb. Her eyes widen. And she slaps a hand over her mouth.

'Belinda,' I say, my bottom lip quivering, 'will you marry me?'

7

SARAH-JANE STRODE THE LENGTH OF HER HALLWAY, AND AS SOON as she set foot into her plush living room she tapped the nurse on the top of his shoulder, causing him to drop the battered paperback of *1984* he had been reading to his patient.

'Didn't mean to startle you,' Sarah-Jane said as the nurse stretched between his own legs to pick the book up. 'Any movement today?'

When the nurse sat back into the floral-patterned chair, he twisted to face Sarah-Jane, his lips turned down, his head somberly shaking.

'Not really. His left arm fell off his lap once. And his mouth popped open a couple of times... but that's pretty much it.'

Sarah-Jane pushed her tongue against the inside her cheek, and then nodded her head over her shoulder, signaling for the nurse to leave her alone with Phil. The nurse placed the open copy of *1984* face down on the arm of the chair he regularly sat on to attend to Phil, then swished his faux-plastic scrubs down the long hallway.

Phil was slouched onto the orange sofa, his lips and eyes shut tight, his breathing loud as it grunted through his hairy nostrils. Sarah-Jane took one step toward him, removed the

black egg-shaped nozzle from her pocket and, holding one of
Phil's temples with her other hand, she pressed the black egg
into the opposite side of his head until the suction took. His
eyes blinked open, but they were glazed over, heavily bloodshot, and unmistakably zoned out. Sarah-Jane placed a hand
under his jowly chin, and then tilted his head backward so she
could stare into those bloodshot eyes, but they just rolled back
into his head as if he were a toy doll. She tutted, reached for the
handheld pad with the pulsating, sky-blue button in the center
of it and then held it flat in her palm as she took one slow step
backward.

'Jesus Christ,' she whispered to herself. She stared around
her quiet penthouse; around her vacant open-plan living room;
around her famous kitchen-cum-studio; and then out of the
floor-to-ceiling windows at New York City twinkling a rainbow
of colored lights back at her, before she faced Phil again with a
heavy sigh and, without hesitating any longer, she tapped her
thumb against the sky-blue button twice.

A sizzle could be heard inside the black egg, and then Phil's
left arm rose before landing itself back down to the orange sofa
with a thump. His head leaned a little forward, and his eyes
popped open, as if they were focusing on the woman standing
in front of him.

'Phil, Phil,' she whispered. 'Phil, it's me. Sarah-Jane. I need
you to do your best to signal to me, okay. Even if you can't talk.
Signal to me, Phil. All I need is one signal. For you to let me
know you can hear me.'

She paused, to give Phil time to respond. But his head rested
back onto the sofa, and his eyes began to glaze over.

'No. No, Phil,' she whisper-shouted. 'Please. Listen to me.
Just listen to me, okay. I want you to move your left arm if you
can hear me… if you can understand me. Just move your left
arm.'

She paused, squinting at Phil's left hand resting on the
orange sofa. It didn't move. Not even a flicker of a finger.

'Sally W. Campbell is the President of the United States, Phil. Sterling Ziu and Max Zuckerberg have agreed to sign the Release Bill. You remember the Release Bill, don't you? Well, Phil… it's real. The Release Bill is real. And she wants me to sign it. Phil… Phil… should I sign it? Should I sign the Release Bill? Move your left arm if you think I should sign the Release Bill.'

She glared at Phil's left hand again. But it remained still; his curled fingers slumped to the sofa. So, she took a step forward, lifted that left arm, and placed it gingerly onto his lap. Then she reached her hand into his pants pocket and pulled out his Sia band. After slapping it to his dry forehead, she took another step back.

'Sia, play Oasis, *Wonderwall*,' she said. 'Sia… share song with Phil.'

Wonderwall was the only song Sarah-Jane could remember Phil actually liking. He wasn't one for keeping up with trends, and never once listened to music on Spotify—even though he owned half of the company. Spotify, for him, was all about podcasts. Heavy interview-led podcasts. He didn't have time to listen to music. Though Sarah-Jane did recall with a squinted side-smile this morning that in 1997 — during the summer they first met as a roving reporter and cameraman slash producer for their local PBS Network — Oasis were receiving a lot of US radio play. And she recalled catching him whispering along to *Wonderwall* one day in the van they would travel the streets of northern Kansas in. It was the only time she had ever seen him try to sing. Phil likely wouldn't remember the story even if he was cognitive again—the moment likely lost on him many years before he had even contracted dementia. Yet *Wonderwall* was the only song Sarah-Jane could think of that might help waken him from his slumber.

As Liam Gallagher began to groan out the opening lyrics, Sarah-Jane exhaled.

'Phil,' she said. 'Phil. I need you to just send me a sign. If you can hear me, I want you to send me a sign. With your left hand. Sally W. Campbell is the President. The Release Bill is real. Should I sign it? Should I agree to sign the Release Bill?'

She paused, listened to the guitar riff, then stepped forward again and lightly touched the back of Phil's left hand with the nail of her index finger.

'Phil, listen, listen to the music. Remember? Back in our reporter's van fifty years ago, huh? I caught you singing to this... remember? This left hand,' she said, circling her finger-nail around his hairy knuckles, 'I just want you to move it. Just try with all of your might to move this hand if you can hear me. I need to know that you can hear me. Please, Phil...' she removed her finger from the back of Phil's left-hand and stepped back again, 'please just move your left hand... to let me know you're still in there. Do it. Do it, Phil. Move it now. Move your hand.'

She held her breath.

For nothing.

Nothing but stillness.

A deathly silence outside of Sia.

Liam Gallagher groaning inside of Sia.

When she closed her eyes with disappointment and exhaled the breath she was holding with a deep sigh, the front door of her penthouse opened, and Sarah-Jane could hear the move-ment of shoes down her hallway carpet, before the clunk of a heavy bag dropped onto the floral two-seater chair behind her.

'How is he?' Erica asked.

'Same,' Sarah-Jane said swiveling to face her daughter, her heavy, green eyes glistening with the threat of tears. 'Even though I used this fucking thing again!'

She threw the handheld pad across the living room where it crashed against the far wall, before landing softly on the carpet, and then she slapped both palms to her face and cried into them.

'Christ, Sarah-Jane,' Erica said, as she rushed toward her mother, enveloping her in a tight hug.

It was the first time Erica had ever embraced Sarah-Jane in such dramatic fashion, but that was because it was the first time she had ever known the media mogul to be this torn, this heart-broken, this depressed…

'Take a seat,' Erica whispered into her mother's ear.

She moved her backward, toward the sofa where she helped sit her down next to a gormless Phil. Erica, took four steps backward, all while staring at her parents, then sat down into the floral chair next to the shopping bags she had just dropped there when she first noticed how upset Sarah-Jane was.

'What m'I gonna do?' Sarah-Jane exhaled.

'About what?' Erica asked.

'About what?' Sarah-Jane said. 'About him. About Phil.'

'Well,' Erica paused, taking the time to cross her legs, knocking the battered paperback of *1984* off the arm of the chair in the process. 'We know the data on LiD. We know that people in Phil's age range, they don't wake up, Sarah-Jane. Not for long. For a second maybe. That's all we're going to get from Phil from now on. Seconds of the day where he looks at us and recognizes us, but then… well, he's just going to get locked back in again, isn't he? Sarah-Jane, it's been months now. And week after week, day after day, he gets more and more locked in. He's not going to wake up. Phil is locked in.'

'He has to wake up. He just has to,' Sarah-Jane said, gripping her lover's left hand and placing it between hers. 'C'mon, Phil. Wake up. Wake up. Just for one minute. I just have one question to ask you… that's all.'

She sobbed, and Erica uncrossed her legs to move toward her, only for her mother to hold a palm up, stopping her. The body language the two of them had begun to speak over the past few weeks was more of a discomfort than a comfort to Sarah-Jane. She didn't want another hug; she didn't want further reminding that she had forgone so many meaningful relationships in her life for the sake of her career.

'Look, Sarah-Jane,' Erica said. 'What Phil would tell you, if he were able to wake up, would be to concentrate on your show. You've a new season launching in eight days' time, and we have slim pickings to launch with. Let the nurse look after Phil, and how about you and I… we discuss the show. Without your show, you lose your voice. Let's concentrate on how you can launch with a bang, huh?'

Sarah-Jane shook her lobbed bob and sighed audibly.

'The show is not that important.'

'The show is everything,' Erica said. '*Everything*. It gives you your voice. The show should always be our number one priority…'

Sarah-Jane held the stare of her daughter for a long moment.

'You think the show is the number one priority when Phil is dying right in front of our eyes.'

'Whoa, hold on,' Erica said. 'Sarah-Jane, Phil is not dying. He is being fed, and he could live for another decade… another two decades in the comfort of this home.'

'He's dead to us, for crying out loud, Erica.'

Erica opened her mouth to reply, but only offered a tired sigh instead. She glanced at Phil, then back at Sarah-Jane, the annoying thought that she inherited more of her father's features than her mother's still not fully receded from her mind, even all these years later. Then she sat more upright in the floral armchair, moving the shopping bags out of her way with a push of her shoulder.

'Look,' she said, 'I know, and you know, that Phil always saw *The Zdanski Show* as the priority. Yes, you own a hundred other shows, but your own show, your own voice was everything Phil worked hard for every day of his darn life. It was his obsession. *The Zdanski Show* was his number one priority from the moment you both signed that contract at CSN back in ninety-ninety-whatever-it-was. If you stop caring about your show, then you know what… Phil may as well be dead.'

Sarah-Jane didn't reply. She, instead, gripped Phil's left hand tighter, between her two hands. Then she leaned over and kissed him where his beard used to decorate his red-rosy cheeks before it got all patchy in his old age.

'What you thinkin', Sarah-Jane?' Erica asked when the silence rippled past a state of comfort—leaving an awkwardness in the air that always seemed to hang when these two were in conversation. They may have spent the past quarter of a century cohabiting and coproducing, but they also spent that quarter of a century co-resenting each other. The fact that Sarah-Jane had given Erica away within minutes of giving birth to her had hovered like a dark cloud over their relationship for all that time; never to be addressed – not with any specificity.

Sarah-Jane brought Phil's hairy hand to her mouth and repeatedly kissed it.

'Sarah-Jane,' Erica said, reminding her she was still in a conversation. 'C'mon. You need to concentrate. You need to get back to work; to start getting excited about a new season of *The Zdanski Show*.'

'Get excited? You want me to get excited,' Sarah-Jane said, dropping Phil's hand to her lap. 'How am I supposed to get excited when he's sitting here with drool hanging from his fuckin mouth every darn time I look at him?'

'Maybe that should be your opening story,' Erica suggested, shrugging her shoulders. 'Let America know what living with LiD is like. It's a growing topic. If folks heard it from you, then they'd really start to believe the LiD epidemic is coming.'

'Jesus, Erica,' Sarah-Jane said. 'If I tell America that Sia causes LiD and that it might be coming to a home near you, I may as well just sign the fucking Release Bill. I may as well admit that everything I own is killing people.'

'Then sign the fucking Release Bill,' Erica said, sitting more upright. 'Make that your opening show. It'd be a smash hit. You signing a document as powerful as the Declaration of Independence.'

Sarah-Jane sighed, making a whistling sound through her pursed lips.

'You really think I should sign it, don't you?' she asked her daughter.

'Look to your right,' Erica said. Sarah-Jane took in the sight of her love slouched on the couch, a fresh bubble of saliva clinging to the bottom of his lip, waiting to leap into the wisps of his gray beard. 'Do you want this happening to other families? Do you want Americans to go through the pain you are going through right now? Look at him. He's gone. He's locked in. You say you've been waiting on Phil to tell you whether or not you should sign the Release Bill, but isn't he telling you everything you need to know right now? Isn't his silence the answer?'

Sarah-Jane flicked her heavy green eyes away from her lover, to take in her daughter who happened to share the exact same eyes as her father.

'You're right,' she whispered.

'Huh?' Erica said.

'You're right. Phil is giving me his answer. Phil being locked in tells me everything I need to know.'

'Wait... what?'

'I'm gonna sign it, Erica,' Sarah-Jane said, 'I've decided. I'm going to sign the Release Bill.'

MADISON MONROE

I couldn't go back to the college after my appearance on *Good Morning DC*; couldn't face the guilt. So, I left a recorded message on the Headmaster's holomail, telling him I was feeling the effects of a virus taking over. The thoughts of facing little Neve's questions was scratching at my brain. She'd have been dismayed watching me lie on TV. And I could just picture her pale face, her bottom lip hanging open, her eyes squinting in disgust at me.

Despite all of those guilty thoughts, my gut is mostly feeling scorched by Laura Trailing telling me I didn't pop on hologram. I thought I'd be nervous by now. Nervous about breaking back into this office and carrying out tasks two and three. But I'm not. Because the burn of not popping in hologram is overriding the nerves. All I wanna do is get this over and done with, then I can go back to my couch and cry at home, waiting on that two hundred and fifty thousand dollars to drop. Once it drops, I'll be fine. I know I will. I don't need to be a regular guest on some shitty breakfast show... I'll be happy when that money drops. Happy and with credit for the first time in my adult life.

I stayed on my couch sniffling tears for three hours after the show, until I felt so tired of crying that I swapped my own Sia band for the untraceable one. A Blynq message was pulsing as soon as I slapped it to my forehead. The hoodie said I was to break into the office again at six p.m. precisely, and from there I was to await further instructions on tasks two and three. He also told me I had to wear what he had delivered in the mail for me. An all in-one paper boiler suit. A boiler suit with a tiny brown bottle of fluid inside its pocket. The boiler suit looks as though it would be uncomfortable. But it's not. It's actually quite light. And airy. But even that isn't stopping my armpits from sweating as I walk around this office again. It's actually a little neater than it was when I first broke in here a few nights ago. I stare at the framed photographs hanging along the wall again; the same men all lined up with their arms around each other, growing older with each passing photograph, grinning for the camera. When I'm squinting at one of the smiles, the yellow light pulses in the top corner of my Sia and my heart drops.

I wink my eye to accept the message, then blink once to begin playing it.

'Madison,' the hoodie's hologram says, appearing in front of me, 'Here's task two. I have sent two emails to the untraceable Sia you are wearing right now. I want you to copy these two emails, then open up that huge computer screen in the office you have broken in to so you can paste them in there. The first one must be sent to the email address written at the top of the email I have just sent. The second email you paste in *has* to be saved to the drafts folder. That is all that is involved in task two. One email to send. One email to save to the draft folder. You have three minutes… off you go.'

He blinks away.

Three minutes? What the fuck? A panic hits me, and I rush toward the big computer screen and wave my hand in front of it. As soon as the screen awakens, I wink at the email icon in the bottom corner. Then I blink, accepting the first email sent to me by the anonymous hoodie before double blinking, AirDropping it to the big computer screen. When I paste the email address into the top bar, I swish my eyes to the left, sending the email off. Then I repeat the process, by winking and blinking the second email onto the big computer screen, before saving it into the draft folder. I think I held my breath through all of that. But it's done. The first email sent to the email address provided. The second saved to the drafts folder. That's it? That's task two. This sure is easy for a two hundred and fifty thousand dollar bid. Although I know task three is going to be a different beast altogether. I take the small brown bottle out of my pocket and stare at it again. As if it's going to change.

When I lean back from the desk, the silence of the empty room washes over me and I walk toward the far wall to squint at the photographs again. I think I like looking at them because I'm wondering which man it is that I'm probably about to kill.

I realize as I stare at the old faces that I am feeling rather calm; calm for somebody about to tackle task three of a big bid on the Dark Web; calm for somebody who was told they didn't pop in hologram this morning.

Suddenly, the door downstairs shakes, then swings open. Now I don't feel so calm. Holy shit! Who the hell is this? What am I supposed to do? I stare up into the top corner of the untraceable Sia, in search of another blue pulse; the final Blynq message from the hoodie. Task Three. But nothing is pulsing. Except my strong heartbeat.

I fall to my stomach and begin crawling and shuffling backward, like a snake wearing a boiler suit, until I'm fully hidden under the large desk. Then the front door slams shut, and footsteps begin to make their way toward me.

VIKTORIA POPOV

I spent the morning walking around little towns outside of Kyiv, looking at small houses I would be able to buy when I get my one hundred thousand dollars. I must have worn the carpet in the motel room out while I was walking around those little towns outside of Kyiv. But that was a better way to spend the day than lying on the bed, because that was making me sleepy.

I did not want to go out scooting again. Scooting around the White House for three hours yesterday was too much. So, I stayed here all day, walking around little towns outside of Kyiv.

The yellow light still hasn't blinked on. But it will. It has to. It's Thursday. Thursday is the day I'm carrying out the hit. And I haven't even been passed a weapon yet. But if I have to use my bare hands, I will. I've done it before. I killed that Russian with my bare hands. All I would need to do is get her alone. I can kill anyone if they're alone. It's easy. You just wrap your fingers around their necks and squeeze so tight that they don't have time to react. They're too worried about sucking in their last gasp of air that their eyes grow delusional, and their face gets very red and looks like it's going to burst. Then they suck in their last gasp of air, and they get all light in your hands.

I have decided I might move to Khotyanivka. It is about

twenty miles outside of Kyiv. My cousin used to live there. Daryna. I hope she still lives there. But I am not certain because I couldn't find her online. If she is still there, we can become friends. It would be nice to start my new life where I know one person. Khotyanivka isn't the prettiest of the towns. But I can see myself there.

As soon as the blue light pulses in the top corner of my Sia, I hold my eyes closed and breathe really slowly. As soon as I open them, I wink once at the blue pulse, before the dark figure's hologram blinks in front of me.

'Viktoria,' he says, 'One hundred thousand dollars will drop into your Sia account as soon as your target's life ends. Listen to me clearly. You were chosen to carry this out because of your experience. You tell us you were one of the deadliest assassins in Boston. *This* assassination requires a deadly assassin. Your target is at this address.' He blinks both eyes twice, AirDropping a map locator into the Blynq message.

'It is about a forty-minute e-scoote from where your motel is. This is your target's home. I want you to arrive at this home and enter the premises. Your target will enter after you. Be patient. This is where I need your experience. Your hit, Viktoria… it needs to look like suicide.'

'Suicide?' I say to nobody, noting I am only talking to a Blynq message and the four walls of this tiny motel.

'Viktoria,' he says. 'I want you to leave now to make it to this address. You will listen to me explain how to make the assassination look like suicide while you walk.'

BOBBY DE LUCA

We woke up smiling in each other's faces. In fact, we didn't really wake up at all. Because we barely slept. Well, I didn't anyway. Not really. I spent most of the night staring down at the top of her white hair, inhaling her smell. It felt like heaven to have her heart beating against my ribs. No feeling can beat the feeling of somebody else's heart thumping against your own body.

We'd already talked about sex not being a motivation for us spending the rest of our lives together; that kisses and hugs would be more than enough to satisfy both of us. I'd hugged hundreds of people before last night. My mamma when I was younger. My poppa. My little sister. My best friends. Heck, the whole Mafia family used to hug each other and kiss each other on both cheeks back in the day. But I ain't ever hug somebody the way I hugged Belinda last night. We were so inseparable that I took the cab with her all the way to the airport this morning where we clung to each other like Siamese twins, until time finally beat us, and Belinda had to go through security to catch her flight back home to Canada.

After she had got through the gate, she spun around to look at me before bringing her hand to her lips so she could kiss her engagement ring. Then she waved it at me and disappeared down the long hallway.

I can't believe I'm engaged. I can't believe I finally asked her; that I finally held her; that I finally met her in person. I know we've met hundreds of times over the months, but it's just not the same in hologram, even though we did fall in love over hologram.

I glance up into the top corner of my Sia to take in the time. The morning has gotten away from me. I need to get some work done. I've barely been around this week for one of my company's biggest and busiest times of the year. Though I guess this is proof that they can survive without me; that De Luca's will continue its legacy while I'm off sunning my fat ass all over the world.

I just need to get this hectic week out of the way, then I'll be free to sun that fat ass all over the world, with the love of my life by my side.

The red circle pulses in the top corner of my Sia and my heart flutters. Because I know it's her. A holomessage. I wink my eye at the pulsing circle, and then she blinks up in front of me, grinning.

'I love you, sweetie,' she says in her cute Canadian accent, before pushing her lips toward me and kissing them. 'I can't believe you're my fiancé.' She gasps, then chuckles before lifting her fingers up and showing me the ring again. 'Bobby, I can't wait to spend the rest of my life with you. I'll forever feel grateful for the day you suggested we meet alone to discuss your products' packaging. As soon as we started meeting together, I knew my life would change; change for the better. And now I am excited that I feel like a little girl all in love all over again. I'll call you when I'm back home, sweetie. Bye... my fiancé.'

Her hologram disappears, and I'm left standing in the middle of my living-room, grinning to myself. I haven't stopped grinning since the moment I saw her head nodding and the tears pouring out of her eyes yesterday when I got down on one knee.

I know everybody is saying America is miserable… but I'm not miserable. Not anymore. In fact, I think I might be the happiest man in America right about now.

TIMMY BUCKETT

I feel for the gun in my pocket. It's cold. Really cold. And heavy. Heavier than it looks.

The guy who's paying me to do this, he just said I have to keep my head down. That I can't let anybody see me. I won't. I'm good at keeping my head down. At keeping a low profile. It's what I've been doing since I moved to DC. Because I couldn't let Scar and his gang catch up with me. If they ever caught me, I know they'd kill me. And they wouldn't do what I'm gonna do to this woman—they wouldn't just shoot me in the back of the head and get away as fast as they could. They'd torture me. Torture me until I drenched my face in tears and my pants in piss. Then they'd end my life.

The guy said the woman I've to shoot in the back of the head is really bad. And that I will be doing America a favor by getting rid of her. That's fine by me. I'd get rid of anybody for fifteen grand. I'd get rid of anybody to make sure Caggie gets rid of that baby growing inside of her.

Cag left a few missed holocalls on my Sia earlier, but I don't want to talk to her. Not until this job is done and I can tell her I have the money to send her off to California. I know she'll get the abortion. Because that girl is obsessed with me. She loves that I'm a bad boy. Because it goes against everything her precious daddy told her she needed in a boyfriend. All chicks are the same. They'll go against their daddy's wishes, just to have some excitement in their lives. Cag is excited by me. I know she is. I know I can control her. Chicks are easy to control. Easy to manipulate. That's why I know she'll be on that flight to California next week. Because I said so.

I squint into the distance to see if the football fields are nearby. I usually use Sia to map out where I have to go. But I've had to find my own way here, because Sia keeps track. And I don't want anyone to track me. That's why my Sia band is lying at home on my sofa. The guy also told me I wasn't to take an e-scoote to the football fields because they can be tracked too. It's a long walk. But I guess it's not much work for such a big pay day. Fifteen K just for walking four miles and pulling a trigger is great work if you can get it. It takes me four months of packing boxes at Markt to earn fifteen K. Now I'm going to be earning that in little more than an hour.

I continue to grip the cold butt of the gun in my pocket as I walk. I wonder who this chick is I'm going to fire a bullet into the back of. Maybe she's the girlfriend of the guy who hired me to do this. Maybe she cheated on him, and he is paying her back in the deadliest way possible. Fine by me. Because her being dead means that thing growing inside Cag will also be dead soon.

I see a glowing sign, pointing the way to the football fields and so I follow the narrow alleyway it leads me down. When I step foot inside the alleyway, I can see that the football fields are overgrown. Most public football fields are overgrown. Cos people don't play football on fields no more. They play it inside their Sia. They play it from the comfort of their own home.

The wind is blowing more now, and it's whistling down the alleyway. I probably should have brought a coat. But I'll be fine. The adrenaline of killing this chick will keep me warm. As soon as I step foot out of the alleyway, I settle behind a tree, my hand still wrapped around the cold metal butt of the gun and then I do what the guy told me to do. I wait. I wait for her to walk across those football fields past me. Then I'll walk up behind her... and bang!

POTUS. SALLY W. CAMPBELL

When I enter the large rectangular dining hall of the hotel to modest applause, I immediately look for her. She's sitting where she always sits at this annual Dinner. At the table in the center of the front row. She doesn't look as heavy-eyed as she has over the past few times I've holocalled her. It looks, to me, as if the light in her green eyes has turned back on. And that light makes my stomach roll over with excitement. Maybe the light is back because she's made her decision. She looks as if a weight has lifted from her shoulders.

When her green eyes catch my brown eyes, I smile and nod at her. And she smiles back. That's the first time I've seen that pretty face smile at me in months.

'Zdanski looks in good spirits,' I whisper to Kyle Borrowland as I take my seat.

I look toward her again and she winks at me before her head moves toward our host, Pete Davidson, who has just walked to the center podium to a much louder and longer round of applause than the one I received when I entered.

'HELLO,' he shouts into the microphone. 'CAN THE TV PEOPLE ALL THE WAY AT THE BACK HEAR ME?' I laugh. So does everybody else in the room. 'I'm old enough to remember the days when the TV people were sitting up here…' He points at the front row. 'Now they gotcha all sitting in the back with the non-VIPs. Is FOX News here?' he asks, holding a flat palm above his eyes and squinting into the crowd. 'CSN? CNN? MSNBC? Lookatchall way back in the shadows there… about as useful as a pair of balls on a dildo.' He gets another huge laugh. 'Speaking of significance, front and center at the Correspondents' Dinner — as always — is Miss Sarah-Jane Zdanski.' A huge round of applause rises as it always does when Sarah-Jane is announced at this Dinner. Which is no surprise. Not when she pays the salaries of seventy percent of the people in this room. 'You're still, *Miss* Zdanski, huh? Forever a Miss. Sarah-Jane, you and I have the opposite relationship history, huh?' A small laugh. 'Not only have you never married, Sarah-Jane, you've never even dated. Get this, Sarah-Jane Zdanski has been in the public eye for half a century now, and no media has ever photographed her on a date. Then again, she owns most of the media doesn't she? So, you know it is likely you're as much of a hoe as I am… Just nobody ever gets to hear about it.'

He gets as many 'ewwws' for that joke as he gets laughs. But that's the way Pete Davidson likes it. He plays for the 'ewwws' as much as he does the giggles. He always has.

While he continues to travel around the room, roasting the most well-known producers and reporters and news executives, I decide I'll wait for my turn to be the butt of the jokes by spending the time studying Sarah-Jane's reactions. She seems to be laughing along at every wisecrack Davidson fires out.

'Zdanksi's in great form,' I lean back and whisper to Borrowland. 'I reckon she's decided to sign the Bill.'

Borrowland turns down his bottom lip and nods his head, then he laughs and claps once at the next Davidson barb, before leaning nearer to me.

'You might be right,' he whispers. And suddenly my stomach ripples with excitement. 'Still,' Borrowland continues, 'you gotta go hard on her in your speech.'

I nod at him before fake laughing at the next Davidson joke, even though I didn't hear it.

'Which brings me to the President,' Davidson says. I take the time the crowd are applauding to beam a wide smile in anticipation of my takedown. When the applause stops, Davidson grins his trademark smirk at me. I know he's staring at my face just so he can study my reaction. 'The second female president in American history.' Another applause. 'The first Black woman president in American history.' Another round of applause. 'The first lesbian president in American history.' He gets a big laugh. It's not the first time he's roasted me for being gay. Even though I'm not. I'm just single. That's all. 'Madam President, I know you have only been in office for three months, but may I ask on behalf of every single reporter here today, how the hell did you manage to get that cancer inside Jarod Wyatt's brain?' I opt to suck air in through my teeth and grimace at that gag. Some of the crowd laugh. But most offer that "ewww" sound Davidson mostly craves. 'Hey,' he says, 'how do we know the President thinks she's ugly?' He shrugs. 'Cos, she hides her face about twenty times a day.'

He holds his hands to his face, doing the peekaboo gag he let me in on during the week while everybody roars with laughter. So, I roar with laughter, too, even though I didn't even think it was worthy of a smile when I first heard it.

'Though in all seriousness, Ladies and Gentlemen of the media, I'm sure you'll agree it's a genuine pleasure to have such a strong woman occupy the White House,' he continues. 'You know why? Because the place has never looked so tidy.' He gets another laugh. Not a huge one. But enough of a laugh to inform us that sexist tropes still work as gags, even in the year 2047. When the laughing stops, Davidson slaps a hand to his heart. 'Despite spending the past three months roasting her on *The Tonight Show*, it is genuinely a great privilege for me to welcome to the podium, Ladies and Gentlemen, the fifty-second President of the United States of America, Miss Sally W. Campbell.'

Davidson grins at me while the who's-who of the national media applaud… anticipating my debut stand-up routine. When I get to the microphone, and the applause slowly dies, I offer a subtle smile to Sarah-Jane in the front row, before whistling a huge exhale through my rosy-red painted lips, causing the overly-large microphone to huff. She winks one of her famous big, green eyes at me in the awkward silence that follows my faux pas, and in that moment I know… I know she is going to sign the Release Bill. We are about to sign the most historic document that's been written in this country since the founding fathers scribbled their names at the bottom of the Declaration of Independence.

'Hey, Davidson,' I say, feeling giddy while I turn to the host, 'You're single, I'm single…' I hold my hands out and with a shrug of my shoulders while the who's-who of American media roar with laughter.

When the cackles and wolf whistles die down, I pull the microphone nearer to my chin, and then lean in to execute everything I have practiced over and over again. This is my moment.

'Ladies and Gentlemen of the media,' I say. 'Asking Pete Davidson for a date will be my only joke of the evening. Because I have a very important and very dangerous set of statistics that I need to share with you today…

MADISON MONROE

The footsteps get louder and scarier, until his shoes appear at the door of the office... where they pause with a creak, before walking off in another direction.

I hold my eyes closed to try to heighten my hearing. Footsteps. A pause. A click. A horrible loud chugging. Then another click. Footsteps again. Louder. And louder. And louder... Until they turn into the office I'm hiding in... Until they sound as if they're right next to me. The stomping stops. And when I peel open my eyes, I notice that not only are his shoes right in front of my face, but the blue light in the top corner of my Sia is pulsing at me. Finally. He gasps out loud, and then farts. A horrible wet fart. I hold my breath, for fear of the whiff reaching me under this desk, when his shoes suddenly spin on the spot, making a horrible screeching sound, before they walk away from me, his footsteps clicking and clacking against the floorboards. The feet stop again, on the far side of the office, and I can make out the knees of his silver suit trousers.

I exhale all that I have been holding in as silently as I can. Then I roll my eyes up into the top corner of my holographics before winking at the blue pulsing light.

The hoodie appears, standing over me.

'Your subject will be arriving home anytime now.' *No shit.* 'As soon as he does, task three will begin… The subject is a very important man. Your job is to end his life. And you're going to end it by making it look like it was all a very unfortunate accident…'

8

Sarah-Jane sat with her hands interlocked and flat underneath her chin, smiling ever so subtly at the President while the media were being drowned in wave after wave of attacks. On occasion she turned to Erica to offer a wink, the subtle smile still evident on the edge of her lips. She was aware most cameras were on her while the President was speaking; but the smile wasn't produced to paint a picture of bravery, she was genuinely smiling because she was genuinely happy.

A weight had lifted from her shoulders as soon as she realized Phil was telling her all she needed to know by not saying anything at all. When she admitted to Erica out loud back in her penthouse two days ago that she was going to sign the Release Bill, she almost became a different person instantly, certainly physically. Her green eyes began to sparkle again, losing the weight they had been carrying, and her perfect teeth were back on show because she began to smile for the first time in months.

Although the subject of the speech they were absorbing was dark, the setting was bright. Bright white. Everywhere. The walls, the tablecloths, the microsilk drapery hanging from the white pillars of the main room of the Heart Hotel were all clean white. As if they were at a billionaire's wedding. Even the cutlery was white; white soup spoons; white dessert spoons; white forks; white steak knives.

Highlighted out of the bright whitewash, standing at the podium, was the purple dress suit and the dark brown skin of the president, whose speech was being met by a still and serene silence by all one-thousand people sat at the bright white tables. The newsmen and women in attendance were all aware they were listening to a speech for the ages. But they were also aware that the speech threatened their livelihoods. It's why the only guest showing their teeth was the one person President Sally W. Campbell had been eyeing throughout most of her speech.

'You keep calling my ideas radical,' the President continued. 'I'll tell you what's radical. Sitting by while humanity continues to decline. That's radical. The fact that you fail to report all of these statistics and facts I've just given to you. That's radical. Americans living their whole waking lives inside their technology. That's radical. What is not radical are the ideas of the people trying to put this right. Trying to roll back the clock. It is you who is turning attention elsewhere while the chances of the American people becoming depressed takes an upward turn every time we measure the data. I am not radical. You, ladies and gentlemen of the American media, it is you who are radical.'

She subtly bowed, tilting her head forward to note the end of her address, only to be met by a stinging silence… until Sarah-Jane began to applaud loudly from the center of the front round table, causing a ripple effect of applause to reach all corners of the bright white room.

By the time the President was walking back to her seat, the applause was almost deafening, and when she finally sat she looked up to see Sarah-Jane aiming her applause right at her, her teeth on full show, befitting of the bright white theme of the room.

'Okay,' Pete Davidson said as soon as his lanky body reached the podium again. 'Can somebody tell me what all that was about, I kinda fell asleep as soon as the President said she wasn't doing any more jokes?'

Davidson received a roar of laughter for his quip and the applause that had rung loudly for the President picked up again… until it got to a stage where folks no longer knew whether they were applauding the President or applauding the host.

'Okay, I've been told it's now time for the White House Correspondents' Dinner to be a, uh… y'know, like an actual dinner. So, bon appetit.'

He raised a glass, then took his seat at the head table, three chairs away from the President, his grin as wide and arrogant as ever, until the applause finally died to an echo of chatter.

'What the hell has the President been smoking?' Cody Williamson shouted out from the far side of the Zdanski table as he was tearing a slice of sourdough bread in half.

'That sure was something,' Annie Brightwater said. 'I think we may have just witnessed a speech for the ages.'

'Bullshit,' Cody sat back. 'That was just speculation after speculation. Sensationalism covered with more sensationalism. Just because a team of three professors run by the President released some unreliable statistics doesn't mean the media are at fault. That speech was a load of trash. How are your journalists gonna handle that, Sarah-Jane?'

He eyed the media mogul as he was dunking his sourdough into his blood red soup before stuffing it into his mouth.

'We're gonna agree,' she said.

'What?' he said, almost choking on his sourdough.

Cody Williamson had been the Zdanski Corp's leading lawyer since its inception as a company back in 2023. In fact, Cody had actually negotiated the company's inception on behalf of Sarah-Jane, so taken was she by his unique legal loopholes. But Cody was now an old man, pushing ninety, and his influence had evidently waned. Though it hadn't waned enough to not be invited to the main Zdanski table at the White

House Correspondents' Dinner. But it had waned enough for Zdanski to stop listening to his outdated opinions.

'I know all the facts the President just threw at us are facts. We all do,' Sarah-Jane said. 'And we're all going to have to do something about it.'

'What the... what the hell do you expect us to do? Stop producing content?' Cody said, before pushing more sourdough bread into his mouth.

Sarah-Jane dipped her white spoon into her blood-red soup, then glanced up at the old lawyer's plastic face, the edges of his eyes as smooth as a billiard ball, his cheekbone implants wide and sharp, his thick lips taut and tight.

'You'll just have to wait to see what we're going to do about it,' Sarah-Jane retorted.

The Zdanski table fell silent, save for the slurping of soup, while all eyes rolled and shifted ominously from one side of the table to the other.

'Sarah-Jane, Sarah-Jane,' a woman roared, approaching the Zdanski table with a rush. 'Can I get your initial reaction to the President's address?'

Sarah-Jane placed her white soup spoon to the side of her bowl, then twisted her neck over her shoulder to see Rene Swaye bending down beside her. Swaye was the main anchor of Bridle News—a left-wing YouTube channel that didn't fall under the Zdanski Corp. umbrella.

'Now, Rene,' Sarah-Jane said, pouting at the anchor. 'Why would I gift you that exclusive?'

Rene squeezed her face into a snarl, then stood back upright.

'Just thought I'd try,' she said. 'Some speech, huh? Aimed directly at all of us. I say we unpack her numbers. We can dig out some dirt on Professor Wickle, stamp his reputation into the dirt. That'll ridicule the numbers.'

'Please,' Sarah-Jane said, turning back to her table, and picking up her soup spoon. 'You may be getting good numbers on YouTube, Rene, but leave the proper journalism to the proper journalists, huh?'

She tipped soup into her mouth while Rene Swaye stared daggers at the back of her lop-sided bob before spinning on her heels and briskly walking to the back of the all-white room where the Bridle News table was stationed.

'So, what are the real journalists going to do about it?' Cody Williamson spat out of his stiff mouth in the resulting silence.

'You'll find out soon enough,' Sarah-Jane responded.

Annie Brightwater glanced across the table at Sarah-Jane's green eyes, unsure of her boss for the first time since she began working for her. She thought she was adept at reading Sarah-Jane Zdanski's intentions, but recently she found the media mogul to possess an undefinable headspace, ever since Phil Meredith had fallen under the spell of LiD. As she squinted across the table at her boss, Annie wasn't sure whether or not the media mogul was going to do something as radical as sign the Release Bill or do something just as radical by ridiculing a President she had known since she was a little girl.

The Zdanski table's eerie silence got distracted by a wave of mumbles and a rush of bodies at the far corner of the all-white room. Being a room filled with journalists, it didn't take long for word to filter through: Florence Galegood — a highly-thought-of reporter at *New York Post Online* — had fainted and was already being cared for by the hotel's medical team.

When the Dinner had settled from the ruckus, the Zdanski table resumed its silence; a silence that was intriguing every-body enveloped in it. Except for Sarah-Jane and Erica. For there was no need for them to feel intrigued. They knew what was going to happen next. They were the only ones aware that Sarah-Jane had decided, forty-eight hours ago, that she was going to sign a Bill that would Roll the Clock Back on America, just as the President had repeated a need for over and over again in her speech. While everyone around the table was trying to decipher Sarah-Jane's non-plussed response to an eye-opening Presidential address, the media mogul turned to her left and leaned her lips toward her daughter's ear.

'I know I'm used to people staring at me, but this is quite intense,' she whispered.

Erica pulled back to beam a huge smile into Sarah-Jane's pretty face, then leaned forward to whisper.

'It's great to see those green eyes come to life again. You've changed since you've made the decision.'

'I didn't make the decision,' Sarah-Jane whispered back, 'Phil did. His silence was deafening. It still is. That is why I need to sign this Bill. America needs to get itself happy again.'

Erica wrapped one arm around her mother's neck and pulled her closer, before kissing her on top of her lop-sided bob.

'I'd miss him being here... if he ever came here,' Sarah-Jane said.

Erica pushed out a laugh. Phil never made it to the White House Correspondents' Dinner. The whole concept of the Dinner had always been absurd to him. He despised the very notion of people patting themselves on the back, which is why he never once attended an awards ceremony in all his years as an acclaimed TV producer—even though he had been nominated for ninety-five awards over his five decades in the industry. When he was approached by the Emmys to receive a Lifetime Achievement Award in 2042, he scoffed at the email before dragging it into his trash can—refusing to even entertain the idea of replying.

'I can't wait until Wednesday,' Erica whispered. 'You're gonna shock America to its very core.'

'I'll let the people know I'm signing the Bill for them,' Sarah-Jane said.

As she was whispering to her daughter, she could feel the heat of the glaring stares of their colleagues sitting around them. So, Sarah-Jane leaned away from her daughter, to break the tension, forcing those eyes to glance elsewhere while she spooned herself more soup. But even though the glares glanced elsewhere, the guests at the Zdanski table were still evidently transfixed on Sarah-Jane's non-plussed reaction to the President's damning speech that their silence was almost loud above the incessant chattering emanating from the other tables.

Sarah-Jane didn't lift her glance to meet the eyes of her guests, instead she continued to spoon red soup in through her red lips and after dabbing a napkin to the corner of those red lips, she turned back to her daughter.

'It's killing me that Phil is locked in, but…' She paused, hesitated, 'I guess I'm happy in a way because his illness has brought you and I closer.'

She leaned her forehead on to her daughter's shoulder, and Erica lifted a hand to comb her fingers through one side of her mother's lop-sided bob.

'Only took us twenty-five years,' she said, blowing a laugh into Sarah-Jane's hair.

The media mogul looked up and smiled at her daughter, staring into the beady brown eyes she had inherited from her father.

'You love me really, don't you?' Sarah-Jane said.

Erica squinted her entire face.

'Nope,' she said, 'I told you… I've always fucking resented you.'

Erica's squint turned into a smile as she echoed the first words she had ever spoken to Sarah-Jane when Phil had led her to the penthouse without any warning whatsoever to be told the most shocking news she had ever been told.

In the silence that was now drowning the Zdanski table, Sarah-Jane leaned forward again, spooning more soup between her luscious lips before shouting across the table to finally relieve the atmosphere of such awkward tension.

'So, Annie,' she said, 'we need to have a meeting on Monday. I wanna talk you through our plans for the new season.'

'Great,' Annie said. 'Have you got big plans?'

'We do,' Sarah-Jane said, placing a hand under the table to gently squeeze her daughter's knee. 'We're going to get all of our viewers back. We're gonna break new records. Trust me.'

She winked one of her glossy, green eyes at Annie, causing her C.O.O. to smile at her before leaning into the table.

'You launching with the Timothée Chalamet interview?' she asked.

'No,' Sarah-Jane said, laughing, 'We've put Timothée on the back burner. We're going to get in touch with his people on Monday and let them know we're pushing the interview back a few weeks. Then I'll call you… to discuss how we're going to tackle this season.'

She tipped another spoonful of soup into her mouth, just as Annie was squinting back at her, intrigue etched all over her narrow, wrinkled features.

'So… are you… you know… Are you going to address what the President just said on the first show?'

'Like I said,' Sarah-Jane shouted over the rising chatter of the other tables, 'I'll discuss it with you on Monday and then we'll—'

Sarah-Jane didn't get to finish her sentence. Instead, she faceplanted her soup. The slapping of her head against the bowl was swiftly followed by a splash as blood-red soup leapt onto the bright white tablecloth.

Her nose inhaled before exhaling out softly, causing bubbles to form and then burst inside her soup bowl. She never inhaled again.

BOBBY DE LUCA

Once Saturday is over, I'll get on with the sale of my business. Then me and Belinda can live the lives we've been talking about for months. Me and my fiancée; me and my soon-to-be wife.

I haven't felt this excited in I don't how long. Maybe ever. In fact, I'm not sure I was this excited about anything, even when I was a kid.

I usually e-scoote home but decided to walk today because when you are in love, even walking can be fun.

'Hey, Sia,' I say, 'call Belinda.'

She blinks in front of me before the ringtone has finished its first pulse.

'Hey fiancé,' she says, smiling at me.

'Hey fiancée,' I say back to her.

'So, I was thinking,' she says. 'We should get married in Italy. Just the two of us and two local witnesses. I found a small church in Rome that would be so perfect.'

I smile back at her.

'Sounds idyllic,' I say.

'Then we can honeymoon for the rest of our lives.'

'I love you so much,' I say.

'I love you, too,' she says.

The two of us continue to smile at each other while I waddle my way back to my house.

'I, uh… I know I might be a little premature, but I've already instructed my lawyers to process the sale of my business,' she says. 'They said in about four weeks' time, the money from the sale should filter into my account. Then I'm yours, Bobby. I'm yours forever.'

'My sale might take a bit longer,' I reply. 'But as soon as this Saturday is over, I'll organize the sale of my business, too. I can't wait. I can't wait.'

'So, the plan is Rome first, to get married, then maybe Venice for the first leg of our honeymoon?'

'You can plan it all,' I say. 'Wherever you want to go, I want to go.'

She smiles at me again. And I smile back.

'Well, that's what I'm gonna do now,' she says. 'I'll email the church, see if we can get availability to get married there in early June and then I'll check around some hotels in Venice.'

'Book the most romantic hotel you can find,' I say.

'I will,' she says.

Then she blows me a kiss, and I blow her one back.

'Call me tonight,' I say, 'let me know how it's going.'

She blows me another kiss.

'Love you, fiancé,' she says.

And then she's gone. In the blink of an eye.

I continue waddling; waddling while whistling; whistling because I am happy.

When I reach my house, it feels weird. Again. As if somebody has been in my home. It's just a funny feeling I always seem to get these days. It scares me. It's not the fact that somebody could be in my home that scares me. It's LiD that scares me. It scares me that I am imagining it all. I just have to remember that the doctor told me I don't have LiD. I have to believe her. I need to stop feeling frightened. Especially now that I am the happiest man in the entire world.

I walk straight to the kitchen, to make myself a cappuccino. It's always the first thing I do when I get home. When I'm finished at the coffee grinder, I make my way to my office... It's another habit I've adopted. I tend to stare at the photos of my dad and all his Mafia guys on my walls while I wait on the coffee to grind. It's funny... It smells kinda different in here. And I get that strange feeling again that somebody's in my house...

I try to shake my head of the feeling as I walk back to the kitchen to get my cappuccino. A cappuccino always makes me feel more calm; more relaxed; more me.

I blow into the mug, touching it to my lips as if I have to test it every time to see if it may be too hot. It's always too hot. So, I leave the mug on the side of the kitchen counter, and I walk toward my bedroom, to get myself out of this suit and into something more relaxing. Only two more days of wearing a suit. Then I'm done. Forever. *De Luca's* will no longer be *De Luca's*. It will have a new name. And a new owner. And I'll have pocketed about one and a half million dollars, more than enough to spend with my beautiful fiancée as we travel the world together on our forever honeymoon.

I step my short legs into my striped pajama pants, then waddle myself back into the kitchen feeling as giddy as a kid at Christmas, before scooping up my cappuccino from the kitchen counter and waddling with it cupped between my two hands toward the sanctuary of my sofa.

MADISON MONROE

I tossed the untraceable Sia band and the small brown, empty bottle into the river as I raced across the bridge. Then I set fire to the paper boiler suit and watched it disintegrate into ash before I tossed the lighter into the river. It's exactly what the hoodie instructed me to do.

It was Rohypnol in the bottle. Untraceable after twenty-four hours. My job was to squeeze six drops into his cappuccino. Then I hid back under his large desk on my belly and waited… and waited. He was stumbling and stuttering to himself before he fell asleep. Then I set to work; to do the hardest task of all my tasks. I stripped him. Folded his clothes neatly and placed them on the end of his bed. Then I dragged his heavy ass all the way to his bath. It was a struggle to get him into it. But I surprised myself. As soon as he was lying flat down in the bath, I ran the faucet. Then squirted some bubble bath into the water as it tumbled out of the faucet .

He died right in front of me. I know he did. The hoodie told me I had to stay to watch. To make sure he drowned. I waited for eleven minutes. He never came up. He's gone. Whoever he is. I don't know. And I don't want to know. All I want is the two hundred and fifty thousand dollars I was promised for carrying out these tasks. Then I can lift myself out of this gloom. I won't feel down about the murder. By the time his body is found, the Rohypnol will have evaporated, and his murder will have looked like an accidental drowning. I don't feel bad about it. I don't. I feel excited. Excited because it was so easy. Exited because I'm about to be in credit for the first time in my life.

I'm trying to convince myself, as I pace away, that I won't get mixed up in the Dark Web again. As easy as that was for two hundred and fifty K, I'm not desperate anymore. I don't need any more money. I'm fine. My misery will lift. I'll become a good teacher again. Somebody who cares about her students because she's no longer bitter and twisted and broke.

But I can't help shake the thought that all I had to do was scope out a premises. Inject six drops of Rohypnol into a steaming mug of coffee, then drag a two-hundred and fifty-pound obese guy into a bath. And I had to send those emails. There's clearly something big in those emails. But I can't wrap my head around what that is. They read very innocent to me; about adding a change of ingredients to some kind of red-pepper soup. Then a notification for the changing of those ingredients was to be left unfinished and saved into drafts folder. Never to be sent. There has to be something in it. But I really need to stop thinking about it. I need to forget all about the Dark Web. I just need to collect my money, then get on with my life. My good life. My better life. I just need to get home. Then do what I usually do: Veg out on the sofa until I feel sleepy. Then I'll go to bed, as if nothing unusual happened to me tonight. I'll wake up in the morning and go into college and face the music with Neve. I'll tell her I only said what I said on *Good Morning DC with Marley and Dom* because they were paying me to say it. And that I'll never say anything like that again. That I'll never put myself in a position where I'll ever be that desperate for money again.

I skip up the steps to my front door, press my finger against the reader and as soon as I get into the hallway, I slam the door closed behind me; leaving everything that happened out there. In the past.

When I kick off my shoes, I immediately feel more comfortable. So, I let my Afro release from the tight balls I had it plaited into, just so my hair could fit under the hood of that paper boiler suit. It was imperative I left no traces of myself. That obese guy wasn't killed. He drowned in his bath. Innocently.

When my hair fully releases, I bounce onto my sofa and rasp an audible exhale from the back of my throat… an exhale filled with relief, relieving me of my fright. Or my guilt. Or my I-dunno-what.

Clause leaps up on my lap to watch my long exhale dissolve into a yawn.

'Hello, girl,' I say. She purrs. Then hisses. It's unusual that she hisses. 'Hey… what's wrong with you, girl?' I say. 'Can you feel my guilt, girl? That why you hissing?'

VIKTORIA POPOV

I have never made a killing look like a suicide. But the figure in the Blynq messages made it sound easy.

I have already gotten into her social media to leave a message on her Facebook and Glint profiles. I just wrote, 'Good-bye.' It is what the figure told me I should type. She was saying goodbye on her socials for a reason. Because she was about to hang herself. He said I would find something inside her flat that I can hang her with. It didn't take long. At first I took a belt from her closet. Then the belt from her dressing-gown hanging on the hook on her bedroom door. But when I found the cable wire of an old computer, I knew it would be perfect.

Right now, I'm hiding on the far side of her bed, near the window I climbed into, wrapping that cable wire around my two gloves, waiting on her to come home.

I don't feel scared. Not like I used to when I killed Mafia guys. Because when you are working in the Dark Web, there is no need to feel scared or worried. Everyone is anonymous in the Dark Web. No authorities will be able to catch me even if they were looking for a killer. Which they won't be. Because this woman isn't about to be killed. She is about to die by suicide.

I unwrap the cable wire from my gloves as soon as I hear a

creak outside, then the front door beeps twice before it releases open. I creep down onto my stomach on the window side of the bed, just in case she comes into the bedroom first. But she doesn't. She shuffles past the bedroom, and into the living room and kitchen where that horrible little cat is.

She sighs. Really loudly. As if she has had a hard day. And I hear the cat hiss as if it's trying to tell her there's a stranger hiding in her bedroom.

'What's wrong with you, girl?' she says. 'Can you feel my guilt? That why you hissing?'

I wrap the two ends of the cable wire around my gloves, leaving about seven inches in the middle; enough to wrap around her neck. Then I'll just pull up. That's what the figure told me to do. Pull up. Because that's where a hanging strangles a person. Up the neck, hugging the jaws. I slowly rise to my feet gripping the cable with both hands held out in front of me and I begin to tip-toe out of the bedroom. When I reach the hallway, I hear that she has turned on the news channels.

'There's just two nights until the debut White House Correspondents' Dinner of President Sally W. Campbell. The event will be hosted, once again, by Pete Davidson…'

I stop and close one eye, so my other eye can peek through the gap in the door. She is sitting up on her sofa, her horrible cat purring at her while she gets lost in the news.

When I tip-toe into the living room, the cat looks up and hisses at me. But she can't warn her owner in time. It's too late.

I wrap the middle of the cable around her neck and pull upwards, as hard as I can. Squeezing and squeezing and squeezing while her body shakes and wiggles. The cat hisses and hisses while I pull harder and harder. But that's all a cat can do. Hiss and purr.

When she stops wiggling and I release the cable, her body falls off the sofa and slaps to the carpet. The cat jumps onto the top of the sofa, then onto my shoulder, hissing and punching its paws at me. It swipes at my neck. And I immediately know it has taken some of me in its claws.

'Little bitch!' I say, swinging it from my shoulder. It purrs up against its owner's body and I push two of my gloved fingers to my neck, pushing at the cut. When I look at my gloves, there is no blood. But she sure did take a little chunk of my flesh. I stamp my foot and make a roar sound at the cat, and it jumps back, wincing. Then I begin to unwrap the cable before I tie it into the tight noose I had been practicing since I started hiding behind the bed. When I drag her body toward her bedroom, the cat follows us slowly, purring and hissing, with every stride it takes.

'Shut up, you little bitch,' I say to the cat as I'm wrapping the noose of the cable around its owner's neck. Then I begin to pull her by the legs as the cat hisses and purrs at me. It takes me a few tries, but I manage to pull her body upward, so I can hang the cable around the hook on the back of her bedroom door. When I let go, she sways a little. But then she stays there. Hanging. Dead.

I shrug at the cat, then turn around and walk toward the window I came in through.

When I pull the window open, I can hear the wind. It has gotten stronger since I was last outside. But that is all I can hear. The wind. Nobody else. No witnesses, other than that little bitch of a cat. So, I step out on to the ledge, and then turn around so I can push the window closed again.

As soon as I jump down to the grass, I stop so I can look around, just to make sure nobody is watching me, and to make sure the only noise I can hear is that wind. When I am happy there are no other sounds, I begin to walk toward the old football fields, taking the long route back home; the route the figure in the Blynq messages told me I should take…

TIMMY BUCKETT

I stand behind the big tree to block out the wind. The tree is at the far end of the old football fields, where the guy told me I should wait… and wait.

I did wait. For about fifteen minutes until I finally saw a figure walking my way from way, way back in the distance.

As she gets nearer, she actually looks like she's quite fit. A hot-blonde MILFy type.

So, I feel for the cold metal of the gun in my pocket again and grip it tight. I try to make out her face as she speed walks toward me, but she has her head down and I can't see just how hot she is. When she paces past the tree I'm hiding behind, I can hear that she is breathing fast. She's definitely trying to get somewhere quick. It makes me stop and think. But not for long. I don't have the time to wait around. I have to almost jog to catch up with her. Because of the wind, she doesn't hear me coming. I lift the gun and aim for the back of her head. Just as I was told to. As soon as the barrel touches her blonde hair, I don't hesitate. I squeeze the trigger, then continue walking, without taking the time to watch her body collapse to the ground. I need to get out of here quick. It's quiet around here for sure. But by the time I get toward Brookland, there'll be houses. There'll be people. There'll be life. I'll just have to keep my head down when I get there. As if I am just a normal guy walking down a normal road in a normal suburb. And not somebody who just took out a hot blonde MILF with a bullet to the back of the head.

The guy said the fifteen grand would be left in my apartment in cash when the job was complete. I haven't had cash since I was a boy and my grandma used to throw some coins into my hand. It's a bit of a stress, having to use cash to book the flights to California. But it shouldn't be a problem. I've worked out how to do it. I can go into an actual travel agency in Maryland, about half an hour scoote away from where I live. You don't have to book flights online. There is an actual travel agent who can do that for you. I never knew that.

I wasn't nervous earlier. But I am starting to get nervous now. Especially about walking out of these fields and back into the real world. I grab for the gun again, then get down on to one knee where I begin to scratch away at the dirt under the overgrown grass. It takes a while for me to get about ten inches down, but when I do, I place the gun inside the hole before refilling it with dirt and grass. Nobody will find that gun in there. Not among twenty acres of overgrown football fields that nobody has played on for about ten years. It'd be like finding a spit in the sea.

When I stand back up, I look around me at the emptiness and darkness, then I put my head down and begin walking toward life, toward Brookland. I hate walking. With a passion. That's why I e-scoote everywhere I go. I guess everybody does these days.

I start to breathe in and out slowly as I begin to see the first lights of Brookland in the distance. It's only another ten or fifteen-minute walk to get there. All I need to do is look like a normal guy. That's all. A normal guy walking down a normal street in normal suburbs.

Soon as I cross the first pathway that leads away from the

fields, a car's light blinks on to my right. It makes my heart thump, and I immediately stare toward the lights with a fright, before I immediately look away. Nobody needs to see my face. Not when there is a dead body slumped in one of the football fields about a mile back. My breathing gets sharp again. And short. And then suddenly the car starts to move slowly forward, panicking me. I think about running. Racing as far away as I can. But I don't. I just stop. Maybe I've been scared stiff. Maybe I am just waiting for the car to pass me by, so that my breathing can get normal again, and I don't need to feel so frightened.

'Yo, Timmy Buckett!' a voice shouts out.

My stomach drops. My breathing stops. And I know now that I am scared stiff. The car lights glow brighter, until they are lighting me up.

I squint toward them, to make out who is calling my name. Then the car stops, and a dark figure gets out. As soon as it starts walking toward me, I know I'm dead. Because I know that walk. I know that fucking walk!

'Holy shit, Scar,' I say. I never thought I'd see that face again. Only in my nightmares. 'Listen, Scar,' I say. Panicky again. 'I'm s-so sorry I stole your drugs. I'll get that money back to you. I swear.'

He grins at me. The way the Joker grins at Batman. And I know there's nothing left for me to do... other than to run. So, I do. I spin around and race off back into the fields, back toward the hot MILF's lifeless body. But the car revs as soon as I start to run, and I can feel it speeding behind me even though I can't see it.

'Time's up, Timmy,' Scar shouts over the noise of the car, 'you keep running, we'll just prolong the agony we're gonna put you through.'

I stop running as soon as the car catches up to me, and I fall to my knees, surrendering. When my head tips me forward and my face slaps against the long grass, I immediately start sobbing; sobbing like I haven't sobbed since I was four years old, and I cut my knee open in the school playground.

The kick to the ribs is painful, and it forces more tears to pour from my eyes. Then he grabs me by the back of the hair until I'm on my feet again, staring at that nasty scar.

'Get in the car,' he says.

'Wh-wh-where you takin' me?' I say.

He grins. Like the Joker again. His scar looking really nasty in the glow of the headlights.

'We're taking you back home, Timmy Boy. To Baltimore. We've got a little torture chamber all set up, ripe and ready to bring the most pain possible to the only little fucker whoever thought it wise to steal from me.'

'N-n-no, just, just kill me now. Do it now. Shoot me. Just do it. Do it now.'

He laughs in my face. Like the ugly prick he is.

'Now where'd be the fun in that?' he says.

Then he grips me tighter by the hair and drags me toward the blinding lights of the car…

POTUS. SALLY W. CAMPBELL

I remove my hands from my face and sigh. Again. I'm boring myself with my sighs. I've been sighing non-stop since the Correspondents' Dinner. As if each sigh is trying to breathe out reality, huffing the living nightmare from my mind.

I've been trying to balance my shock with my work. But it's not easy. I made one statement to the American people in the early hours of Sunday morning, then I boarded Air Force One headed for Kansas. To where I felt most comfortable. I'm scheduled to be in Berlin this week, meeting with the German Chancellor to discuss our countries' lack of progress when it comes to Net Zero. But I couldn't make it. Not while I was suffering with so much shock. And so much grief. I felt Kansas was the best place for me to be. It's where we both grew up, even though she doesn't have any family here anymore. Her only attachment to the town she grew up in is the distorted memories some of her old neighbors still possess. One elderly woman I met this morning told me she knew Sarah-Jane was destined for stardom from the time she was a toddler. "She shone like no girl I ever seen shine," the neighbor told me. She was heartbroken, crying and sobbing on my shoulder, even though she hadn't seen Sarah-Jane in person for over sixty years.

Half of the nation are, like her, heartbroken. The other half are almost gleeful. But that's the way it's supposed to be with Sarah-Jane Zdanski. She was the queen of dividing the nation. In life, and in death…

I'm standing at the spot that brought the two of us together some fifty years ago: the dilapidated building that was once Median High School—where my sister and six others were gunned down, gifting Sarah-Jane a story that would catapult her to stardom. I don't blame Sarah-Jane for her successes. Of course I don't. She would have become a star with or without the Median High School shooting of 1997. Tragedy would have eventually come her way. Tragedy comes every reporter's way.

'Madam President,' Borrowland calls out as he somberly walks toward me. 'I've just had an update. Florence Galegood is making great progress in Sibley Memorial Hospital. She's expected to make a full recovery.'

'Oh, thank God,' I say, slapping my hand to my heart even though I don't believe in God. The American people think I believe in God. Of course they do. They believe every American president believes in God.

'Our intel says she reacted as well as the doctors could have hoped to her adrenaline transfusion, and they expect her to be discharged within forty-eight hours.'

'Great news,' I say, smiling. It feels wrong to smile. As if two people didn't die right in front of our eyes just four nights ago, shocking not just us in attendance at the Dinner, but the entire population of America, into a numbness.

I soak in the good news about Florence Galegood as I look up and down the quiet, flat roads of Lebanon, then I spin on my heels to walk down the embankment that leads me to the iron-framed window, with my two tallest Secret Service guys tailing me. I've only peered through this window once before. About a week after it happened at the candlelit vigil the local mayor had organized. For some reason I thought it would be wise to stare through the window and into the classroom my sister was killed in. As though I wasn't going to hear the gunshots pierce through my ears. I try not to hear them now as I squint through the dusty window, but it's hard not to, even though I'm now just staring at a concrete room and not a classroom with one of my sister's posters hanging on its back wall.

It's probably viewed in some quarters as selfish that I've retreated to Lebanon since the Correspondents' Dinner. Especially as Sarah-Jane wasn't the only one to die on Saturday. Michael Williamson's life ended too. He was a long-time researcher at CSN who just happened to suffer from the same nut allergy as Sarah-Jane. It was the same allergy Florence Galegood suffered from, too. Luckily for her, she hadn't eaten too much of the soup before she collapsed off her chair. They were the only three people at the Correspondents' Dinner to suffer with such a severe nut allergy. Which I've been informed by Borrowland was actually a fortunate statistic. Because the national average suggests five people should have been struck down by the amount of nuts that were shaved into that soup.

'Madam President!' Borrowland shouts, distracting me. 'Erica Murphy is holocalling. It's the call you've been waiting for.'

'Drop her in my Sia,' I say, as I remove my translucent band from my coat pocket and slap it to my forehead.

'Madam President,' Erica's hologram says, nodding as soon as her hologram blinks in front of me.

'Erica' I whisper, 'I want to extend my most sincere and deepest sympathies to you. And my most sincere apologies. We're looking into everything. But it seems... it seems a little...'

'A little what?' she asks.

'As I'm sure you've heard, the soup served at the White House Correspondents' Dinner had peanut shavings in it. It was never flagged as containing nuts on the menu. But, uhm... there's something else I need to share with you. The caterer, who changed the menu... he, uh... he died, too. He drowned in his bath two nights before the Correspondents' Dinner, before he could provide the hotel with details that the soup contained peanuts.'

'What the fuck?' her hologram spits at me. 'I knew it! I fucking knew it. I knew this was murder. Someone knew. Someone knew Sarah-Jane had that nut allergy.'

'We're looking into everything,' I say softly to her, trying to calm her rage; trying to calm her grief. 'There were emails sent. From the caterer's computer. One was sent to notify the change of ingredients to the soup. Then there was another email written up that was supposed to be sent to The Heart Hotel to notify them the soup should be marked as a high-allergen item, only... only the email was unfinished. It was never sent. It was saved in his drafts folder.'

'Jesus Christ,' she says, shaking her head. 'I knew it!'

She blows out through her flushed cheeks, then begins pacing in a frustrated panic, shock upon shock mounting on her shoulders, until she eventually stops walking. Stops sobbing. And shakes her head again.

'I understand how shocking such a tragedy can be,' I say. 'I am so, so sorry.'

'Did you put the peanuts in the soup?' she asks me.

I clasp my fingers over the navel of my black dress suit and squint back at her, my head subtly shaking.

'Course not.'

'Exactly,' she says. 'So, with all due respect, Madam President, stop apologizing to me.'

'I'm sorry,' I say.

Then I hold my eyes closed. Because I can hear myself.

'Find out what the hell is going on here, Sally,' she demands, her finger pointing, her jaw swinging with disdain. 'Make sure you have the best of the best on this.'

'They are already on it,' I say. 'I promise. We'll get to the bottom of exactly what happened, Erica.'

She stares down toward my black high-heels, her jaw still

swinging, her nose sucking up the tears that are threatening to flood her face.

'Poor Phil,' I say. 'He has no idea.'

'Phil?' she says. 'Yeah. He knows. We told him. We had to tell him.'

'Sorry?' I say. 'Phil came through?'

'Yeah,' she says. 'We have one of those Ripple Stimulus Machines. We

brought him through on Sunday, to tell him Sarah-Jane died. He started ranting and raving and crying and sobbing and… well, then he just collapsed back on to the sofa, and got locked in again.'

'Really?' I say squinting at her hologram. 'The Ripple Stimulus actually works in patients like Phil?' She shrugs her shoulders at me. And in that moment I desperately want to ask her about the Release Bill. Especially if Phil came through. But I shouldn't. I can't. Not while she's still grieving. 'Did, uh…' I say, before hesitating. I decide inside my hesitation that I *have* to ask her about it. The well-being of America depends on it. 'Did Phil say anything else when he came through?'

Erica glances up at me, then rubs the cuffs of her sleeves into her crying eyes.

'Oh,' she says. 'You wanna know about the Release Bill, don't you? Two people died at the dinner you were hosting, and yet all you wanna know about is your fucking Release Bill.'

'No… it's not that… I…I…' I stutter before gripping the bars on the window with frustration while I shake my head at Erica's hologram that is now standing inside the vacant classroom.

She stares downward, then her eyes suddenly flick up to me before she swipes her sleeve across her face again.

'Well, if it puts your mind at ease, I can tell you,' she says. 'We won't be signing no Release Bill.'

My heart drops. And I let go of the steel bars.

'Sorry? What?' I say, panicked. 'You… wait. What. Who's *we*?'

'We? Me and Phil. We run Zdanski Corp. now. When I brought him through, I asked him, I asked him about the Release Bill. Wanna know what he said? He said, 'Over my dead body'.'

'What? I…I…' I stutter again, then I bring my hands to my face. 'Erica, you can't do this. Sarah-Jane would have signed that Bill. I know she would have. She gave me the impression at the Dinner that she was ready to sign that Bill.'

I notice Erica, through the gaps of my fingers, shrug her shoulders at me again. Then she folds her arms.

'Well,' she says, before huffing out an audible sigh, 'Sarah-Jane ain't here anymore… is she?'

9

WHEN THE BLACK EGG WAS STUCK TO PHIL'S LEFT TEMPLE, HE always looked more gaunt, more disabled, more locked in. As if the black egg was a beacon, shining its bright light to highlight his body's demise.

Despite his appearance, the bristling of breath rasping through his hairy nostrils was slow. Slow and steady. And calm. He was the calmest one in the room. Because he was the only one in the room who didn't know what had happened.

The penthouse had been deathly dense since Saturday night. Although Sarah-Jane had, on occasion, spent months at a time away from her New York home, the penthouse always retained a glow and a sheen in the knowledge she would return. But the illumination and atmosphere of the penthouse seemed to die when she herself had died. Although the bright white light in the kitchen was stark, the living room, where Phil was slouched into the orange sofa with the black egg to his temple, was thick with shadows of musk and murk.

Silhouetted in front of Phil's slumping body, the grungy figure of Erica stood, her feet astride, her fingers lightly gripping the edges of the handheld pad of the Ripple Stimulus as if it were an old-fashioned cell phone.

She sucked one gulp of breath down the back of her throat, then slowly whistle blew that breath out through her lips. When she palmed the pad in her left hand, she stabbed the index finger from her right hand to the blue pulsing button twice… and waited.

A sizzle could be heard hissing from the black egg, as Phil shot bolt upright, frightening Erica, before his left hand fell from his lap, and dropped on to the orange sofa.

'Phil,' Erica said, stepping forward. She palmed the device again, then stabbed at the blue pulse two more times. The sizzling lasted longer this time, and a sizzle of smoke floated from the egg and rose into the darkness toward the ten-foot-high ceiling. Phil's eyes widened, and he shrugged his shoulder, as if his whole left-side was shaking its way out of numbness. 'Sarah-Jane is dead, Phil,' Erica said, somberly. 'Somebody didn't warn The Heart Hotel that there were nut shavings in the soup.'

Phil blinked his bloodshot eyes, and when they opened they were evidently moist. A deflated huff forced out through his hairy nostrils, then his body relaxed, except for his left hand that was trembling against the sofa as if it were icy-cold.

'Which was pretty genius,' Erica continued. 'But in truth it was a bit of a no-brainer really wasn't it? She was gonna sign the Release Bill. Can you believe it? She was gonna sign the fucking thing! She was gonna sign away everything we own… everything we control. As soon as you got locked in, I knew how I was gonna do it. Jesus, I've daydreamed about killing her with nuts from the moment I learned nuts could kill her. I used to think I'd get to the head chef of Sosa Restaurant, y'know? Kill her that way. But when I realized the Correspondents' Dinner was coming up, you know me, Phil, I'm like you… Like father, like daughter, huh? I just couldn't resist turning the story up to its highest level. So… we got to the guy who runs the catering for The Heart Hotel. A soup with peanut shavings that came with no warning that peanut shavings were in it. How fuckin' simple is that? How fuckin' genius is that?'

The glisten of moisture in Phil's eyes instantaneously dried and his eyelids threatened to close, as if he was locking back in, even though his left hand continued to tremble, shuddering up and down against the sofa.

'Hey, Phil, look here,' Erica said, taking a step toward him and bending down, meeting him face-to-face, her narrow straight nose inches from his bulbous, hairy nose. 'Can you hear me? Phil? C'mon, Daddy. I gave you four blasts of that Ripple Stimulus Machine… You should be as awake now as you ever will be again. You'd have been proud of me. You'd be proud of how I'd done it. How we done it,' Erica says, glancing over her shoulder, to glare into the shadows of the murky living room. 'Daddy, you remember Mykel, don't you?' A figure stepped forward, the pants of his plastic faux scrubs swishing. Phil's eyes blinked rapidly. And his left hand formed into a ball, as it continued to bounce off the sofa. It swung for Erica. But she was too swift and ducked away, laughing.

'You'd have been so proud of her, Phil,' Mykel said, his voice soft, his words deadly.

'Tell him,' Erica says, 'tell him what we did.'

Mykel bent his neck down, to stare into Phil's bloodshot eyes.

'Well,' he said. 'Where shall I start? Like your precious little daughter said, we got to the caterer who provided the soup. He happened to change the recipe by email, but didn't get to warn the hotel… because, well, because he happened to drown in his bath before he could finish the email. The woman who put him in that bath and made him drown? Well, she was a manic-depressive teacher out of some college in Washington—a hundred and sixty grand in debt. She hung herself in her bedroom after saying goodbye to her remaining few friends on social media. Oh,' he said, puffing out a laugh while eyeballing Erica, 'the woman who made that teacher's death look like suicide… well… she was killed. She received a gunshot to the back of the head. Her body is still lying out in some open football field in the back ass of DC somewhere. Hasn't even been found yet. When she is finally found, the victim's past will lead an investigation to the Boston Mafia. She used to work for the Boston Mafia. The guy who put that bullet in her head? Well, we're not sure where he is. I arranged for his past to catch up with him… Which gave us a cover for a cover for a cover for a cover.'

'Get it, Phil?' Erica said, stooping down to mirror Mykel, the two of them glaring at Phil's bloated face. 'Nobody will ever solve Sarah-Jane's murder. Her death will be a conspiracy theory Americans will talk about for decades. Like the JFK shooting. Or the fuckin' moon landing. The guy who changed the recipe forty-eight hours before the Correspondents' Dinner happened to drown in his own bath just after changing the recipe. Sounds suspicious, don't it? Yet suspicion won't lead anybody anywhere. Mykel here planned it all.' She patted her former foster brother on the back of his scrubs and winked at him. Then she turned back to Phil's slumping body. 'Well, I planned it all. Mykel carried out the leg work. Now come on, Phil. Tell me. Just nod at me once to let me know. It's fuckin' genius, right?'

Phil's eyes were dry, and his breaths had returned the slow and steady inhales and exhales that made him the calmest person in the room. His chin was threatening to tuck back into his neck. But it hadn't. Not yet. Not while his left hand was still trembling.

'Zdanski would've wanted it this way, don'tcha think, Phil?' Mykel said, 'She will be as famous in her death as she was in her life. Or infamous… is that the right word? What's the difference between those two words anyway?'

He stood back upright, and Erica followed him.

'He's fucking gone, isn't he?' she said. 'Has he heard one word of what we said?'

'He definitely understood Zdanski was dead. S'why his eyes watered, isn't it? It's why he tried to grab you.'

Erica stuck her bottom lip out and rounded her chin before she gripped the pad in her hand again and held her thumb over the pulsing blue light in the center.

'No,' Mykel said, grabbing at her elbow. 'You've already given him four shots. If you roast his brain with another shot of that, and he dies right here, right now, that will undo everything we've done. Leave him. Leave him locked in. It's time anyway... four minutes...'

Erica sucked on her teeth, stewing and chewing on the thought.

'I want him to hear this,' she said. 'He has to hear this.'

She tapped her thumb twice against the blue pulsing light, then stepped forward as a thin pirouette of smoke rose from the top of the black egg toward the deathly dark high ceiling.

As soon as she stepped forward, Phil's left hand rose upward, and his head began to shake.

'Hey, Phil,' she said, loudly. 'Can you hear me? Can you fucking hear me? I want you to hear me. I'm gonna do it. I'm about to do it...' she glanced over her shoulder at the bright white lights of the kitchen, then back at her biological father, to see his left fist curling into a ball, juddering against the orange sofa. 'I'm gonna tell America everything. I'm gonna tell them Sarah-Jane was my mother. And you... and you were my father. I'mma tell them everything. Now how good a fuckin' story is that to open a new season with, huh? In one hour's time, I'll be the most famous face in America. Who also owns the most famous name in America. Zdanski. Zdanski Corp. It's all mine now, isn't it?'

She cackled a menacing laugh from the back of her throat, then took one step toward Phil before leaning down and grabbing at the jowls of his face where his beard used to be before it turned white and patchy, exposing more of his bloated, blotched skin.

'Can you hear me, Dad?' she said. 'Make sure you can hear me... I need you to hear me. I was just on a holocall to the President before I came to wake you up. Y'know what I told her? That there's no fucking way we're signing any Release Bill. Why would we? When we hold all the power in this country.'

Phil's gloomy glare shifted, and Erica squinted, pausing for a quick moment, wondering if his eyes had met hers.

'You can hear me, can't you, Phil?' She shook his jowls when no response was forthcoming. 'Watch me. I want you to sit there and watch me. This is gonna be a bigger launch show than anything you and my precious mother ever launched with. What were those numbers you liked to boast about? The Median High School shooting? Thirty million. The Benji Wayde murder? A hundred and twenty million. Well, I'm about to blow those numbers outta the fuckin' park.'

'C'mon, Erica, its time,' Mykel said, tugging at her elbow.

'Sit him more upright,' she instructed Mykel, nodding toward Phil's slumping body. 'Make sure he's watching me. Make sure he's facing that kitchen island.'

Mykel walked to the back of the orange sofa and yanked Phil's heavy shoulders backward, ensuring the bloated former cameraman-slash-producer was sitting as upright on the sofa as he possibly could be. A gurgle could be heard in Phil's throat, but when Erica spun around to glare at him, she realized the gurgle was not a sign that her father was becoming lucid again, but rather a sign that his battery was switching off. His chin was slowly tucking back into his neck, and his bloodshot eyes were zoning out.

She tutted quietly to herself, then turned on the spot to march confidently toward the stark bright-white light.

When she stepped up and sat onto Sarah-Jane's stool at the end of the kitchen island, *The Zdanski Show* logo glowing warmly in neon orange behind her, she squinted into the murky living room to see Phil's silhouette facing her way. Front row. Front and center. Even if his eyes were staring downward at where the marble tiles of the kitchen floor rounded into the butt of the most famous kitchen island in America.

'How am I looking?' she asked Mykel, calmly.

He swished his plastic faux scrubs toward the Sia camera that would, in just ninety seconds, beam Erica's glowing holo-gram into every Sia band in America, then nodded his head once.

'You look great,' he said. 'Now remember… look somber. Sad. As if you haven't just lost a boss. But lost a mother. Then tell America that you literally lost your mother.'

'Please,' she said to Mykel. 'You've been working in news for ten minutes. I know exactly what I'm doing.'

Mykel grinned to himself behind the Sia camera then shouted out: 'One minute.'

He twirled a small knob on the side of the Sia camera, making Erica's hologram glow even sharper, then he stepped back into the shadows of the kitchen-cum studio, to the spot where Phil usually stood when Sarah-Jane was addressing the nation.

Erica cleared her throat twice, then swept up the fake notes lying in front of her and bounced the butt of them off the marble top of the kitchen island.

'Okay, let's make history,' she said.

She licked her lips, then sounded her opening two sentences over and over in her head.

That was when Phil gurgled and shouted. She watched as his silhouette rose, then immediately slumped to the carpet.

'Holy shit,' Erica said, stepping down from her stool and racing Mykel toward the slumped body in the middle of the darkly-lit living room. She knelt down beside her father's bulbous head and leaned into him. She could hear his breath whistling coolly and calmly in and out through his disgusting nostrils. 'What the fuck did he say?'

'I-I,' Mykel was laughing. 'Did he say something about the

Release Bill? Sounded to me like he shouted 'something, something Release Bill.'

'What the fuck?'

Erica laughed.

'I dunno…' Mykel said, as he scooped Phil's body back upright into a seating position.

Erica stood behind the sofa to wrap both hands under his armpits and drag him back up onto the orange sofa.

'Are you fucking serious? Did you hear him say Release Bill?'

'I honestly don't know,' Mykel said. He was still laughing; laughing from the fright. And the shock. When he sat Phil more upright, facing the bright- white light of the kitchen, he grinned at Erica. 'He shouted something that sounded like Release Bill… or maybe I'm just imagining it.'

Erica held her mouth open with shock.

'Fuck, fuck, fuck,' Mykel said, 'Twelve seconds… go, go.'

The shock dropped from Erica's face and she turned to march toward the kitchen. When she stepped up onto the stool, she leaned her forearms onto the cold marble top and glared into the Sia camera, watching the holographic numbers countdown to single figures… until they reached the numbers her father used to always shout out to her mother before she went live to the nation.

Three… then two… then one…

'Good evening, America,' she said. 'And welcome to the show…'

Today, only six companies own 90% of America's media output. By the year 2047, only three companies are projected to own 90% of America's media output.

COULD THIS REALLY BE OUR FUTURE?

Watch an interview with author David B. Lyons on YouTube now in which he discusses:

- Whether life will really be like this just twenty-five years from now

- How he came up with his vision for the future

- How we can put a stop to such a possible insular life for the next generation

Use the link below to watch the video now:

https://www.subscribepage.com/murdersthatkilledamerica

David B. Lyons is the author of three trilogy sets.

The Tick-Tock Trilogy

The Trial Trilogy

The America Trilogy

Visit here to get your next David B. Lyons read now:

http://theopenauthor.com/my-books/

ACKNOWLEDGMENTS

This book is dedicated to the memory of one of the closest friends I'll ever have—Thomas 'Bomber' Healy.
From the cul de sacs of Cabra, to the national stadium wearing green, to the jaws of Mountjoy prison, to the movie studios of Hollywood, to the many pubs of Emmet Road.
It may have been a short life. But it sure was a short life well lived.
Thomas, the impressions you made on me will live within me for the rest of my days.
So, too, will the memories.
Oh man, those memories!
Thank you for being my friend.
It was as much of an honour for me as it was a pleasure.
I love you, brother. And I'm gonna miss you forever.

*

The publication of *The Murders That Shook America* would not be possible without the hard work of a fantastic creative team of people.

My agent:
Joanna Swainson at the wonderful Hardman & Swainson Agency

My editorial team:
Lisa Gellar

Brigit Taylor
Maureen Vincent-Northam
Deborah Longman

My beta readers:
Eileen Cline
Margaret Lyons
Kathy Grams

My designers:
MiblArt*

*MiblArt are based in Ukraine and are currently working through energy rations and fear of a murderous bully entering their town. A lot of my thoughts this year have been with Julia Rozdobudko and the team of world-class creative designers at MiblArt.
May peace, love and freedom shine on you soon.

Made in the USA
Middletown, DE
09 April 2023